Howdy! Hola! Bonjour! Guten Tag!

Book One
Touchables: A Dystopian Trilogy

Face-to-Face

Terry Sanville

Branching Realities
Independent Publishing, LLC

Face-to-Face
Terry Sanville

Face-to-Face is a work of fiction. Names, characters,
places, and incidents are products of the author's
imagination. Any resemblance to actual events or
persons, living or dead, is entirely coincidental.

Story copyrights owned by Terry Sanville
Original cover illustration by Enrique Meseguer

First Printing
July 2020

Branching Realities Independent Publishing aims to
find the best in fiction of all genres from independent
authors all over the world. To find more about us visit
our website or send us an email. Please support the
independents of publishing and writing.

Website: branchingrealitiespublishing.com
Email: branchingrealities@yahoo.com
Store: irbstore.co

1

Tony Matteson and Fox Slade hustled down Main Street, past the boarded-up Courthouse and the torched movie theater, heading toward home. On a side street, a police crawler rattled toward them, its knobby tires rolling over decades of debris, its blue and white roof lights flashing. Tony slung the half-full can of paint into a gaping storefront and took off running. Fox matched his speed, her flyaway red hair complementing the indigo latex spattered across her coveralls.

The 'Forcers turned onto Main. "Hold it right there, you two," blasted from their crawler's speaker.

The pair ran faster, dodged around junker cars, piles of refuse pulled from long-abandoned shops, around mounds of books outside a place called "The Phoenix," the volumes turning into mush from years of sun and rain. The crawler gained on them. They cut through an overgrown park near the creek, past the ruins of Mission de Tolosa. Tony glanced at Fox and grinned. They'd been sixteen when the 'Forcers had last put up a good chase. Now, a couple years later, they still could outrun them. Another crawler pulled from a driveway and skidded to a stop directly in their path. Winged doors shot upward from its beetle-shaped fuselage and two officers jumped out. The 'Forcers made a grab for them but missed. Tony and Fox angled through a parking lot, and clawed their way over a rotting fence into a back alley. A skip loader rusted where it had last worked on some kind of construction job. They slid past it and reached the edge of the town's old commercial district.

A warm September wind blew eastward along the boulevard, pushing them toward the Garage, a half block down. More flashing lights. The Police closed in. The couple bobbed and weaved around grasping hands, past hastily-aimed stun guns. Something slammed into Tony's shoulder. He tucked his compact body into a ball, rolled once, and came up running. Reaching the entrance to the five-level parking structure, the pair sprinted inside. The Police didn't follow, wouldn't follow. Tony and Fox climbed the stairs two at a time, passing dark floors full of the Touchable Clan's campsites. At the top level open to the sky, they rushed to the parapet and stared down at the Police. Fox flashed her burning blue eyes at Tony and grinned, her chest heaving. The officers stood with hands on hips in the littered street, calling through their megaphones for the teenagers to surrender.

A few of the new arrivals that lived on the roof joined the pair, shouted insults at the 'Forcers, and waved antique rifles and handguns in the air. An old guy with dreadlocks and his son emptied their waste buckets over the side and the patrolmen scattered. The Roofies laughed.

"They almost got us," Fox said. "Are you all right?"

Tony grinned. "Yeah, I'm fine. But I told you one of those Untouchables would call the Police. You have to paint quicker."

Fox glared at him. "You're the one that wants details. You can't rush details. You can't force art."

"Yeah, yeah, I know. We'll let things cool for a few days then go back and finish it. How's our paint supply holding out?"

"We'll have plenty," Fox said, "unless they find our stash."

They descended the stairs to the second level and moved to their campsites, shoved side-by-side against the Garage's east wall where the morning sun warmed them and the thick concrete walls blocked the Pacific winds. Tony stood on his toes and kissed Fox, a soft one on the mouth that lingered, then ducked inside his tent. His mother looked up from her reading and scowled.

"Where the blazes have you been? You missed your afternoon session. We were going to talk about Descartes and the other philosophers."

"Sorry, Mom, I was out helping Fox—"

"Yes, I'll bet you were."

"We're just having fun, Mom."

"Uh huh. That girl's a fine artist. But if the Police catch you kids painting those hillside homes, your old mother's gonna be lonely for a long time."

"It's just a game, Mom. Gives the 'Forcers something to do. Besides they'll never catch us. You should see the big houses above the hospital. The murals really tell a story."

"Do they show two teenagers behind bars?"

Tony laughed. "No, but we can work that in somehow if you want. We're mostly painting landscapes, you know, camouflage... so that the buildings disappear against the hill."

"Well, enough art for one day. Come on, it's suppertime and you know how quick the line forms when they serve meat."

Tony retrieved his mother's cane and helped her to her feet. They joined Fox and her parents and climbed the stairs to the roof where the communal kitchens stood beneath an open-sided shed. That day, the cooking crew had plucked and roasted chickens taken from their coops south of town. The meat smelled wonderful and at least half of the Touchable Clan's three hundred members had already lined up, plates in hand, awaiting their ration of chicken, green beans, salad, and beer brewed on the third level by a half dozen enthusiastic families. Every adult contributed something to the clan's life. Tony's mom taught school, from the smallest tykes to the most advanced adults. Fox's Dad helped take care of the community garden. Her mother worked in the rooftop food prep area, tending the drying trays filled with apples, almonds, and cabernet grapes scavenged from abandoned orchards and vineyards.

The families sat at long tables and ate their meals. The head of the clan climbed onto a packing crate and yelled for their attention.

"Listen up, clansmen. Just a reminder, tomorrow is autumn cleaning day. Public Works will be here bright and early to charge the sprinklers with disinfectant. For you new folks who just joined the Roofies, they'll be pumping cleaning fluid through the standpipes and flooding the top deck. So everyone needs to clear out by 0800."

"Why'd they ever start doing that?" a new Roofie asked Tony's mother.

"Back in 2080 there was a cholera outbreak in the Garage. Ever since then, it's been drenched with Pine-Sol on each solstice and equinox day. It's a real pain, but after more than thirty years we've had few health problems."

"You kids better leave early tomorrow morning," Fox's mother told the teenagers. "You really pissed off the Police with that cat-and-mouse act of yours. They'll be waiting for you."

Tony nodded. "Fox and I can hole up at the Library."

Fox smiled at him, her face smeared with chicken grease. "While we're there, we can grab some more books for you, Mrs. Matteson."

"Thank you, Fox. Some of my students need reference materials. I'll give you a list."

The two families chatted about the day's events and

complained about having to spend half the night packing everything onto rickety carts to haul from the Garage the following morning, only to drag it back near sundown.

After dinner, the teenagers carried their families' waste buckets south through the deserted industrial district to the sewer farm, an expanse of downwind pastureland managed by the Roofies and Romero, their leader. Tony remembered when he and his mom had turned up at the Garage a decade before and had joined the clan. All new members had to live on the roof and work at the sewer farm—afternoons spent pouring caustic lye into the waste ditches and covering it with fresh soil, all under the watchful eye of King Dave. They had camped on the roof in a leaky tent for three years before a space opened up on the second level next to Fox.

After dropping off their buckets and picking up clean ones, Fox and Tony moved north to the creek and their favorite pool hidden beneath a bridge and a tangle of willows. They stripped naked and slid into the black water, scrubbing hard at their bodies to remove the grime and the paint stains. Afterwards, Fox laid her slender body on the long grass under the trees. Tony slid his muscled arms around her and they spooned. In the warm Indian summer evening, night herons squawked and egrets and great blues beat the air above them. The couple made slow love, slept, then woke and hurried back to the Garage to prepare for the morning move and their next scrape with the Police.

∿∿

"Wake up, Tony. We're late."

He opened his eyes and looked up at Fox. "What time is it?"

"0530. We should have been outta here an hour ago."

Tony glanced at his mother, slumped on a cushion and snoring. "Just let me roust Mom and I'll come get you."

In a few minutes he joined Fox outside her family's tent. They snugged their backpacks tight around their shoulders, pulled on black knit caps, and descended the stairs to the Garage's main entrance. Three crawlers with lights flashing waited outside. At the rear and side exits, they found more 'Forcers with stun guns drawn.

"We're screwed," Tony muttered.

"Not yet, come on." Fox led him to the roof. A few of the families had started edging their overloaded carts toward the first ramp and the precarious descent to ground level. The couple moved to the south wall and peeked over its edge at the Police.

"What are we supposed to do, fly?" Tony asked.

"No, stupid. See that old utility line?" She pointed to a thick black cable attached to a metal stanchion on top of the parapet. It angled downward into the gray dawn.

"You're kidding me," Tony said.

"No, it's our way out. When I was a kid, I hooked myself up to that thing and slid down the block. It passes through some trees and ends at a pole maybe a hundred meters away."

"But you were smaller then and..."

"You calling me fat?" Fox said, smirking.

"God, no. But I'm not sure that line will hold."

"Quit worrying. We'll go one at a time. I'll meet up with you at the Library... at our normal spot."

Before he could say anything more, Fox removed her belt and tied it in a loop around the utility line. "Now listen. When you hit the tree branches, grab hold."

"You're not gonna get stuck out there dangling, are you?"

Fox grinned. "Relax. This line drops quickly and you'll be going fast enough to reach the trees."

"Be careful," Tony said and kissed her.

She pushed off from her perch on top of the parapet. The line sagged and she disappeared. Tony listened but heard nothing. He laid a hand on the wet cable. It jounced a few times then stilled.

The sky continued to brighten. He hurried to hook his belt around the line and stuff his jacket down his pants. He slipped one arm through the loop. Sucking in a deep breath, he dropped off the parapet and slid through grayness, passing over the crawlers' flashing white and blue lights. An ocean fog had pushed inland and hung at treetop level. It wet his face. He continued to slide, his arms numbed from clutching the belt loop. Something brushed his side. He smashed into a mat of small twigs, reached out and grabbed hold with one hand, stopping his forward motion. He couldn't see the ground. But he released his other arm and pulled himself up the slender branches to a large limb, across the limb to the trunk, then down, the tree's bark digging into his flesh. Dropping onto the sidewalk, he backed against a church with shattered stained-glass windows, his chest heaving. Something touched his arm, and he jerked, struggling to hold back a yelp.

"You made it without breaking your stupid neck," Fox said.

"What are you doing here? You're supposed to—"

"Yeah, well I couldn't leave you behind if you crash-landed."

He hugged her, could feel her body tremble, or maybe it was his own, he couldn't tell. He also felt his pants slipping down his thighs, yielding to gravity since he had abandoned his belt on the overhead line.

"Not now, Romeo," Fox said and backed away from

7

him. He yanked up his trousers and tucked in his shirt and jacket.

They walked along quiet streets, cutting a zig-zag route to the brick Library, across the square from the boarded-up City Hall. The pair found the hole cut in the chain link fence at the rear loading dock. Fox struggled to slide her long body through it while Tony easily slipped between its jagged edges. His mother liked to call him her wire terrier because of his curly brown hair and compact features. But so long as Fox loved him, he didn't care what others called him.

Tony kicked at the metal service door then yanked it open. The inside smelled of dust. Moving along a carpeted corridor, they emerged into what must have been the main lobby, with reading rooms opening off it.

"Where do you want to start?" Fox asked.

Tony pulled a scrap of paper from his pocket and they stared at his mother's clear handwriting. "Most of what she wants is medical reference, geology, with a few bug books. Let's start upstairs then move to special collections if we need to."

They climbed to the second floor. Sunlight poured through wire-glass windows, allowing them to move easily between the stacks. Thick dust covered the volumes. The pair pulled on painting masks before dislodging anything from the shelves. Tony always enjoyed this part; it felt like a treasure hunt. It wasn't long before he and Fox had stashed the desired books in their backpacks and had returned the ones his mom had finished with to their rightful places. His mother felt adamant about taking back what she'd borrowed. "Someday, libraries will be important again," she'd said.

They moved to an open balcony off the third floor, sat on rusting chairs, and watched the sun move across the valley, chasing the retreating fog toward the

Pacific coast.

"So do you want to go paint?" Fox asked.

"Naw. We should wait until they're done cleaning the Garage and ditch these backpacks. Besides, the 'Forcers will be looking for us. They know we've been painting on that house, so we need to take a break."

"Then, what do you want to do all day?" Fox grinned at him and he grinned back.

"You could try reading something. You can read, can't you?"

She stuck out her tongue at him. "You know I'm more of a visual and tactile person."

"Great. Let's go look at the special collections."

Tony took her hand and they pushed through a series of doors into a musty room with a bank of tinted windows across one wall. He opened a wide drawer and removed a stack of large pages, black ink on fragile paper. On the first page, a colored photograph showed a mob of smiling people, standing elbow-to-elbow. The caption read: "Farmers Market Draws Thousands."

"What's that all about?" Fox asked.

"My Mom says the farmers used to bring their goods to Main Street one night a week. They'd close it off and sell all sorts of stuff."

"It looks like they're having fun. Are they from a clan or are they Untouchables?"

"Look," Tony said, pointing to the top of the sheet, "it's from 1995, the beginning of the Gadget Age."

Fox nodded. "Yeah, now I understand. Your Mom taught me about the Change, when people began to shift from face-to-face contact to remote contact... for just about everything."

"It must have been wild before the Change... when everybody moved all over the place, met each other, went to schools, gathered to listen to music or poetry."

Fox stared absently out the windows. "The internet

replaced all of that... and people got lazy, then scared after the *Nouveau-Polio* and *Indonesian Plague* outbreaks killed millions. They figured they could live out their lives without contact."

"Yeah. All those gadgets that connected everyone eventually left them... alone."

Fox paged through the stack of sheets and paused to stare at photographs of streets clogged with cars, and people speaking in groups. She clapped a hand over her mouth. Full-sheet pictures showed masses of people lying on cots in football stadiums, in parking lots, in auditoriums, with masked medical staff wandering between the rows.

Fox slid the drawer shut and shuddered. "Have you ever met an Untouchable?"

"Only once, near the airport runway where the supply drones land. The guy scared the hell out of me. Actually, he looked more upset than I was."

Fox grinned. "Well, with that wild hair of yours, who could blame 'im."

They ate their lunch of soda bread, carrot sticks, dried apple slices, and beer on a shaded balcony overlooking the downtown. A red-tailed hawk had built its nest at the top of a building's vent pipe. The bird's hoarse cries echoed down the corridors between decaying facades, bounced off plaster walls of dull gray and ochre that hadn't felt fresh paint in almost a century. Tony sat and read an illustrated book about the Chumash Tribe of Native Americans and their slow and peaceful demise. He was always reading something, but especially liked history. Fox covered page after page in her sketchbook with detailed pencil portraits of crumbling parapets, cracked walls, shattered windows, sidewalks with weeds sprouting from fissures caused by the roots of monstrous trees and their seedlings left un-pruned for decades.

"Someday, I'll make a book about all of this," she

said.

"That would be great. But you'd need to find a way to get it digitized before anybody would see it. You can't exactly sell them door-to-door to the Untouchables."

"Hey, quit stomping on my dream. At least I have one."

Tony knew she was right and shut up. In addition to painting, he liked playing his homemade guitar and performing with a group of other guys at the clan's weekly beer fests on the roof. The band hung out on the fourth level under the stairs, practiced tight harmonies for songs that they'd taught each other, and whaled on their homemade guitars, banjos, tambourines, and on Jimmy's bass fiddle. But Tony would turn eighteen in a few days and would have to join a work detail to help the clan. Fox had a few more weeks of freedom. Both had talked about running away, but to where, and to what?

As the sun set, they worked their way across the downtown and approached the Garage. Crawlers parked on the surrounding streets with officers watching the entrances. Midnight passed before they finally cleared out and the teenagers re-joined their parents. The camps smelled of disinfectant and full waste buckets. Tony couldn't wait until they painted once again in the clean air of the upper highlands.

⌣⌣⌣

Four days later after breakfast, they climbed the foothills that formed one side of the town's valley. Traffic in the Untouchable neighborhood was mostly remote-controlled vans and trucks serving each home, depositing groceries, medical supplies, clothing, or whatever had been ordered on the web. The vans moved fast, their cameras normally ignoring wayward pedestrians. But Fox and Tony took no chances and ducked behind shrubbery or abandoned cars whenever they heard the high whine of an electric vehicle.

They each carried four big cans of paint with brushes shoved into the pockets of their coveralls. The house they sought stood high in the foothills near the edge of town. Its wide glass windows had been replaced long ago with solid plaster, its sloping yard overgrown with chaparral plants covering the concrete walkway and steps that had once led from the street to the front door. But the solar panels on the roof looked new, along with four wind turbine units. Their mural covered half of the house facing the valley, a hillside scene that spread over walls, old window openings and part of the front door. After trudging up the steep hill carrying their paint, Tony and Fox collapsed in the shade of a manzanita, sucked in deep breaths, and wiped the sweat from their faces. Fox had forgotten to bring her water bottle. They took turns sipping from his canteen and watched the heat shimmer above the asphalt.

With the street clear, they hurried up the driveway and slid along the house's wall to the front door.

"Be quiet," Tony whispered. "Whoever's inside is probably real twitchy."

"It's worth it. Will you look at the definition I'm getting?" Fox pointed to the mural.

"Yeah, it's some of your best work. But just be quiet. We can finish up and be outta here by lunch. You did bring the lunch, didn't you?"

Fox grinned and patted her backpack. They set to work, opening paint cans, mixing the colors in cups, and rising to dab blotches of green, blue, yellow, and ochre onto the smooth plaster. They worked fast, with Tony laying down big blocks of color with his four-inch brush. The latex paint dried quickly, allowing Fox to come through and create images out of the seemingly-random pattern of colors. They worked steadily, not talking, the sun burning their backs.

Fox worked on the fine points of a rock outcropping that covered the front door, concentrating, a small paint brush clenched between her teeth. She rose from her squatting position and swayed, her face flushed. Tony grabbed hold of her just as she collapsed. He stretched her body out on the concrete pad, her long red hair forming a blazing corona around her head. Fox's arms and legs twitched and her eyes rolled back in her head. He grabbed his canteen and placed it to her lips. But she pushed it away, moaning. He splashed water on her face. Her whole body shook.

Tony stood and stared at the vacant street with not a van or even a garbage truck in sight. In the distance, the Garage rose above the town's skyline. He thought about running for help, but didn't want to leave her. He turned and pounded on the front door. Silence. He continued pounding.

"My girlfriend is sick. We need help."

Tony repeated his plea over and over. Finally, the metal slab cracked open. From the looks of it, the door hadn't moved in years. A green eye peered at him.

"Please, help us. We won't hurt you."

"How... do I know that?" a man asked in a raspy voice.

"We're artists, not criminals. Please help."

"So you're the ones that have been messing with my house."

"Yes, yes. Just let me bring her inside. We won't hurt you."

The green eye looked down at the redheaded girl shuddering on the concrete. The man chanted under his breath, "to do good or do no harm... to do good or do no harm... to do good or do no harm." Tony recognized the phrase but couldn't remember where it came from.

The door scraped open and a towering blond guy, with muscular arms and wearing some kind of head-set, motioned him inside. Tony bent and grabbed Fox underneath her arms and dragged her through the opening onto clean carpet. The Untouchable slammed the door behind them.

"Bring her in here," he directed.

Tony followed him into a large room with banks of video screens streaming a dozen or more different images. The room felt like the Garage did in wintertime after a rain. His sweat turned cold and he shivered.

"Lay her on the sofa." The man pointed to a long cushioned chair and Tony did as directed.

"Wait here."

The Untouchable moved to another room and returned with plastic bags filled with clear cubes. Tony touched them and drew his hand back.

The guy frowned. "What's wrong? You've never seen ice cubes?"

"Ah, no," Tony muttered.

The man took three small bags of cubes and placed one under each of Fox's armpits and one down her shorts. She moaned but continued to tremble.

"What's wrong with her?" Tony asked.

"Heatstroke. You're crazy to... to be outside in that sun."

He left the couple but returned shortly with a thick cut-glass pitcher of water. He poured some into a cup and handed it to Tony. "You'd better drink some yourself. You don't look so good... but then I haven't seen anyone face-to-face in... years."

Tony gulped the water, then held a full cup to Fox's mouth. "Come on," he murmured, "you gotta drink."

She opened her blue eyes, grabbed the cup and emptied it. After a while her flushed face returned to its normal color and she sat up, casting off the ice bags. "What happened? One minute I'm painting and the next I've got freezing water between my legs."

The Untouchable's hoarse laughter echoed throughout the house. Tony had noticed that the guy talked too loud, as if he wasn't used to speaking with people in the same space.

"Excuse me for laughing. I believe what you... you had was a heatstroke."

"How would you know about heat?" Tony said, glowering. "You probably never go outside this... this refrigerated bunker."

"Quite right, Mr. Painter. I moved to the CenCal Coast eight years ago from the Northeast. I haven't been outside since."

"So what do you do?" Fox asked. "Do you have, ya know, a wife? Girlfriend?" She massaged her cramping arms and legs, stood and moved unsteadily around the room, leaning against countertops for support while staring at the flickering vid screens.

The man watched her nervously. "I'm CEO of a physicians' consulting service, and a licensed doctor. This hillside spot gives me good satellite access, great for data and video uplinks and downloads."

The couple stared at each other. Tony had read the terms in books. But no one at the Garage had a computer or web access. It was all part of the weird stuff that the Untouchables did.

Tony asked, "But don't you have to meet your... your patients?"

"Good God no," he said. "We can do all our work in cyberspace, and leave the rest to the regional hospitals and labs. Hell, I haven't talked to... to another body in months. The drone vans unload supplies directly into my storage unit. If I need something repaired or serviced inside this house, I go to my safe room while the work's being done."

"But why?" Fox asked. "Why not go outside? There's lots of cool stuff to see and do. Aren't you lonely?"

"To answer your previous question, no, I don't have a wife, and no, I'm not lonely. I can get everything I need from the web."

"Everything?" Tony asked, and gave Fox a quick squeeze.

"Yes, even sex," the man shot back. "Today's pornography involves all five senses, and I can direct the action and have my choice of thousands of partners."

"But, don't you want... want friends?" Fox stammered.

"I have thousands of friends. I write or speak to dozens of them every day. And I can choose when to be alone and when to link up."

"Sounds... frightening," Tony said and frowned.

"On the contrary. Your world is the scary one... where nothing is certain or controlled... where people do cruel things to each other. As a consulting physician, I've viewed what your kind is capable of."

"But what about love?" Fox asked. "Do you love any of your cyber friends?"

He looked away. "I'm afraid that emotion is pretty much useless. Some of my fellow physicians are married. From what I can tell, love is a temporary condition, not worth the long-term investment."

Tony grunted and poured himself another glass of water. "So, thanks a lot for helping us, mister. We'll get out of here and leave you and your house alone."

"I don't think so," the man said, a faint smile spreading his lips for the first time. "You've been trespassing, defacing my house and lowering its resale value. I can't let that go unpunished."

"But why?" Tony asked. "You don't go outside, don't even know what we've painted."

"I know. I can see everything." He muttered something into his headset and a bank of vid screens clicked on, showing images of the outside of his house from various angles. One screen showed Fox and Tony dabbing away with their paint brushes.

"So you've known all along," Fox muttered.

"Yes... and now I have you."

Tony and Fox glanced at each other then bolted for the door. But it wouldn't open. They ran throughout the house but didn't discover any other opening to the outside. Returning to the video room, they found the Untouchable standing with his bulging arms folded across his chest, waiting.

"Why don't you have some more water, kiddies, while I contact the Police? They should be here momentarily."

"Wait, wait," Tony pleaded. "What if we repainted your house so it looked like it did before?"

"Nice try. But once outside in that savage world of yours, who knows what you'll do. I'm afraid that you don't have anything to bargain with... except maybe..."

"Except what?" Tony asked.

"Except maybe the affections of your girlfriend. The porn vids are good, but there's still room for improvement."

"You want to... to..." Fox clenched her fists and stepped forward.

"Easy, girl. I can break you and your pipsqueak boyfriend like twigs."

"Who's being savage now?" Tony muttered and moved next to Fox.

The man lunged at her, grabbed the front of her coveralls at the neckline and yanked downward, ripping the material away, exposing tanned flesh. She screamed and lashed out with a leg. But the guy twisted sideways and the blow glanced off his hip. Tony threw himself at the attacker, his fists swinging. The Untouchable held him off with one massive arm. A huge fist shot toward Tony's face, a burst of light as if a star went nova, then blackness.

He came to, sprawled on the floor across the room with a throbbing jaw, loose teeth, and a mouth full of blood from a mangled lip. Fox lay naked on the sofa, screaming. The attacker pinned her down with a knee and roughly fingered her groin. She flailed at him with clawed hands, trying to reach his eyes, her body bucking and heaving. He raised an arm and back-handed her hard across the face. He hit her again, and again. She lay still and moaned. He stepped back, removed his headset, and stripped naked, a hulking white and hairy man. He stretched out next to her. She remained motionless. The guy rolled on top of her and propped himself up, one massive paw around her throat and the other caressing her breasts.

On hands and knees, Tony crawled across the carpet and pulled himself up on a table leg. He grabbed the near-empty water pitcher, crept to where Fox and the Untouchable lay, and slammed it against the back of the man's head. It struck with a dull thud. Sucking in a deep breath, he drew it back and swung again with all his might. This time the pitcher came away smeared with blood. The attacker collapsed onto Fox. She pushed him off. He rolled onto the floor and stared up at them, his eyes fixed. A large crimson puddle stained the carpet.

Fox staggered to her feet and fell into Tony's arms. They stood trembling. Finally, when they had calmed, Fox tied what remained of her clothes onto her body, her chest bloodied from where the man had scratched her with his fingernails. A red mark covered most of one cheek. Tony bent and checked the Untouchable for a pulse. He couldn't find one.

"Are... are you all right?" he asked Fox.

"God, I can still smell that creep," she said and shuddered. "We gotta get outta here."

"I know, I know. We'll figure it out."

They stared at the bank of video screens that

flashed printed information, graphs and charts, photographs and written messages from around the world. Tony put on the man's headset and tried various voice commands, pressed several buttons. But nothing he did unlocked the front door.

"Wait here, I got an idea." He disappeared down a hallway and returned with an old-fashioned fire axe. "I think I can cut through the wall where the windows used to be. Stand back."

A short time later he stood with his hands on his knees, panting. They both stared out the hole that he'd slashed in the wall, then squeezed through it into the sizzling afternoon. After being trapped inside the cold house, the air felt like fire. Tony grabbed his canteen and splashed both of their faces. The high whine of a police crawler moving in their direction sounded in the distance. They raced downhill into the old commercial district. At a shady spot next to the creek, they talked about how much to tell their parents, and afterward, where to run.

Tony dipped his head in the stream then ran his figures through his tangled curls. "When the 'Forcers drive by that house, they'll know something's up. Besides, we left our paints behind. They'll know it was us."

"Maybe if we go to the Police and tell them our story..." Fox began, but stopped when Tony scowled.

"Who's gonna believe that an Untouchable invited two clansmen inside? That sounds crazy."

"Yeah, and there's no evidence that he tried to... to rape me."

"But there's plenty of our cells and prints around that place. We're pretty much screwed." Tony covered his face with his hands. "And when somebody who pays the 'Forcers' salaries gets killed, the Police will never let up."

They ran back to the Garage. Tony dreaded telling

his mom and the Slades about what had happened. But once he started, he recounted the full story, leaving out nothing. His mom sat stunned while Mrs. Slade hugged her daughter and cried. Mr. Slade disappeared and returned with the clan leader. The adults huddled and grumbled to themselves. Finally, they broke apart and scattered, except for Tony's mom.

"You two come with me," she ordered. They followed her hobbling form across the second level to the barber's camp. Inside the tent, the teenagers sat side-by-side, while Mr. Bochum clipped Tony's curls, shaved off his mustache, and bleached what was left of his hair blonde. He cut Fox's scarlet hair short then dyed it black, along with her eyebrows. As they finished up, three other couples that Tony and Fox didn't know well entered the tent.

"So these are the fugitives," one of the boys cracked. "It's about time us small guys get some recognition."

Mr. Bochum ordered the couples into hastily arranged chairs. The guys had their dark locks curled into bouncy mops, while the girls had their hair dyed crimson.

"What's this all about?" Fox asked.

"Does the word 'decoy' mean anything to you?" one of the new redheads answered.

"Don't worry, kids," Tony's mom said, "I'll explain it all when we get back to camp."

Once inside their tent, she poured the teenagers herbal tea and laid out the plan. The couple sat in stunned silence as shadows lengthened and sunset approached.

Outside, a fleet of police crawlers encircled the Garage. They'd been parked there since shortly after the fugitives had returned, barking out orders for Tony and Fox to surrender. Vans full of reserve officers had pulled up behind the crawlers and formed a gapless perimeter, their stun guns held at the ready. The blue and white flashing lights lit up the entire block and half the Garage's interior. An armored truck with blacked-out windows parked behind the vans and waited silently.

Inside the Garage, the clan members huddled in groups at the exits. Each group included one couple with a red-haired girl and a curly-headed boy. On the roof, the snickering Roofies knelt behind the parapet, fingered their full waste buckets, and waited for the signal.

Tony and Fox stood silently with one of the groups and listened to his Mom's final instructions.

"Your packs are stuffed with food and the canteens are full. Head south into the foothills. Stay away from the roads. You'll be too easy to spot if you use them. Keep moving and don't stop until you run out of food."

Tony hugged his trembling mother, her tears wetting his neck. Fox's father folded his daughter into his arms, his face gray and set. Her mother sobbed.

Tears streaked Fox's cheeks but she tried to smile through it. "Don't worry. We're gonna have a grand adventure, aren't we Tony?"

Tony's mother brushed away her tears and lowered her head. "And one more thing, Anthony," she murmured. "Don't ever come back."

Outside, a new voice blared through a loudspeaker. "Listen up, Touchables. This is Lieutenant Statler speaking. We don't want any trouble with your clan. Just send Tony and Fox out and we'll leave you alone. They'll be treated fairly. But if you don't cooperate, we're coming in to get them. You have five minutes to decide."

The rumble of voices within the clansmen groups grew then died. Tony grasped Fox's hand and squeezed. She kissed him. The minutes dragged by.

Then, it started with a whistle blast.

The Police advanced on the Garage.

"Who are the savages now?" Tony muttered.

As the 'Forcers neared the building, the Roofies stood and emptied their waste buckets over the parapet. The line of Police fell back, the officers using every swear word Tony had ever heard. But they regrouped and advanced again, yelling, their stun guns raised, face masks lowered, shields up. From inside the Garage someone struck the old school bell. The clansmen charged from the exits and ran in all directions, rushing the police lines, darting between them. The officers broke ranks and chased after the red-haired girls and their curly-headed companions. Some of them knelt and emptied their stun guns into the crowd. Dozens of people lay in the street, moaning.

"I got 'em, I got 'em," an officer bellowed and other Police joined him and hustled one of the decoy couples into a van. When the bell had sounded, Tony and Fox had held back and watched the mêlée develop. Now, they sprinted from the rear exit and cut a serpentine path down the boulevard until coming to a side street. A beanbag round hit Fox in the back of her thigh and she went down hard. Tony grabbed her and they hobbled away. Fox moaned, her face streaked with tears. But they kept moving. At the south edge of the city, they followed a drainage swale across open fields and climbed into the coastal hills, not stopping until they reached the ridgeline. Staring into the valley, they could pick out the cluster of crawlers, their lights still flashing. But another orange light poured from the Garage's openings. A haze of smoke hung over the building as the campsites burned.

The couple watched the flames for a long time. The crawlers retreated. A loud explosion shook the valley. A dust cloud engulfed the Garage. When it cleared, there was a new gap in the skyline, one less building for Fox to draw. The crawlers disappeared and the town once again became a black abyss in the center of a valley where only security lights twinkled from the hillside homes of the Untouchables.

"There'll be more of us heading south," Tony said.

Fox shook her head. "No, they'll take over the Library or find a school with a good roof. They're not leaving. It's their town too."

"We're losing a lot, ya know," Tony muttered and dropped his head.

"Yes, I... I know."

She encircled him in her arms and squeezed, his head pressed against her shoulder. He kissed her and they swayed together, their hearts pounding steadily, resolutely. Tony shuddered. Stepping back, he asked Fox gently to drop her trousers. He lightly touched the angry-looking red welt on the back of her left thigh. She jerked away from him.

"If we just keep moving, it'll feel better in a while. But you'll have a fist-sized bruise there in a day or so."

They slid down steep canyon slopes, heading south and west toward the half-submerged and abandoned beach towns, toward the rumored communes on the Channel Islands just off the Pacific Coast, where Chumash Indians had long ago worshiped their gods, painted strange images on rocks, and enjoyed their face-to-face lives.

2

They hiked through the night under a nearly-full moon, scrambling along game trails or crashing through chaparral until collapsing beneath a massive oak on a ridge overlooking the Pacific. They awoke in mid-afternoon and stood gaping. A rolling green sea stretched westward and slid beneath a fog bank several kilometers offshore. A beach town lay a couple hundred meters below them, divided by a broad free-way, its cracked concrete lanes studded with shrubs and trees.

"We gotta find some water," Tony said, shaking one of their empty canteens. "We guzzled most of our supply just getting here."

"We might find some down there."

"Yeah, maybe. The Untouchables probably live in those hillside mansions. But the rest of the town..."

The sea had flooded many of its streets, reminding Tony of library photographs of Midwest towns along the Missouri River after winter storms. In this ghost town, some buildings had folded into the black water, others showed only their roofs. Offshore, the remnants of a pier poked above the rolling waves. Closer to shore, the top three floors of what looked like a hotel rose above the ocean. Tony stared hard at some kind of canoe tethered to its fire escape. Smoke drifted from a pit on the roof next to a green patch of garden, a couple of spinning wind turbines, and a bank of solar panels.

"Someone's down there," he said, pointing. "Let's go... but be careful."

They pushed their way downhill through shoulder-high wild mustard until reaching the upper hillside neighborhoods of the Untouchables.

"I'm surprised they get enough sunshine here to make those solar panels work," Fox said and pointed to the homes.

"Yeah, but they'll always have the damn sea wind, not to mention the smell of rotting kelp, salt air, the stinky fish."

"Ah, come on, give it a chance," Fox scolded. "You should love the ocean. It's so... so open and wild."

Scrambling downhill and across the freeway, they came to the flooded area bordered by coarse gray sand, a new beach that carpeted the old streets.

"Do you think you can swim that far?" Tony asked and pointed to the hotel.

"You're kidding, right? I can swim a lot better than you. When I was a kid, I hung out at the lake and swam every day."

"Good, 'cause I don't see anything we can use as a boat."

Fox pointed. "Grab that tub to put our backpacks in."

She waded into the cold sea and headed toward what had once been the shoreline. Tony retrieved the plastic tub and hurried to catch up. The cavernous storefronts on either side of the corridor stared at them, like a skull's empty eye sockets. They pushed forward, without stopping, being careful to skirt old cars and piles of junk partially hidden by the water. About a hundred meters from the hotel, they placed their backpacks in the tub and began swimming. Tony pushed at the water, feeling clumsy but strong while Fox slipped through it, hardly making a ripple. They nudged their cargo before them and quietly app-roached the hotel's fire escape.

From inside the building came a high-pitched

shriek. Two floors up a little boy ran onto a railing-less balcony and jumped into the sea. A bigger girl followed him, laughing all the way down. The children surfaced immediately and pulled toward the ladder. When they neared Fox and Tony, they stopped to tread water.

The little boy asked, "Who are you? Are you Inlanders?"

Fox smiled, "I guess we are. We've come from over those mountains." She pointed to the golden hills studded with oaks.

"What are you doing here?" the girl asked.

"We're traveling," Tony said. "Are your parents here? Can you ask them if we can visit?"

The children climbed the ladder and metal stairs, agile as squirrels, and disappeared through an open window two floors up. In a moment, a bare-chested man with a scraggly beard and long hair clambered down. The man grinned at them, but his eyes stared coldly.

"You gotta be really hurtin' to swim out here," he said.

"Can we join you?" Tony croaked. "My legs are killing me and..."

"Oh sure, sorry. Give me your stuff and climb on up."

Tony felt nervous about handing over their supplies, but figured they'd never make it anywhere if they didn't trust someone. He pushed the tub toward the man, stepped onto the ladder, then turned and pulled Fox up.

"I'm Tony and this is Fox."

"I'm Noah, just like the guy in the Bible. You've already met Jonathan and Sarah. My wife Margaret is upstairs. Come on up and have some tea."

Tony and Fox climbed to the balcony and let the wind and sun dry their clothes a bit before ducking inside the apartment. The huge room had windows spaced every few feet. Paintings and crafts hung on the walls between the openings.

"Welcome, welcome," said Margaret, a graying middle-aged woman with a flat face and large bare feet. "Come sit and tell us about your journey." She stared into their battered faces and raised a trembling hand to her cheek. "What... what happened to you two?"

Tony glanced at Fox and noticed the dark bruises shadowing her face. He sucked in a deep breath. "We ran into a bit of trouble."

"Yes, I can see," Margaret murmured.

"Sit down and tell us about it," Noah said and motioned to chairs that looked like they had been scavenged from different houses. The teapot and cups on the low table looked handmade.

"You know," Noah continued, "I was listening to my radio this morning. The Police are looking for a young couple that killed a citizen up in de Tolosa. You know anything about that?"

The color drained from Fox's face, making the bruises stand out even more. She nervously fingered her damp hair, the black dye coming off on her hands. The foursome sat quietly for a few minutes until Tony spoke.

"Yeah, we know about that. The 'Forcers are looking for us."

Margaret frowned and pulled her squirming kids to her side. "You killed a man?"

Tony stared into her eyes. "Yes. The bastard tried to rape Fox."

The building shook and Tony shuddered.

"Don't worry," Noah said. "It's just the incoming tide. The bottom floor of this place was built like a massive seawall that goes down to bedrock. Only a tsunami could take us out."

"How did it happen?" Margaret asked.

In a halting voice, Fox recounted the events of the previous day. The family listened in wide-eyed silence, even the children. Afterward, Margaret whispered something in her daughter's ear and the kids moved off to play at the other end of the room, where huge cushions covered the floor.

"We tell our children *everything*," Margaret said, "the good and the bad. But rape and killing... I'll talk with the kids later."

Noah gave Tony and Fox the careful once-over and Tony wondered if he had the guts to jump off the balcony into the sea if they had to leave quickly.

Noah relaxed into his chair. "We don't get many travelers passing through. You're the first in more than five years."

Tony nodded. "Do you belong to a clan?"

Noah chuckled. "Nah. There aren't enough people in this town... just a few families that hung around after the sea flooded the place. It came up fast... was all over with by '57. There's a group called the Dunites that set up camp down the coast. But they don't have more than a couple dozen families."

"What about the Untouchables?" Fox asked.

"The what?" Margaret looked confused.

"You know, the people who stay inside."

Noah grinned. "Oh, them. We call 'em the No-see-ums 'cause we never see them outside. There are a few dozen that live on the hill. But we're a ways from the nearest drone supplyport and the vans only make weekly drop-offs."

"So where are you folks headed?" Margaret asked.

Tony looked at Fox and wondered if this couple would tell the Police. Would he and Fox be captured, hauled off to the regional jail before they even escaped the district?

"We're heading... heading south," Tony said.

"Huh," Noah grunted and scratched his beard.

Outside the sun had dropped into the western fogbank and a gray mist moved onshore, enveloping the hotel. The two kids jumped up and ran around the room, closing all the windows. In a few minutes the outside world disappeared into a swirling whiteness.

As the room darkened, Margaret switched on strange-looking electric lights, moved to a far corner and took down plates and glasses from a cabinet. "I hope you two like rock cod and vegetables. I grow what I can in our garden and Noah does the fishing."

"Where do you get your water to drink and grow stuff?" Tony asked.

"We've got a solar unit on the roof that turns sea-water into a fresh supply. Ya know, the sun actually does shine here."

"We're almost out of water and appreciate any you can spare," Fox said.

"That's not a problem," Margaret said. "Give me your canteens and I'll fill them."

"Our son Jeremy should be back soon from scavenging," Noah said. "You'll like him. He's about your age and did all those paintings on the walls."

Fox looked around the room at the artwork and grinned. "They're really good. Where did he find oils and acrylics and the painters' panels? I've been searching for years."

"Are you an artist?" Margaret asked.

"Yes, Tony and I have painted murals all over de Tolosa. That's how we got in trouble with the Police... and with the... the man we..."

"Jeremy found all his paints in a shed across town," Margaret said. "This place used to be an artist colony before the Change. Noah's great grandfather built the hotel for tourists who traveled hundreds of miles to buy original artwork of this coastline."

"Yeah, now the... the No-see-ums get everything from the internet," Tony said and scowled. "I've read that they can download an image at almost no cost."

Noah disappeared to the balcony and climbed the fire escape. In a few minutes he returned with a charred piece of something laid out on a wooden plank.

"I hope you like cod. I caught it this morning and she's been smokin' most of the afternoon."

Tony stared at the smoldering blackness. "We Inlanders don't get a lot of fish... maybe a few trout or bass from the lake, but not..."

Noah chuckled. "Just spread some of Margaret's salsa on it. But watch out for the bones."

The children gathered around the table, their mother handing them plates and pointing out where to sit. Fox and Tony devoured the food, downing the green salad like rabbits raiding a cabbage patch. No one at the table spoke, as if paying silent homage to the world that gave them food to survive and prosper. The adults sat back while Margaret poured beer into stout mugs. The couple sipped the bitter brew and watched the soft fog darken. Near sundown, the sound of someone climbing the fire escape rousted the children. They ran to the balcony.

"It's Jeremy, it's Jeremy!" they called and jumped up and down. "What did you bring us, Jeremy?"

A tall boy climbed through a window opening and dropped a full sack onto the floor. He wore nothing but shorts, his tanned body slender like his father's, blonde-haired, his face bare of beard or mustache.

"Come here and meet our guests," Margaret called. "They're from de Tolosa and are traveling... south."

Tony stuck out his hand and the boy stared at it for a moment before taking it into his own.

Noah laughed. "My son hasn't had anyone to shake hands with for a long time, if ever."

Jeremy grinned. "Sorry I wasn't here when you arrived, but I found some really neat stuff scavenging down the coast and lost track of time."

"Yeah, I know how it is," Tony said. "I used to spend hours doing the same thing."

Jeremy knelt and wolfed down the food his mother had held back for him. He guzzled two mugs of beer, all the while staring at Fox.

Margaret nudged him. "Jeremy, slow down enough to talk with our guests."

"That's okay, Margaret, let him eat," Fox said. "We know what it's like to be hungry."

"Yeah, but talking... with a pretty girl... is much nicer... than this cod," Jeremy said between mouthfuls.

Fox laughed and Tony glanced at her. She stared at the tall boy, smiling while pulling at her ragged hair ends.

"So why are you guys here? How long can you stay?" Jeremy asked.

Fox told him their story, including a summarized version of the killing of the Untouchable. Jeremy sat up, reached forward and touched Fox's arm.

"I'm sorry you had to go through that. I always knew the No-see-ums were a bunch of horny bastards."

"Yeah, I have no problem killing anybody who tries messing with my... my girl," Tony blurted.

Both Fox and Jeremy gave him a strange look.

Noah grinned. "Sounds like the alpha wolf howling to me," he said and slapped Tony on the back. "Relax. You'll just have to get used to living with a pretty woman."

Tony shot him a dirty look, felt his face burn with embarrassment. The conversation lagged.

Jeremy dragged the sack to the center of the room and began unloading it: bolts of cloth found in the attic of a shopping mall to the south; sealed containers of salted nuts from a partially submerged grocery; and swim fins for the children.

"I got the fins from the underwater warehouse," he explained. "Looks like it was used to house diving equipment. There's a bunch of kayaks there too."

"What's a kayak?" Fox asked.

"It's like the one tied up to the fire escape."

"Ah, like a canoe," Tony said.

"Yeah, but you use a paddle with blades at both ends. The ones I found are ocean-going craft that can seat two. I dragged a couple home. Tomorrow I'm going back for more stuff that's submerged, but it's tough. My lungs really ache and the water's gettin' colder."

"I'll come with you," Noah said and refilled everyone's mug with beer. "I have some marijuana if anyone wants to toke up."

Fox laughed. "Nah, I'd better not. That stuff makes me..." She looked at Jeremy and giggled. "Besides, us Touchables are beer drinkers."

After dinner Jeremy took Fox on a guided tour of his paintings hanging on the wall. He didn't invite Tony to join them. Margaret sat on a cushion next to Tony.

"You'll have to forgive my son, Tony. There are only a handful of girls anywhere near Jeremy's age within a day's walk of this place. He's a bit... a bit..."

"I get it," Tony muttered. "But Fox and I have been together for a long time."

"I can tell that," Margaret said and smiled.

Tony turned to her and Noah. "I really appreciate your kindness, but we'll need to leave tomorrow. I don't want to get you folks in trouble if the Police come looking for us. If we found you guys so easily, they will too."

Noah nodded. "The 'Forcers patrol this area regularly, but normally stay outta the water. You'd better avoid the roads and travel the coast. The inland areas have lots of eyes as you get closer to the supplyport in

Santa Maria."

"What about using one of those... those kayaks that Jeremy found?" Tony asked.

"Yeah, you could make good time by sea," Noah said. "But the afternoon winds come up strong and the waves whitecap. Unless you're an expert boatman..."

"I'm a quick learner."

"I'll bet you are," Noah said. "I'll take you two out early tomorrow morning and show you the basics."

"Great, I wasn't looking forward to walking much farther. My feet are killing me."

Noah laughed. "Paddling a kayak is easy on the feet... but hard on the back and arms. But both of you look tough enough."

Fox and Jeremy finished their tour of his artwork and rejoined the group. "Jeremy really is a wonderful painter," Fox said excitedly. "I could really learn a lot from studying his work and—"

"I'm sure we both could," Tony said, "but we need to leave tomorrow."

Both Jeremy and Fox frowned. "Why so fast?" Fox asked.

"The Police must be onto our disguise by now and will be looking for us."

"But, can't we stay just a day or two?"

"I'm sorry."

"You don't look sorry," Jeremy growled.

"Hey, we're the ones on the run, not you. You just want to mess around with my—"

"Tony, cut it out," Fox said, her face darkening.

Noah laughed, stood and let out a good imitation of a wolf call. "I'd better put together a pack of supplies for you two and figure out how to lash it to the kayak."

Fox slumped next to Tony but wouldn't look at him. The family moved to different areas of the apartment. Noah and Margaret read Ellery Queen novels, the kids working on some kind of puzzle and Jeremy sulking in a corner, sketching on a tablet with the nub of a pencil and staring at Fox the whole time. Outside the incoming swells rumbled against the hotel's foundation, causing a slight tremor that kept Tony on edge. Finally, the family turned in after showing the couple the latrine, a hole cut in the deck of one of the hotel unit's balconies, directly over the crashing surf. Tony shuddered when he remembered that he and Fox had swum through that same area to reach the fire escape. But, he figured, it's a big ocean.

He lay next to Fox on a thin pad, her back to him. When he placed a hand on her shoulder, she pulled away. Finally, she rolled over and faced him.

"I'm so mad at you I could spit," she hissed.

"I know. I'm sorry I got jealous."

"Jeremy is a nice guy, but he's not..."

"Look, I can tell that he wants you."

"Yeah, well so did most of the guys back at the Garage."

"It's just hard for me to watch, ya know? We're gonna run into guys that haven't talked face-to-face with a... a beautiful woman for a long time."

"Well, do you trust me?"

"Yes. But..."

"But what?"

"But remember, we're not with the clan anymore. There are no rules out here. This is like the pre-Change Wild West. We just gotta play it, you know, smart."

"Nice save," Fox said. "I was wondering how you were gonna get outta that one."

She dug him in the stomach then kissed him gently, avoiding the mangled part of his lower lip. He wanted to take her right then, but would feel embarrassed if he woke any of the family. He wrapped his arm around her and pulled her close, felt her warmth soothe the ache in his muscles as he dropped into a dream-filled sleep.

In the morning, Margaret fed them thick slices of coarse bread spread with wild berry jam. They washed it down with herb tea. Tony chewed carefully, his jaw swollen and throbbing from the Untouchable's blow. Noah took Tony and Fox out in one of the two-man kayaks, a sky-blue craft that almost disappeared against the blue-green Pacific. He showed them how to paddle and steer, to run shoreward with the waves, to run against them, and gave them tips for what to do when they capsized. Their slender craft looked about six meters long, had a molded and sealed plastic hull, with two seats and a central storage area set into a depressed cockpit. A hatch located at the raised bow opened to a watertight compartment. A similar compartment occupied the stern.

"You will roll this thing," Noah said, "especially with all your gear strapped to it. So ya gotta know how to save the paddles, right the boat, and get back in."

After a few fun rolls in the morning sea, they returned to the hotel. The family said their goodbyes, with the exception of Jeremy who stood sullenly on the roof and watched. Noah helped them gather their things and secure their backpacks and new provisions to the tie-downs at mid-ship. They stowed their food in the watertight compartments. With a thank you and wave, Tony and Fox pushed off and paddled out beyond the surf line. Fox sat in the front seat with Tony in the rear, working the rudder with his feet to keep them tracking in a straight line. A north wind blew cold but not hard and the sea stayed flat. Fox twisted around and grinned at Tony.

"Where to, my Captain?" she called.

"South, matey, south."

3

They turned the boat toward a point of land that lay far beyond a coastline of towering sand dunes and scrubland. The sun rose and the fog burned off. As the wind picked up, so did the size of the swells. Tony felt like they rode the back of some slow-bending serpent, one minute in the trough, out of sight of land, and the next riding high on the crest, surveying the broad sweep of the CenCal coast. He remembered inspecting a copy of a painting in the Library titled "Gulf Coast" by Winslow Homer. For a while he felt like the black man on the deck of that derelict sailboat, slanting through a treacherous sea with the boat's mast snapped and the water filled with sharks. Tony studied the sea's textured surface and the sky above, relieved to find only brown pelicans flying in long single-file lines, skimming the surface in search of a meal.

The fugitives didn't talk, paddled steadily. Tony thought about his mother, imagined her hobbling along the streets of de Tolosa with the other Touch-ables, looking for another home. He tried to put it out of his mind, focused on counting each stroke of the paddle, the cadence of his deep breaths. He figured Fox must be doing the same, her head rolling with each pull of her two-bladed paddle. By noon, the hotel had disappeared into the haze. They moved farther offshore and paused for lunch, chewing on nuts and berries that Margaret had packed and part of their own apple and raisin supply from the Garage.

They bobbed gently on a flat sea. "How far do you

think we've come?" Fox asked.

"I don't know. Can't be more than a few kilometers. But my shoulders feel like it's been a few hundred."

"Why don't you let me paddle for a while and you can take a break. With this southern current, we'll still make good time."

Tony grinned. "Thanks. I'll do the same for you when you get tired. Have you seen anything onshore?"

"Yeah, a few drone crawlers blasted past on the beach. They were really screaming. Didn't look like any normal patrol I've seen inland."

"I wonder why they're even out here? There's nothing but scrub land and dunes, no place for the Untouchables to live."

Fox frowned. "I'll bet they're looking for us. We're lucky we blend in with the waves."

"Yeah, but if they spot us, we've got no place to run."

They paddled in silence all afternoon, stayed well offshore, and kept a low profile whenever they spotted crawlers on the beach. After a day on the sea, Fox moaned and muttered to herself. All of Tony's joints ached from the constant twisting. The sun hung just a few centimeters above the horizon, and the wind freshened. They decided to go ashore for the night. Tony hadn't spotted a drone crawler for quite some time.

Turning the boat, they paddled toward shore. Ahead lay a narrow beach backed by tall dunes, with smaller ones closer to the water. Spindly-legged birds strutted along the shore, probing the wet sand with their long upturned beaks. A colony of seagulls bedded down for the night, their beaks tucked under their wings. Tony studied the beach in both directions. The shore angled steeply from the waterline and the surf thundered before them.

He sucked in a deep breath and rolled his shoulders. "Okay, when I say go, paddle as hard as you can."

The swells pushed them toward the beach. At the crest of a wave Tony yelled "Go!"

They paddled furiously as the wave broke, rocketing them forward. Fox let out a long whoop. A section of the wave sent a wall of whitewater roaring toward them from their starboard side. The kayak lurched sideways. Tony held his breath. Their world turned upside down. He grasped his paddle tightly and let the roaring foam smother him. Something banged his head and he realized it was the unsinkable kayak, bouncing over the water toward the shore. He struggled to stand in the waist-deep sea, the undertow pulling at his legs. Fox stood a few meters away, laughing. The kayak rested hull-up near water's edge.

"We gotta practice our landings," Tony called and grinned at her.

They quickly righted their boat and stood wet and shivering. Tony checked the hatches of the bow and stern compartments; they'd remained watertight and their food dry.

"Look." Fox pointed to the north.

A sand cloud bloomed on the horizon and he could just make out flashing blue and white lights.

"Crawlers! Come on," he yelled. Grabbing the kayak's bow line, he began hauling it toward the dunes.

Fox joined him. "We'll never make it. They'll spot the drag marks. We'd better carry her."

"They'll spot our footprints no matter what."

"Crap."

They could just make out the outlines of the crawlers, the high whine of their engines audible above the wind and surf noise. The couple lifted the kayak by its bow and stern and staggered across the beach, gasping for breath. The crawlers' screams grew louder. From out of the dunes scrambled a band of natives wearing ragged clothes and short capes made out of some kind of animal hides. Fox and Tony froze in their tracks, open-mouthed.

A tall man sporting a full beard but with clipped hair reached them first.

"What the hell are you gawking at?" he said, laughing. The group tore the kayak from their arms and ran inland, disappearing into the dunes while other natives followed behind to erase their tracks with tree branches. Fox went down on her knees. But two of the natives, one of them a dark-haired pretty woman, bent down and hauled her upright and spirited her along. They passed through gaps between the dunes, the band muttering to themselves, and headed toward a dense eucalyptus woods.

"Keep moving, keep moving," the tall man yelled and the group doubled its pace, charging through deep sand without pausing, half-carrying, half-dragging Tony and Fox along with them. At the tree line they set the couple down and ran between the closely-spaced trunks, across scrubland and into a dense willow thicket that bordered a small dune lake. The inside of the thicket opened up into an encampment.

Tony and Fox knelt on all fours, gasping for breath. *This is nothing like running on pavement*, he thought. He sat next to a heaving Fox and watched her red face gradually return to its normal color, watched the clansmen go about their business as if they had just returned from a stroll down the beach. They had set the kayak, paddles, and their gear in a small clearing. The camp had a central fire pit where various pieces of meat and fish roasted on spits. A dozen or more cone-shaped huts constructed of reeds surrounded the fire. Tony recognized their design from a history book he'd read on the Chumash Indians. The huts' sides were adorned with animal skins, shells, and flotsam from the sea. The ribs of a huge animal, probably a whale, formed the frame of the largest hut. The tall man emerged from its low opening and walked toward them. Tony stood to greet him.

"My name is Dunham," the man said and extended a hand.

Tony grabbed it and gave it a hard shake. "My name's Tony and this is... is my girl, Fox."

"I'm glad to see that some of you travelers still know the old traditions."

Fox leaned forward and grabbed Dunham's hand and squeezed it hard. Dunham grinned. "Ah, another strong woman. We have a few around here, my wife included."

"Thanks for helping us," Tony said. "I was surprised that the crawlers didn't chase us inland."

"The trees stop 'em... and they normally don't have any reason to bother us. There are no Hide-a-ways living around here that need protection."

"Yeah, we call 'em the Untouchables," Fox said and smiled for the first time since the chase.

"What's the name of your clan?" Tony asked.

"We call ourselves the Dunites, after the original group that camped near here back in the 1930s. We live off the land and only trade with the Floodies for tools that we can't make and for medicines."

"Floodies?"

"You know, the people that live in the flooded cities up north."

"Ah, yes." Tony nodded. "We stayed with one of the families last night."

"I'll bet it was Noah and Margaret," Dunham said. "Nice people... but I'm worried about their boy. Jeremy's gonna need a wife soon... and that could be a problem."

Fox's face darkened with the mentioning of

Jeremy's name but she stayed quiet.

"Why don't you two come to my hut and let's talk. You can meet my wife."

On entering the shelter, Tony realized that only he could stand upright while both Fox and Dunham had to bend over. They sat on grass-filled cushions.

"This is my wife, Jane," Dunham said, grasping the hand of the dark-haired woman Tony had seen on their dash inland. "We both grew up with the Dunites and I've been their leader for five years."

"Do you want some tea? I make it from wild mint." Jane poured a greenish-amber liquid into earth-colored cups.

The group sipped the tart liquid in silence before Jane finally asked, "So what are you two doing here in our little piece of paradise?"

"We come from de Tolosa and are heading south," Tony said.

When Tony didn't say anything more, Dunham cleared his throat, "But why are you running from the Police? Normally we see maybe one beach patrol a week. But there's been ten times that many in the last couple of days. And that last one wasn't drones."

Tony hesitated before answering, his mind spinning. *Maybe these folks would turn them in to the 'Forcers just to reestablish the peace. Maybe they hated outsiders of any kind. Maybe they're cannibals and would roast them over their fire.* With that last crazy thought, Tony burst into nervous laughter.

Fox's mouth dropped open. "What's wrong with you, Tony? Go... go ahead and tell them. Dunham and Jane seem like good people."

Tony nodded and sucked in a deep breath. "Both Fox and I are artists. We were painting a mural on an Untouchable's house when Fox had a heat stroke. A man took us inside. He seemed nice enough, gave us ice and water. But then he tried to rape Fox. I... I killed him."

The crackle from the fire pit and muted voices outside made the only sounds. The silence lengthened. Finally, Dunham pulled his fingers through his scraggly beard and muttered, "Killing someone is serious shit."

"Yeah, I know that," Tony said too loudly. "The 'Forcers blew up the Garage where our clan lived, probably because they wouldn't turn us in."

"Your clan sounds like a fine group of people," Jane said.

The foursome sat very still, as if letting the reality of the killing settle in. Tony wondered how often he'd have to explain it on their southbound odyssey. Maybe he needed to cook up a good lie and avoid the whole trauma because it upset Fox. She sat with her face buried in her hands, shaking. It grew dark inside the hut.

Dunham cleared his throat. "Well look, you're welcome to stay the night and share a meal with us Dunites. It's music night and should be fun. But we can't risk you staying longer. The Police already treat us like squatters. There's a group of Hide-a-ways back east that own the dunes. They want to build sand bunkers and run a road out here for the delivery vans, use the shore wind for power. They'll use any excuse to sic the 'Forcers on us."

"I understand," Tony said. "We'll be gone before dawn."

"I'm sorry," Jane said. "It must be hard on you two." She reached forward and gently touched the deep bruises that had formed on Fox's face. "But you've got the right idea about heading south. We've heard good things about the communes down there."

Outside, a bell rang. The babble of voices grew louder. Dunham rose and pulled four plates and mugs from a hutch shoved against the wall. He handed a set to Fox and Tony and they moved outside to where a line had already formed near the central fire pit. He moved to the head of the line and cleared his throat.

"Listen up, fellow Dunites. Tonight we have two Inlanders visiting us from de Tolosa. They'll be sharing our food and staying with Jane and I until the morning. Maybe we can convince one or both of them to share some of their fine Inlander music after supper."

Dunham returned, grinning. "You two do know how to sing or play something?"

Fox chuckled. "The gulls sing better than I can. But Tony is... is great."

They sat on logs surrounding the fire pit and ate the meal with their fingers: strong-tasting meat of some sort, steamed clams, and a broad-leafed vegetable with red veins that had a spicy taste. Tony watched the clan eat, a quiet group that talked in soft tones. He noticed that there were few children; most families had only one or two.

"Where are all the kids? In our clan, there was always a horde of 'em swarming the Garage."

Jane smiled. "We encourage people to control their family size. We want to remain here in the dunes. If our clan grows too much, we won't be able to sustain ourselves and will have to move somewhere else or forage longer distances for food."

Fox asked, "So how do you manage to, ya know, keep girls from getting pregnant?"

"Well it's certainly not by abstinence." Jane laughed and dug Dunham in the ribs. "But seriously, we trade deer meat to a Floodie who lives over an old pharmaceutical warehouse. They have a stash of BC pills and condoms that should last a few generations. By keeping our numbers down and being careful, we should be all right. How about you two?"

"Ah, we... we handle it just fine," Tony said and

dipped his head, conscious for the first time that other Dunites around them listened in on their conversation.

Fox grinned. "Yeah, as if *you* pay any attention to birth control."

After supper, several people disappeared into the trees and returned with flutes, large and small drums, and a variety of strange contraptions with thick gut strings. But one gray-haired woman with a dolphin tattoo across her chest and a flower behind her ear brought a guitar. When she took it out of its ragged case, Tony's jaw dropped. He had only seen pictures of such instruments in hundred-year-old magazines. The Martin had steel strings that looked almost as ancient as the instrument and were covered with a greenish patina. But when the woman strummed its strings, it made a sweet rumble that caused Tony to yearn for his own homemade guitar and the tight harmonies of the Garage boys back in de Tolosa.

After everyone more-or-less got in tune, the musicians played instrumental music that he'd never heard, followed by small groups singing what sounded like their own compositions, songs of the sea, of dune life, of the face-to-face world before the Change, before the rising oceans, before the rise of the Hide-a-ways. While the musicians played, women filled their mugs with beer. It tasted sweet, like it had been made from wild honey. Tony gulped down a mugful and the serving ladies refilled it immediately. As the night came on, a high cloudbank rolled onshore, blotting out the stars and the moon. Many of the Dunite couples staggered to their feet and danced in circles in front of the musicians, their arms flying above their heads, faces wet with sweat, mouths grinning. Those not dancing pulled their log seats closer to the fire pit. The singing got louder. Dunham leaned over his wife toward Tony and Fox. "Here comes the best damn part," he slurred.

"You'd better get ready."

The dancers stopped their gyrating and moved back to their seats. The woman with the guitar adjusted one of the strings then handed it to an old geezer to her left. The guy and his wife sang an ancient blues song that Tony recognized as Saint James Infirmary. Afterwards, the crowd clapped and hollered and the guitar got passed to the next person around the circle. When the instrument reached Tony he tuned each string carefully and played notes and chords in rapid succession, buying himself time. The crowd settled down.

"What should I play?" he whispered to Fox.

"Jeez, I don't know—what about that old song with the strange words, 'It's all right Ma, I'm only bleedin'.'"

"Yeah, that might work."

Tony retuned the strings and began to sing. The cold night air stung his throat but he forced himself to sing through it. In between the verses he stared around the circle. Most of the Dunites seemed to be dreaming, thinking about something far beyond what they knew and understood. When he finished the song, the crowd whooped and hollered. Jane looked at Tony and shook her head, wiping away a tear. "We could use your music. It's a shame... a real shame."

The guitar continued around the circle. The crowd got drunker and drunker. Tony pulled Fox toward him and kissed her. Some of the Dunites cheered. The fire had almost burned out when the foursome stumbled back to the hut. Tony and Fox slumped onto a soft mattress that Jane said was stuffed with tule down and seabird breast feathers. In the darkness they waited until they heard the other couple's snores before struggling out of their trousers and making quiet love, their bodies shuddering like wind-blown eucalyptus leaves. Afterward, Tony wrapped his arms around Fox and stared into the darkness, his mind

45

already spinning, thinking about the morning, the dash into the sea, heading toward someplace as unknown and wondrous as... the Southland.

4

Captain Hanpian slumped in his home-office chair and stared dully at the vid screens for the umpteenth time, watching the record of the unmitigated Garage disaster unfold. His men had failed to capture the young punks. Instead three decoy couples waited in holding cells to be released, since it wasn't a crime to dye your hair red. Then Lieutenant Statler had given the order prematurely to blow up the Garage. Hanpian had hoped to use its destruction as leverage to convince the clan's leadership to disclose which way the fugitives had run and a description of their disguises. Lieutenant Statler, now Sergeant Statler, had screwed that up big-time.

A video screen bleeped and Hanpian bent his aging pale body forward and pushed a button. Commander Pynard glared at him from her rooftop office at Regional Headquarters in Goleta. The building once housed University Administration before all the colleges went to online systems and had shut down their campuses.

"So what the hell is the status of your murder case, Ben?" the Commander asked. "I need some good news. The brass in Sack City is all over my ass about it."

Hanpian drew a mental picture of the commander's imposing ass and shuddered. "I can imagine. We haven't had a murder in this District in three years, and homicides are way down statewide."

"Damn it, tell me something I don't know."

"There's not much to tell. The clan members might have scattered throughout de Tolosa and we're having a hard time questioning anybody. I'm still on the look-out for the boy's mother. But I don't have the staff for a building-to-building search. A couple of nights ago, a shore patrol spotted something strange along the coast, south of the Floodies. The vids are too fuzzed to get detail, but it looks like two people in some kind of craft coming ashore."

"I knew it, I knew it," Pynard said excitedly. "They're heading down coast."

"Yes, that would be my bet too... and staying away from the roads. But we don't have many eyes on that area since Vandenberg Air Force Base shut down."

"How fast can they move? If they reach El Lay, they'll be gone forever."

The Captain sighed. Pynard always stated the obvious, as if that could solve anything. She depended on the creativity of her District chiefs, then took credit for their work. *Typical*, he thought.

"Satellite weather shows some storms coming on-shore in the next week. That should slow them a bit. I'm thinking maybe we should station a squad at Gaviota Pass and intercept them before they get far-ther south—if in fact that was them on the video."

"Just do it, Ben. At least I'll have something to tell the brass. So who was this citizen that the punks killed anyway?"

Hanpian bit his lip and swore under his breath, angry that he didn't have more to report on a citizen who lived in *his* Patrol District. "We don't have much of a file here—and Central Records had even less. He was the CEO of a consulting physicians' service of some sort. His psych profile hasn't been updated in years, but his last one showed problems with women. I figure there was something going on between the girl and the citizen and that the boy killed him over it. But the citizen had disconnected all the vid coverage inside his home, so we have no digital record."

"But you have the couple's prints and cells, right?" The Commander sounded impatient.

"Oh yes. It may be a bit old school but they're the murderers, all right. Their motive is still unknown."

"Keep me posted. Your District has been quiet for a long time. I hate to see that change."

The Commander's image disappeared from the screen before he could reply. Hanpian let out a deep breath, glad that he could get back to actual police work. He studied his map screen of the coast, picked a spot to set up base camp for the intercept squad, and then sent various messages to his subordinates to make it happen. With 120 kilometers of coastline between the dunes and the intercept point, he knew he had plenty of time to plan carefully. He sighed and pressed another button on his console.

"Sergeant Statler, what have you learned about the boy's mother?"

The sergeant's sharp voice boomed throughout Hanpian's home-office. "Nothing much, Captain. Because of her... her disability she'll be easy to spot. But we haven't found where the Touchables are holed up."

"Have you staked out their gardens and sewer farm?"

"Yes sir. But they've staying away."

"They can't hide forever. Tomorrow start a grid search of the downtown, then fan out from there."

"But Captain, we only have—"

"Just do it. Roll in the quiet drones to scan the streets first, then follow up on likely sites—schools, churches, commercial buildings—that could hold a crowd."

"Are you sure they've stayed together?" Statler asked.

"No. But that clan has been together a long time... and they're tough. Just keep looking."

"Will do, Captain... and again, I'm, I'm sorry about

the—"

Hanpian cut him off before he finished and shifted his gaze to the map screen, wondering what it would feel like to sail south through the rolling seas, along such a treacherous stretch of coastline.

5

They walked slowly through the dunes, not speaking, a fresh onshore breeze pushing at them, blowing the sand in their faces. Four Dunites carried their kayak between them, its storage area crammed with supplies, including some wild mint tea in an old plastic jar. Tony and Fox had said their goodbyes to Dunham and Jane back at camp. The rest of the clan slept.

Reaching the shoreline, the Dunites laid the craft at water's edge and faded into the dunes.

"Not very friendly of them," Tony muttered.

"I think that's what some clans do," Fox said. "We're outsiders and haven't gained their trust—like the Roofies in our clan. Besides, the less they know about us, the less they can tell the 'Forcers."

"Yeah, I guess. At least Dunham gave me this map." He held up the folded paper relic sporting a red AAA logo at one corner. He moaned. "Ouch, my head still hurts."

Fox smiled. "What a child, can't even hold your beer. A few hours of paddling will take care of that."

They shoved the kayak into the sea and clambered aboard. With the extra supplies, their craft rode low in the water. They easily pushed beyond the surf line and rested in calm water.

"So, where to, Captain?"

"Other than south, I don't really know. I think maybe we can make it around the next couple of points and reach the old Air Force base by nightfall."

"Won't there be Police at the base?"

"Yeah, maybe. But let's paddle out a kilometer or so. I don't like being so close to the beach patrols."

The sky turned a soft gray color. The sun peeked over the coastal mountains, warming the air. They made good time and in a short while turned southward. The coastline disappeared and reappeared between the swells. They put their shoulders into the paddling and didn't slow for lunch until the sun hung high above their heads. From out of the west a humongous cargo ship with Asian markings steered in their direction by its onboard guidance system, monitored remotely, Tony guessed, by some Chinese official on the far continent. As the craft came within a couple kilometers, it gently altered course to a southward bearing. Within an hour it had disappeared around the point of land that the couple aimed for.

The sun grew hot. They fashioned hats and scarves from pieces of canvas that the Dunites had given them to shield their heads and shoulders. But after only two days of paddling, their hands had become chafed and blistered. They used strips of the rough cloth to wrap their painful palms and fingers. As they slid across the ocean, a great blowing sound startled Tony. They stopped paddling and stared seaward at the massive slow-rolling bodies of a pod of humpback whales less than thirty meters from their kayak, moving north toward the Big Sur Coast and Monterey Bay. The whales' huge eyes stared at the seafarers, as if to say, "What the hell are you two doing out here?" or maybe "Why are you heading in the wrong direction?" Questions that Tony had been asking himself.

He started to groan softly with each pull on the paddle. His arms and shoulders ached and his butt had gone numb hours before. But Fox showed no signs of letting up.

"I'm starting to feel that walking wouldn't be so bad," Tony said.

Fox turned around and grinned. "Yeah, until you walk for a few days, much less a couple of months. I say we stick with this boat as long as we can, then figure something else out."

Tony nodded. Fox looked beautiful, even wearing her strange disguise. The dye in her hair had partially washed out and reddish-purple patches were mixed amongst the black. The sun had burned her face a deep sandstone brown along with her bare arms. He watched her shoulders roll with each stroke, thought about their lovemaking the night before, and paddled harder, focusing on the horizon.

In the late afternoon, the wind freshened and the swells began to whitecap, swamping their craft and dousing the pair. They angled toward shore somewhere south of Point Purisima. The remains of the Air Force base caused them to stop and stare. Huge metal structures towered above the scrubland. They hadn't seen a shore patrol in hours.

"What do ya think?" Tony asked. "The surf looks low and the beach is broad."

"Yeah, I say land here. And let's try staying in the boat this time."

Pushing off hard and with Fox's characteristic whoop, they rode a gentle comber ashore until the bow nudged the sand. They climbed out and toppled onto the wet sand, laughing, stiff from sitting all day. Tony's hands stung from the salt water washing across his cracked fingers. His feet looked prunish and encrusted in brine. They crouched beside the kayak and stared up and down the shoreline, listening for the high-pitched whine of the drone patrols.

Groaning, they lifted their loaded craft and stumbled inland to a hollow hidden by sand dunes. Out of sight and the wind's blast, they stretched onto the hot sand, rubbed their backs, and let the warm sun cook them dry. With a couple hours of daylight left, they tore dune grass from its roots and brushed away their footprints into the dunes.

"I gotta walk some," Tony complained. "My muscles need to loosen up if I'm gonna sleep tonight."

"Let's explore whatever-it-is." Fox pointed to one of the abandoned structures just inland from their sand hollow.

"It's called a gantry. The Air Force used it to house and launch rockets back before the Change."

The pair moved slowly inland through the dunes, following what looked like a faint game trail. The gantry stood in the middle of a field covered by cracked and crumbling concrete slabs. One side of the structure still displayed the pale image of a painted-on American flag. Pieces of metal littered the ground. A series of stairs with rusted-through railings climbed the tower to walkways that extended into its cavernous interior. The couple edged inside the building. Sea birds flew in and out of its dark corners. A colony of gulls called the roof home and had covered the ground below with bird droppings.

"So why did they, ya know, abandon these things?" Fox asked. "They look expensive."

"My Mom says that when our country's population dropped after the Change, there wasn't as much interest in war. Military bases closed."

"But there's still a military."

"Yes, but it's much smaller. Besides, this place was used to send spy satellites into space. There got to be too much space junk above us. When the U.N. stepped in and took control of what gets launched, this base was abandoned. Only some place in Florida still launches rockets."

As the two stood in awe at the towering bird sanctuary, Tony noticed that the blue sky had disappeared. A thick fog pushed by a cold wind rolled onshore. He zipped up his windbreaker and pulled Fox close as they headed toward the beach. The fog continued to thicken, blotting out the dunes and the shoreline altogether. They stood clutching each other with the gray swirl wetting their faces.

"I can't see a damn thing," Fox said, "and the sun's going down."

"Come on, hang onto me and don't let go."

Tony clutched her hand and they followed their rapidly disappearing footprints in the soft sand. The fog grew even thicker and Tony bent at the waist and studied each step, afraid that one wrong turn would leave them on the dunes, blind and cold until dawn, or later. Just before the light failed he almost stumbled over their kayak's bow. Groaning with relief they slumped next to the boat.

"Okay, from now on, you're in charge of watching the weather," Tony said and Fox dug him in the ribs. "Aye, aye, Captain."

Tony hurriedly unpacked the supplies the Dunites had provided: mostly twigs and small sticks to build a fire and some blackened meat wrapped in deerskin. In the darkness, he fumbled with the wood and the antique spark lighter. But in a short time he had a tiny fire going. They skewered pieces of the meat onto the ends of sharpened sticks and held it over their meager fire. The foggy night closed tighter around them—their first out in the open, away from any other humans.

"This is almost like being an Untouchable," Fox whispered as they sat shoulder-to-shoulder.

"No, it's not like anything I remember. We're not surrounded by vid screens and I'm touching you." He leaned over and kissed her sunburnt cheek. They gnawed on their tough meal until the fire burned down to nothing, deciding to save the rest of the wood for the next night, wherever that might be spent.

"The sand is our bed tonight," Tony said and smoothed out a place for Fox to lie beside him.

"Just wait, I need to, ya know… "

"Don't go far. This fog can get you turned around."

"Shut up. I know how to pee by myself."

In a few minutes, Fox returned and removed a long woolen cloak from her backpack. Lying next to Tony, she spread it over them. In the distance, coyotes yipped in the foggy darkness. Tony pictured the thick-tailed creatures with their pointed snouts to the ground, skirting the dunes, looking for easy prey. The couple kissed and Fox snuggled into his arms, pressing her tired body against his. Tony shuddered once then fell asleep almost immediately. He dreamed of a massive rocket resting on its launch pad, orange fire blasting from its base, the ground shaking as in an earthquake, seagulls circling high above, coyotes howling at the rising starburst, and through a small port in the rocket's nose, someone waving to them on the deserted beach below.

The high whine of crawlers woke them in the morning. The couple slid on their bellies to the dune top and peered over. Three police drones approached from the north. Tony pulled Fox away from the dune top and placed a finger to his lips. The two waited, ready to run for it, to where he didn't know. But the drones didn't hesitate and continued southward until their sound disappeared.

Tony took her hand. "They've got cameras and sound equipment on those things that can detect a field mouse farting."

"Yeah, I know, I know all about drones. We had them in de Tolosa long before you showed up."

"Sorry, didn't mean to insult you."

"I'm just cranky from being woken by the 'Forcers."

Tony stared at their map. "Yeah, well we gotta get offshore fast. They've got only a few kilometers of beach to run before they gotta turn around. I don't want to be here when they return."

"Won't they spot our tracks if we leave now?" Fox asked.

"Hmm, that's a good point. All right, we'll stay here. If they turn inland, we'll head for the gantry and hide in the rafters like the birds. Maybe the crawlers hate bird poop and will stay away."

"Very funny," Fox muttered.

The couple grabbed a quick breakfast of dried fruit. Tony wished he had time to brew some of the wild mint tea. His throat felt scratchy and he yearned for something hot. They had just enough time to take a latrine break before the crawlers returned. The machines slowed when they passed the couple's hiding place and almost stopped, but picked up speed again and continued on their route north. The fugitives waited tensely, listening. Tony climbed to the top of the dune and swept the shoreline. No crawlers in sight.

They lifted the kayak and hurried across the beach and into the surf. The cold water stung their legs. The fog had withdrawn a few kilometers offshore and the wind blew strong. Bracing themselves, they paddled hard, crashed into the oncoming surf, but managed to stay straight and moving outward. In a couple minutes they were clear of the breakers and paddling west before turning to port and the next point of land to the south. The cold sea soaked Tony's feet and hands. He groaned with the pain of salt water pouring into open blisters and splits in his skin. He was sure Fox felt the same. A few more days of this and they'd look like shipwrecked sailors from some Spanish galleon, waylaid on a barren beach far from their home.

They paddled steadily all morning and into the afternoon with the swells pushing them toward shore. Tony stared at the map and figured they had reached Point Arguello because the coast fell away from them to the east and the wind strengthened as it funneled into the Santa Barbara Channel.

"Fog," Fox shouted and pointed to the west. A great wall of grayness rolled toward them. In seconds they were enveloped, with visibility barely beyond the end of their kayak.

"Go slow. I don't like this," muttered Tony.

"Aye, aye, Captain."

As they continued southward stronger swells came at them from a new angle. They stopped to listen. Over the howl of the bitter wind, the boom of waves crashing against nearby rocks grew louder as each swell pushed them shoreward.

"We gotta get out of here," Tony yelled over the roar.

Fox nodded, and they turned the kayak to starboard and paddled hard, fighting the swells, and left the shore break behind them. They continued beating the water until the sea flattened somewhat and they turned to port again. But the fog hadn't lifted and, if anything, had thickened.

Tony tapped Fox on the shoulder with his paddle blade and she turned around. "We should let the current take us south. I'm afraid if we keep paddling we'll either wind up being sucked out to sea or we'll tangle up in the surf and can't get out."

For a moment Fox looked scared. "Yeah, we should listen carefully. When we hear the shore break, head on out."

Tony snorted. "If I can tell what direction 'out' is."

They sat tensely, letting the sea take their craft. The dampness soaked through their clothes and they hunched over in their seats, shaking. As the afternoon grew long, the fog pulled away from the shoreline, exposing a coast that looked like something from a different continent. Dune and scrubland had given way to a ridge of tall mountains. Their slopes fell steeply toward a narrow terrace of land and unfriendly-looking cliffs, shoals, and jagged inlets where every wave sent whitewater skyward. Offshore, sea stacks and rocky islands defined where the old coast-line must have been before the sea level rose. The ocean pushed them at an angle toward land.

"What about there?" Fox pointed. "See where that valley cuts through the mountains? There's a beach and..."

"Yeah, looks like some kind of camp."

With the land in clear sight, they paralleled the coast, paddling hard, the effort warming their bodies, until they stood directly offshore of the encampment. A series of broad pointed-tipped boards painted bright colors formed a fence around a compound located on the sandy shelf just above a narrow beach. A railroad line skirted the camp at the base of the mountains and extended up and down the coast. Inside the fence, Tony could make out a crowd of people moving around a fire pit, most of them naked to the waist, including the women.

"Let's move in slow and check them out," he said.

"Yeah, I thought you'd want ta get a closer look," Fox complained and he laughed.

But they had to get through the surf first. Given the slant of the beach and the size of the swells, Tony felt sure they'd be rolling in whitewater again just like their first landing. Tired and cold, they let a swell push them shoreward, then paddled hard. Tony steered the kayak straight and they shot through the sea. On the beach, a crowd of natives jumped up and down in their long shorts and yelled. The kayak skidded across the wet sand and up the shingle. A dozen men and women with tanned skin, streaked blonde hair, and wearing necklaces of tiny shells and bits of mother-of-pearl grabbed their craft. They lifted it from the water and crossed the beach to the base of the shelf.

The natives spoke slowly and used words foreign to Tony and Fox. Once they set the kayak with the couple onto the dry sand, they backed off and stared silently.

"The way we look probably scares the crap outta them," Tony muttered and grinned.

The pair still wore their ratty canvas hats and shoulder scarves with their hands bound and covered with the same material. Fox's hair had a red streak down its center with purplish patches on either side.

Their arms had been burnt the color of Mission tiles, the skin crusted with salt and blistering.

"Jeez, dude, where ya comin' from, man?" one of the natives asked.

Tony rolled out of the kayak and stood, his legs trembling, his lower back in complete spasm. "We're... we're from up north," he replied through gritted teeth.

The group closed in around them. Tony tried not to stare at the big-breasted girls that stood unabashedly before him. Questions came rolling in.

"Where up north?"

"Ah... de Tolosa."

"You came through the Graveyard in that thing?" A man pointed to their kayak.

Fox joined Tony, rubbing her shoulders and peeling off strips of bloodied canvas from her fingers. "What's the Graveyard?" she asked.

A middle aged woman spoke up. "It's the, ya know, coast, north and south of Point Arguello. In the old days, dozens of ships wrecked on the rocks on either side of that point, including some Navy Destroyers. But the storms are even worse now."

"Yeah, it's a really gnarly place, man. The waves are crazy and the wind screamin'."

"So what do you call your... your clan?" Fox asked. She looked uncomfortable facing off a crowd of half naked people.

"We're the CenCal Surfers, and we call this camp 'Surf City' after Huntington Beach, the original Surf City in SoCal."

"Can we stay with you guys for a day or two?" Tony asked. "We've been paddling hard and need the rest."

A curvaceous blonde and a tall man with brown skin and eyes to match stepped forward. "The In-landers can stay with us," the woman announced and took Fox's hand. Fox winced and rolled her eyes at Tony. The couple led them into the compound as others picked up their kayak and set it against the fence. Several dozen open sheds with thatched roofs made from palm fronds circled a central cooking area and fire pit.

"My name is Tasha and this is my husband, Jessie," the blonde said and slumped into one of four overstuffed chairs facing the fire pit.

"We're Tony and Fox. Thanks for taking us in."

Tony gaped at the chairs, which looked like they'd come from de Tolosa's Library reading room. Across the rear of the shed rested two full beds, circa early 21st Century, complete with foam mattresses and pillows.

Jessie caught Tony gaping and grinned. "Yeah, I suppose the furniture looks strange out here in the middle of nowhere."

"Well... yeah," Fox said. Tony tried not to stare at Tasha's boobs.

"Our clan trades weed to the Shut-ins for supplies. They get high and we stay, ya know, comfy."

"Weed?" Fox asked, raising a purple eyebrow.

"Ya know, smokin' Mary," Jessie said.

"You guys look really cold," Tasha said. "You wanna take a hot bath before supper?"

"Good God, yes!" Fox blurted.

"See those two tubs next to the fire? Get in the cool one first and wash off." Jessie tossed Tony a bar of scented soap and a rough piece of cloth. "Then soak in the hot one. We got an hour before dinner, so relax."

"Is it salt water?" Tony asked.

Jessie grinned. "Naw. We have a pipe system that collects fresh water from the valley stream and drops it into a holding reservoir. An underground heat exchanger ramps it up to 40 degrees Celsius."

"Sounds complicated," Fox said.

"Yeah, well the Shut-ins give us what we need in exchange for our Emerald Magic. We grow great weed... the best from Fort Bragg to Panama."

Tasha and Jessie slumped into their soft chairs and stared at Tony and Fox. Around the compound others were doing the same thing, watching, grinning, and sucking in smoke from skinny little cigarettes. Tony noticed Fox's face darkening.

"You sure you wanna do this?" he murmured.

"Are you kidding? I'd hike naked to El Lay for a hot bath."

They stripped quickly. Leaving their salt-incrusted clothes next to their chairs, they walked across the clearing toward the tubs. The Surfers responded with piercing whistles and high yelps. When Fox stretched a leg to dip a toe into the water to test its temperature, applause erupted from the crowd, mostly from the guys. But Tony felt the eyes of the women checking out his compact muscled body. No one laughed.

When the couple slid into the lukewarm water, the Surfers seemed to lose interest and the level of chatter from the sheds increased. Tony and Fox scrubbed themselves and each other hard, applying the soap only after the first scraping. Their hands looked like those of old people and their faces almost glowed in the dusk from days of constant sun. After washing her hair twice, the remains of the black dye disappeared and Fox changed back into a redhead. They climbed into the second tub slowly, the water hotter than anything Tony had ever felt, sat side-by-side on a bench, clasped hands underwater, and let the heat soften the knots in their muscles and back. Tony stroked Fox's thigh, moving upward.

"Not here," Fox murmured.

Tony grinned. "The Surfers would probably cheer us on."

"I'll bet they would. But I'm not a native girl yet."

When the heat became unbearable, they slid from the tub and stood in the cold wind, their skin pink and goose-bumped. Back at the shed, Tasha handed them towels. But their soiled clothes had disappeared.

"Where'd our..." Fox began to ask, looking alarmed.

"They're being washed," Tasha said. "You can wear these."

She handed Tony and Fox folded pairs of long khaki shorts which they slipped on quickly.

"What about tops?" Fox asked.

"We don't wear tops here," Jessie said. "It's a clan tradition."

"I'm sure that one was thought up by the men," Fox snapped.

"Yeah, maybe at first," Tasha said. "But it's a sign that we prize the beauty of bodies in all their various forms."

"But how can you wear only shorts?" Tony asked. "The wind feels freezing to me." He and Fox stood with their arms wrapped around themselves, teeth chattering.

"Part of the challenge for new clan members is to get used to the weather. Most of these people have been here for years. Jessie and I are some of the newest. Besides, the Native Americans didn't wear shirts."

"I don't care. I'm still freezing my ass off. Besides, the natives lived here long before the Change." Fox strode through the compound's entrance with most of the Surfers taking no notice. She returned with her long wool cloak and sat in a chair clutching Tony, the cloak draped over their shoulders.

For supper they ate garden vegetables, roasted

fish, and some kind of cake made with carrots and raisins and sweet icing. Jessie explained that their trade arrangement with the Shut-ins included food supplies—from the same provisions provided to most Untouchable households in the southern region.

That night they slept on a bed softer than anything Tony had ever felt. The wind had died and the moon formed a small fingernail slice of light in the sky. Throughout the camp they heard the unmistakable sounds of people making love, including Tasha and Jessie just a few meters away. Fox rolled on top of his taut body and stayed there, rocking back and forth in the darkness. Tony tried to control his breathing, stay quiet, and enjoy the touch of her flesh. Fox increased her cadence and pressed her breasts against him. When they climaxed, she let out a soft moan.

They jumped when Tasha called to them, "Hey guys, you don't have to stay quiet. It's a natural thing, ya know."

"Thanks for the tip," Tony muttered and Fox giggled into his ear.

In the morning, they found the camp deserted. The fence of pointed-tipped boards that surrounded the compound had disappeared. They climbed from bed and pulled on their shorts. The eastern sun was still hidden by the coastal mountains. The air felt cool, still wet with mist. They munched pieces of cake they found on a plate on a short table in the corner. Staring seaward, Tony's mouth dropped open. Dozens of Surfers dotted the water, riding their wide boards down the faces of waves, hollering to each other, laughing.

"Looks like fun," Fox mumbled between bites of cake.

"Yeah, we can barely steer our kayak through the surf while these guys can dance along the waves."

When Tasha and Jessie returned, laughing and playing grab-ass, they took the newcomers on a tour of the area. The sun had risen above the mountains and felt warm on their bare chests and backs. They followed a worn trail next to a creek up the valley and into the mountains. Once away from the ocean wind, the air became hot and humid. On the lower slopes of the valley amongst groves of oaks, Surfers worked in lush garden patches of head-high plants with pointed jagged-edged leaves.

"Does your clan smoke marijuana?" Tasha asked.

Fox shook her head. "We live... well, we lived in a city where the Police are always watching. They still treat it as illegal for us clansmen even though the Untouchables use it... their dirty little secret."

"Yeah, we're mostly beer drinkers," Tony added.

"Beer will make ya fat," Jessie said.

Fox laughed. "Yeah, you should see the families that brewed the stuff. They definitely drink a lot of their product."

Returning to the camp, they hiked uphill to a point that gave a broad view of the coastline.

"You can see that there are no roads through this sector," Jessie said. "They were destroyed when the sea rose and the coastline moved inland. With no roads and no beach, the crawlers can't easily get to us."

"But what about satellite surveillance?" Tony asked and pointed skyward.

"Yeah, I'm sure the Police watch us on a screen somewhere. But we get fog cover here a good part of the year and they have no good reason to worry about us. There are no Shut-ins living anywhere near us."

"So without the vans or roads, how do you get your supplies?" Tony asked.

"We'll show you after lunch."

After a meal of bean salad and smoked salmon, Tony and Fox followed their guides south along a broad trail that skirted the coastal bluffs. When they came to the creek that drained the valley they turned inland and stopped where a railroad trestle crossed the steep-sided gulch. A crudely-built platform stood on the far side of the trestle. Three burly Surfers sat on a cart loaded with neatly wrapped sacks of marijuana. The center rail hummed with the surge of electricity.

"I'll bet that this is the same line that cuts through de Tolosa," Tony said.

"I'm sure it is," Jessie said. "It gets its power from the old nuke plant not far from your town. They converted the reactors to use thorium instead of uranium. They've got a couple centuries worth of the fuel on-site before they run out."

"So this is how you get your supplies?" Fox asked.

"Yeah, sort of," Tasha said and grinned. "The daily drone makes an... an unscheduled stop here."

"How do you manage that?" Tony asked.

"The elders of our clan know some people," Jessie said and grinned. "As long as there's demand for our Emerald Magic, that train will stop at Surf City."

"But how do you load and unload?"

"Just watch," Tasha said and pointed southeastward along the line. The steel rails began to creak and pop in the afternoon heat. The high whine of a train's electric engines sounded above the ocean's background rumble. The train streaked across the sea terrace. As it approached the trestle and platform its engines shut down and it slowed silently to a stop. The polished door on one of the cars cracked open. From inside, hands grabbed the door and slid it wide. Three Surfers, including a bronzed Amazon of a woman, greeted their fellow clansmen waiting on the cart. The cart boys loaded the marijuana then clambered aboard while the on-train crew offloaded supplies onto the cart and jumped onto the platform.

The whole operation took only a few minutes. The

train's engines engaged and it accelerated smoothly away from the platform, heading toward de Tolosa and points north.

"We deliver most of our product to folks in the El Lay basin," Jessie explained. "So our load tomorrow heading south will be twice as big. But the supplies we get from up north are better. So it's a real balancing act."

The unloading crew pushed the cart across the railroad trestle and joined the foursome.

"Hey, dudes, how was the trip?" Jessie asked.

"Totally cool," a tall guy with a graying beard answered. "We got the medicines that the Ehrbars and Hopkins needed and scored some pretty decent supplies."

Tasha introduced Tony and Fox to the crew as visiting Inlanders. The unloading guys stared at them, grinning, taking in Fox's bodacious body and her flaming red hair. The Amazon girl looked bored.

"So which direction are you guys heading?" Terry, the bearded guy asked.

"We've got this bitchin' kayak. We plan on paddling south tomorrow and—"

"You're not running from the 'Forcers, are you?"

Tony stared at Fox before answering. "Why, is something going on?"

Steve, a long-faced boy with a pug nose answered. "When we rolled over the trestle at Gaviota just south of here, I cracked the inland door. A bunch of crawlers, vans, and what looked like jet boats are parked on the knoll overlooking the old campground."

Fox's face turned pale and Tony stayed silent.

"So what's up, guys?" Jessie asked. "Is there something you're not telling us?"

"Look, we don't want the Police to hassle you folks," Fox said. She turned to Tony. "Maybe we should leave right now."

"Relax, relax," Terry said and grinned. "Let's talk with the clan elders over dinner and we'll figure something out."

"But you gotta come clean with us," Jessie said, "if you want our help."

Tony clutched Fox's hand and nodded. They made their way back to the compound. Tony wondered: *maybe tonight I'll smoke some weed to relax before our next escape. But this time, they'll be waiting for us... and where can you run in a kayak on the open sea?*

6

Captain Hanpian stared at the woman's smooth face and dark eyes that filled one of his many vid screens. Even with braided gray hair and a cane, she looked beautiful, mysterious, someone he'd want to meet—if he ever left his home-office to meet anybody. It had taken his drones and manned patrols three days to find Ms. Matteson holed up in an old mill yard next to the creek at the southern edge of de Tolosa.

"I know where your son and that girl are," Hanpian said into the com.

She jounced her cane against the holding cell's concrete floor and pulled a shawl around her strong shoulders. "So?"

"So, we'll have them in custody shortly."

"Then what do you need me for?"

"Just let me ask the questions," Hanpian snapped. "We know that Anthony killed the citizen in his hillside house. We have his prints on the weapon and cells he left behind. We just have a couple of questions."

The woman glared into the screen, eyes flashing daggers. "Doesn't sound like you need anything from me. You've already tried and convicted Tony."

"Well, not yet, but yes, that will happen," Hanpian said smugly. He sat back in his chair and watched the woman's reaction. She buried her head in her hands, shoulders shaking.

Waiting for Ms. Matteson to settle down, Hanpian went over the status of the case in his mind. He knew Commander Pynard would make her daily call and wanted something positive to report. Two days before, a drone patrol had picked up a scrap of cloth off the beach at Vandenberg Air Force Base. They ran the cells and identified the donor as Fox Slade. Hanpian had been amazed that the kids had made it that far. He studied his maps of the coastline, the jagged coves near Point Hondo where seven Navy Destroyers ran aground way back when, and decided that if they hadn't been sucked onto the rocks at Point Arguello, they'd probably hole up at Surf City.

When he talked about the situation with Statler, the sergeant wanted to send an overland force to the Surfers camp and capture the fugitives. Hanpian had quickly rejected that idea; too many routes of escape into the coastal mountains. Statler then suggested that they ask the SoCal District to fly in a few skimmers to approach the Surfer camp from the air. But Hanpian would have to ask Captain Peterson for help, and he wasn't about to get that idiot involved in *his* pursuit. Snatching them from the open sea would be much easier. His forces just needed to be prepared and patient.

The National Weather Service forecast clear skies for the Gaviota Coast. Hanpian ordered infrared surveillance of the ocean in case the fugitives tried to slip by at night. He also had land-to-sea radar set up near the railroad trestle, had constant daylight surveillance, and had jet boats ready to launch within minutes of a sighting. The Police had to be vigilant and wait it out.

Ms. Matteson sat up and blew her nose into a soiled handkerchief. She glared at the vid camera and swore under her breath. "So ask me your questions, Captain, then release me. You have no basis for holding—"

"Oh yes we do," Hanpian cut in. "It's called harboring a fugitive. Whether you are released or not will depend on how much you cooperate."

"But you already have the evidence you need, what

more do you want?"

"I want to know *why* Tony killed that man."

"If I tell you, it'll mean that I'm admitting to his guilt."

"We don't need your admissions. I'm just trying... trying to understand why an artistic boy would do such a thing."

"Have you ever loved a woman, Captain, or are you just partial to other male 'Forcers?"

Hanpian ignored the insult and smiled to himself. "Yes, once, a long time ago, before I joined the State Police Force."

"Then think way back and try to remember how it felt. My Tony loves Fox Slade. They've been together since childhood."

"So, what's love got to do with this case?" Hanpian asked.

"It's the answer to your question."

"You'd better explain," Hanpian snapped, tired of talking in riddles with the rambling woman.

Ruth Matteson sucked in a deep breath. "The kids were painting a mural on the Untouchable's house. It got hot and Fox had a heat stroke. My boy pounded on the door and the man let them in, a doctor of sorts, and treated Fox with ice and cold water. But when they asked to leave, the Untouchable refused. He was a big man and could easily kill both of them. They tried to escape but found no unlocked doors. The man knocked Tony out and attacked the girl. He was just about to fuck her when..."

"When what?" Hanpian asked, impatiently. The Captain felt his face burn. He hadn't heard that term used by a woman and discouraged vulgarity among his staff.

"When my... my son came to and..." The com line hummed as Ms. Matteson again covered her face with her hands.

"That's a very interesting story, Ms. Matteson," Hanpian said. "But there's no evidence that there was ever a sexual assault."

"Really? You find a guy naked on his floor with his head bashed in. That doesn't tell you anything? And didn't they find the girl's skin and blood under his fingernails?"

"That's circumstantial evidence at best. But it doesn't prove anything. For all we know, the two of them could have attacked the citizen and he was only trying to defend himself."

"And you wonder why we don't go to the Police," Ms. Matteson snapped back. "You make up your mind what happened then gather evidence to support your conclusions. What the hell kind of police work is that?"

"The kind that's kept our District crime-free for years," Hanpian said.

"And you don't think that demolishing our home was a crime?"

"That... that was unfortunate. But you Touchables were squatters, had no rights—"

"Exactly," Ms. Matteson interrupted. "We have no rights. Think about that when you proclaim your purpose to 'protect and serve.'"

"Look, I have a couple more questions, then you may—"

"I'm done with your questions. Lock me up or let me go." She backed away from the table and sat with her arms folded across her rising and falling chest, her jaw set, chin raised.

Hanpian sucked in a breath and felt a shiver run down his spine. "Do... do you know if your son has recently talked about your ex-husband, Wayne?"

At the mention of the name, Matteson leaned forward. "No... no. Why the hell would he even... "

"You tell me. You were the one that deserted Wayne. Maybe the boy wants to see his long lost father. You know, Wayne's been looking for you and Tony."

She shuddered. "That's the last place Tony would go. If you know anything about Wayne, it's that... "

"What?"

"Nothing. He's just another damn Untouchable, not fit to live with anyone. You should know about that. Now let me out of—"

Hanpian reached forward and clicked off the com. Leaning back in his chair, he fingered his graying mustache. The boy's father wasn't important anyway. They'd have the pair in custody long before the punks could even get near the Southland and attempt contact. Besides, good ole Wayne had agreed to cooperate with the Police. The woman had been right about the guy, a real idiot. Hanpian studied her face in the vid screen and closed his eyes, wanting to remember everything about her.

7

Tony and Fox slouched on the soft chairs in Tasha and Jessie's shed, not talking. They watched the Surfers bathe in the tubs and begin to prepare the clan's evening meal. From across the compound, Terry, the tall gray-bearded guy from the train crew, approached them, grinning. He motioned to the couple and they followed him to a large shed with chairs arranged in a circle, occupied by older men and women. Terry slumped into a chair and motioned toward two vacant seats.

A small fire burned in the center of the circle. Terry reached for a burning twig and held it to the end of a cigarette as thick as his thumb. He inhaled deeply and passed it to the woman on his right. The marijuana made the rounds until it was gone. Tony leaned back and watched the flow of adults and children around the compound's central fire. The sun hung low above the horizon. It shone through the cracks in the surfboard fence, creating golden stripes on the darkening ground.

"It's time," Terry said, "Time for you to tell your story. If we believe you, and if the majority of the Council agrees, we will help you."

Tony sat forward. But before he could say anything, Fox began speaking. In a halting voice, she recounted every detail of the attempted rape and the murder. Tony felt stunned to hear it laid out so plainly, hear how the attack had made Fox feel, the revulsion, the fear, the hatred, the joy of vengeance. The couple hadn't talked about it much, had concentrated on fleeing, on ignoring the reality of the killing. But it all flowed back to Tony as he listened. He could almost feel the cut-glass pitcher in his hand and its impact with the Untouchable's skull.

Fox stopped speaking. The woman next to Terry shuddered. The silence returned. The sun rested on the horizon and the air cooled. Finally, the group roused themselves and discussed Fox's story in whispered tones. After a few minutes, the Council took a unanimous vote to support helping them.

"This is not going to be easy," Terry said. "The Police are expecting you, so we need to keep them guessing as long as possible."

"But how can we outrun jet boats and radar in our funky little kayak?" Fox asked.

Terry grinned. "You won't."

As the sun disappeared the Council discussed the details of the plan until the dinner line formed and Fox and Tony rejoined Tasha and Jessie in their shed, glad that they had some sort of answer for what came next. That night, Tony reached for Fox in the darkness. Her body jumped at his touch, like it had been stung by a bee. He apologized and lay quietly beside her. The cat-and-mouse game that he and Fox had played with the Police back in de Tolosa had somehow changed into a life or death struggle. Tony still couldn't exactly figure out how that had happened. But the State Police would follow them anywhere, wouldn't give up. He fell asleep thinking about escaping to Central or South America, to Tierra Del Fuego, to some corner of the world that lacked surveillance, lacked drone patrols, lacked Untouchables, where the knot in his stomach could loosen, and he and Fox could return to their art, his music, and to their long slow lovemaking.

In the morning, Tony noticed that their kayak had disappeared. He asked Jessie about it.

"We hauled it inland and it's hidden. When the

Police finally come, and they will come, they won't find it and we'll deny you were ever here."

"Good. I don't want you folks to get into trouble."

"Don't worry. As I said before, so long as there's demand for our Emerald Magic..." He grinned, ran to the fence, grabbed his board and charged into the waves to join the rest of the clan in their sunrise surfing ritual.

At lunch, Fox and Tony forced themselves to eat. They had carefully restocked their backpacks, dumping their old clothes into the central fire pit and packing new garments provided by the Surfers, only keeping Fox's long wool cloak. They sat in the soft chairs and waited, sporting straw hats and Hawaiian shirts worn by the loading crews.

"Just keep the hat on when you're outside," Tasha told Fox. "That red blaze of yours is like a target. Any surveillance will pick you out."

"Thanks. You guys have... have been great." Fox's lips trembled and she grasped Tony's hand and squeezed it so hard that he yelped.

A couple of hours after lunch they hefted their backpacks and joined the loading crew, heading southeast along the railroad until crossing the creek trestle and resting on the loading platform. Their cart was heaped twice as high as the previous day with bags of marijuana. No one spoke, all eyes focused on Point Arguello and the first sign of the southbound freight.

"Do they have any surveillance on the train?" Tony asked Terry.

"No. But they've got lots of eyes at the main stops, like El Lay. That's why it's better for you to get off the train at the north Santa Barbara platform."

Tony remembered studying maps of the Old Mission City at the de Tolosa Library. According to Terry, the town had about half of its pre-Change population, with the lower part of its downtown, the bar district, flooded after the sea level rose. Most of the Untouchables lived on the high Westside Mesa or across town in estates along the eastern foothills. Some clans occupied the old hotels and public buildings in the flooded part of town.

"You don't want to mess with those dudes," Terry had said. "They're into really bad drugs and are constantly killing or raping each other. The 'Forcers just stay clear and let it happen."

Waiting at the loading platform, time passed at glacial speed. Then the train appeared at the western edge of the sea terrace, its front engines bullet-shaped with solid chrome sides extending downward to cover the wheels. It stopped at the platform and the on-board crew unloaded their supplies, while the cart crew loaded their packed bags of marijuana.

"All aboard," one of the loaders hollered. Fox and Tony stepped inside the car stuffed with freight, pre-packed into coded containers that, according to Terry, allowed the drones at the main terminals to offload and distribute the goods to central distribution points. Someone slid the door shut and total cold darkness enveloped them. One of the crew clicked on a hand light and they slumped onto the tops of the freight containers.

"How long until we reach Santa Barbara?" Tony asked Terry.

"Maybe twenty minutes. These trains really haul ass. They're twice as fast as the pre-Change freights."

The train accelerated smoothly, its wheels hardly rattling as it passed over the concrete rail bed. In just a few minutes, Terry pressed a button next to the car's door and it cracked open a few centimeters. "Let's see if the Police are still at Gaviota Pass." He stared through the opening, then let Tony take a look. Below the train trestle a flooded valley opened into the sea.

On one knoll above the valley, a cluster of crawlers, vans, and racy-looking boats parked. Tony backed away from the door and grinned.

"My bet is they'll wait a day or two," Terry said, "before they come looking for you at Surf City."

Tony nodded. "Yeah, by then we should—"

"Just follow the plan, man. They'll be checking every train stop from here to the Mexican border."

Fox nodded, gave a shudder and wrapped her arm around Tony. "You guys have been great. I wish we would have found you before we were on the run. You seem to... to really enjoy life."

Terry smiled. "We enjoy our simple pleasures, work hard, play hard, smoke wonderful Emerald Magic. I never could understand how the Shut-ins can live the way they do. I don't care how good the vids are, there's nothing like the feel of a woman or the thrill of riding waves."

Fox said, "Yeah, it's as if they fear the sense of touch and have lost the ability to cope face-to-face with the world."

"Well put," Terry said. "You sound like my mother. My parents were part of the first commune that settled on Santa Cruz Island. But there wasn't enough water to support them and they moved the clan north, eventually settling at Surf City."

"I noticed that you have plenty of children," Tony said. "How do you keep from, ya know, getting too big?"

"We're real careful about who can join the clan... and we maintain the old traditions of children leaving for other places when they're old enough. Sometimes they come back. But most of the time they disappear. Some stay and marry into other clan families. So far, we've kept a good balance. We're not so incestuous that our kids are cross-eyed or grow six toes." Terry laughed then fell silent as the train sliced through the air with hardly a wiggle.

In a short while the pull of the engines slacked off. The crew rose from their seats, ready to offload some bags of grass for their Santa Barbara customers and scoop inside their in-kind payment, according to Terry mostly medical supplies from an abandoned hospital and pharmacy on the west side of town.

"Now remember," Terry whispered, "head for the creek and hole up, then follow the streets into the northern mountains."

"Thanks, guys. You've been great," Fox blurted too loudly and everybody laughed.

The train slid to a stop and the crew pulled the door open and jumped onto a long platform next to a deserted freeway that cut through burned-out housing tracts, old wooden homes that had been incinerated by one of the many fires that ravaged that city in the decades after the Change. Tony remembered seeing a few photographs in the Library's Special Collections Section of entire blocks going up. But the people had already left, or died off. So the fire department had just let them burn.

The couple watched the loading crew work and scanned the surrounding streets for crawlers or police vans. At other spots along the platform, train doors had slid open and drone loaders pulled freight from the cars, transporting it to waiting trucks. Stepping cautiously into the sunlight, Tony and Fox waved at Terry and the crew and moved off at a trot. They passed through a road tunnel under the freeway and slid down the bank of a low-flowing creek shaded by sycamores, oaks and laurel.

Tony said, "We've got maybe three hours of light. We'll hit the streets at sundown. Terry said they don't have infra-red detection but that the roads are patrolled during the day with eyes everywhere."

"So do we even know what we're looking for?"

"Something about a reed house in a field of flowers, in the hills above the Mission." Tony grinned sheepishly. "I didn't get it when the Surfers told us last night. I was sort of, ya know, stoned and didn't want to sound stupid by asking questions."

"Yeah, nobody likes a stupid fugitive," Fox said and smiled.

They picked their way along the rocky creek bottom to a grassy slope hidden by willows. Stretching out on the ground in the warm afternoon shade, they watched white egrets stalk their prey in the shallow pools. Old houses bordered the creek along one side, their black windows staring and somehow beckoning to them. The deserted freeway bordered the other side of the creek. An occasional drone crawler screamed by and the couple burrowed farther into the undergrowth until the willows shielded them from the outside world.

"I... I wanted to thank you for telling our story yesterday," Tony said. "I didn't realize how... how bad it was for you... ya know, the whole thing with the Untouchable."

Fox reached across his body and laid a finger on his lips. "Shush. We'll talk later. Right now just hold me."

At sundown they ate a meal of dried fruits and smoked fish that the Surfers had given them. Backtracking along the creek bed, they climbed its bank to a street bridge and headed inland toward the massive range of mountains, the tops of which still glowed pink in the twilight. They moved slowly, carefully, aided by a nearly-full moon and only using their hand light when they couldn't see where to step. Following the road uphill, they came upon a huge clearing.

"That must be the Old Mission," Tony said, pointing to a massive church with two tall towers, one of them having collapsed, its stones scattered across the field. The couple sat on one of the stones to rest.

Fox said, "Your Mother told me that all the churches pretty much closed when the Untouchables shifted to online worship. With no money to keep them up and with a few strong earthquakes, they ended up like this." She pointed to the Mission's downed tower, the sagging roof, cracked walls, and lifeless interior.

"Yeah, all those centuries of history pretty much gone. Some of the clans now use them... but to live in, not for praying."

"What's the use of praying?" Fox asked. "God only seems to listen to the Untouchables."

Tony smiled. "Yes, but I'll bet we're happier. My Mom used to talk about how she and her Mother went to church every Sunday, how they'd sing hymns and gossip with the members afterwards. Now only clansmen do anything like that... and the Untouchables... they can have their sanitized version of heaven. I'd rather enjoy mine here."

"Spoken like a true Touchable," Fox said and dug him in the ribs.

They continued inland, picking up a creek just past the Mission and following it into the foothills. In the darkness, they moved carefully and by midnight fell to their knees, exhausted. In a clearing under tall trees, they spread Fox's wool cloak and lay on ground softened by years of built-up leaves. The wind blew off the mountains, rustling the oaks with its warmth. They fell asleep almost immediately.

In the morning, they broke camp quickly. The sun burned hot in a clear sky. Under the trees, the heat felt like a wet mist with no wind to stir it. They took long pulls from their water bottles and continued to follow the creek upslope through an oak forest. Fox stopped, stripped to the waist, and stuffed her shirt in her backpack.

"Those Surfers had a bunch of good ideas," she

said and laughed.

"No complaints from me," Tony said and followed her example. "But stay out of the underbrush. That shiny three-leafed stuff will give ya a rash where you don't want one."

The climb grew steeper and they struggled over huge boulders, small cascades, following what looked like a game trail along one bank. At mid-day they stopped to soak their sweat-covered bodies in a waist-deep pool of cool water. Huge birds that looked like vultures, only twice as big, circled above them.

"I'd like to hitch a ride with one of those guys," Tony said and pointed.

"I think they're condors," Fox replied. "They were almost extinct. But when the State outlawed guns, their numbers increased. They're a type of vulture—just real big ones."

They pressed on. In the back of Tony's mind crouched the fear that they had followed the wrong creek and headed into the wild hills, to wander lost for days until their food ran out and they collapsed in the heat.

"Hey, check it out," Fox said and pointed.

Twenty or so meters ahead, a stone-faced dam with a bridge on top crossed the creek. A gap in the center of the dam let water flow downstream rapidly. At the base of the wall, some kind of spillway had been constructed of concrete.

"This could be it," Tony murmured. "Let's check it out quietly. I don't want any surprises."

A trail took off from the right side of the dam and wound upslope. They followed it to the canyon ridgeline. From behind a huge boulder they stared at an open field full of color.

"This must be it," Tony said and pointed to a two-story reed house at the far end of the field.

Fox said, "I've never seen flowers that... brilliant.

They musta been planted decades ago. God, I wish I had my paints."

"Somebody takes good care of 'em. And look at that vegetable patch."

As they watched, a large woman and a young teenage boy and girl emerged from the house and moved into the gardens, using short hoes to chop weeds and watering cans to irrigate the vegetables. When their cans were empty they moved to a hand pump next to the house and refilled. The family only wore clothes below the waist.

"At least we dressed right," Fox whispered.

Tony stared at the girl, a brunette, until Fox dug him in the side.

"Is there supposed to be a father?" she asked.

"Yeah. According to Terry, he's probably smoking weed in the house. Let's go."

The couple stepped from behind the boulder and walked from under the trees.

"Hello," Tony called.

The woman jumped to her feet, and shouted at her kids, "Go on, get inside."

The teenagers jogged toward the house, checking out Fox and Tony as they ran. The girl smiled at Tony. The woman brandished her hoe and moved toward them.

"We didn't mean to startle you," Fox said as the woman advanced.

"We're friends of Terry Sanders," Tony said. "He told us you and... and your husband might be able to help us."

With the mention of Terry's name, the woman's scowl turned to a smile. She slowed her pace and extended a hand to Fox. "Hi, my name's Maryann. My lazy-ass husband, Glen, is inside taking a nap. Those are our kids Amy and Ryan."

After a round of handshaking, a balding bearded

guy with a hairy chest stumbled out of the house and joined the group.

"I heard you say that Terry sent ya," Glen said.

"That's right. We just came from Surf City."

"Boy it's been years since we've been up that way," Maryann said. "I'm not sure the kids were even born when we were there last."

Glen smiled, showing off two rows of jagged teeth. He seemed to be in a daze, although not too deep to miss out on Fox's fine figure. The young teenagers poked their heads from the house and slowly joined their parents.

"Sorry I freaked out when you first showed up," Maryann said. "We haven't had visitors in over a year and the last ones Glen had to run off with his gun."

"Not to worry," Tony said. "We're here in peace. But we need your help. Terry said you were Surfers at heart and wanted you to have this."

He removed his backpack, opened the top compartment, and took out a kilo bag of Emerald Magic. Glen's eyes got huge when Tony handed it to him.

"Jeez, thanks man. I haven't smoked anything so good since Maryann and I left Surf City. I try growing my own here. But the soil must not be as good and I can't get fishmeal to fertilize the plants. You tell Terry thanks when you see him again."

Tony glanced at Fox and frowned. "We're on a one-way trip south."

"Come in out of the sun, have some cool tea," Maryann said and motioned to their home. A huge boulder formed the back wall of the structure with beams extending outward to support the second floor. Willow branches had been woven together to form walls between the support posts, and the roof sported some kind of thatch. Stone chimneys extended well over the roofline along two of the outside walls. They entered through an arched opening into a main room that included a fireplace and was furnished like the sheds at Surf City with soft chairs and tables. The place felt cool and airy.

"How did you get all this stuff up here?" Tony asked in wonder.

"Easy, I carted it up the road from the old down-slope houses." Glen stared at Tony. "Ah, how did you guys get here?"

"We slogged our way up the creek."

Maryann grinned. "Yeah, that sounds like directions Terry would give. He never did trust roads."

"But aren't there eyes?" Tony asked.

"Not in these hills. I've taken them out with my pea-shooter." He pointed to some kind of rifle hanging on a wall. "The Police know I'm here but aren't interested enough to replace their surveillance."

Fox leaned forward. "But don't the Police hassle you about your... your gun?"

"Nah. I never take it with me when I go downslope and they hardly ever come up here. I think the last drone patrol rolled past a couple of months ago. It could be months until the next."

Outside, the canyon shadows grew long on the flower field. Glen rolled a cigarette of Emerald Magic and sat puffing and grinning into the waning light. The teenagers returned to their garden chores, leaving the adults to savor the upcoming sunset. Tony felt the knot in his stomach begin to relax. The couple had asked them no questions, just graciously accepted their presence based solely on their association with their friend Terry.

Finally, Maryann murmured, "So why are you here?"

Tony glanced at Fox and nodded. She repeated their story. Glen and Maryann sat quietly and took it all in without comment. Afterward, Maryann rose and moved to another room to prepare supper. Tony could smell meat roasting over a fire. Glen sucked on his cigarette.

"That's heavy, man, really heavy," he said finally. "The Police aren't gonna stop looking when a citizen gets killed. And I'm sure the eyes at the train platform picked you guys up."

Tony leaned forward. "Look, Glen, if you don't want us here, I understand. We can head out in the morning."

"No way. It'll take the 'Forcers a few days to figure things out. So we've got time to get ready. Do you know where you want to go?"

"Ah, not really. My Mother talked about the communes on the Channel Islands. But Terry told me that the one on Santa Cruz disbanded long ago. Besides, I don't have a clue how to get offshore... and something small like a kayak seems way too dangerous."

Glen tossed the remnants of his cigarette into the fireplace. "Don't worry about it, man. I know some good people down south. Meanwhile, while you're here, you can help us with the garden while we get ready."

"I gotta ask about that," Fox said. "Why all the beautiful flowers?"

Glen grinned and held two fingers up in the form of a V. "We're flower children, sister. Don't ya remember your history of the 1960s? It's where the folks down south got the idea for the communes."

"My Mom is the teacher for our clan," Tony said. "She taught both of us all about it."

"Well, there's actually another reason for the flowers," Glen said and chuckled. "This land used to be the City's Botanical Garden. The plants are descendants of the annuals and perennials that covered this place."

"Wow, I wish I had my paints to do something with all that color," Fox said.

"Talk with Maryann tomorrow. We may have something you can use."

Maryann returned from the kitchen with a stack of bowls and platters full of steaming vegetables with some kind of meat. "It's venison," Maryann said before Tony or Fox could ask.

Glen explained. "Yeah, the black-tailed deer wander down to the creek for water and into the field to chew up our garden. They end up as dinner."

"Fresh meat, delivered on the hoof," Tony cracked.

Maryann lit candles placed strategically around the main room. Glen retrieved an ancient Kay guitar and Tony entertained the family, the teenagers grinning the whole time.

"It's like, great to hear some different songs," Amy said, chewing on the ends of her brunette strands. "Mom and Pop sing the same old stuff and won't let us near the guitar."

Tony smiled. "Back in de Tolosa, I had to build my own. But it was worth it. Along with Fox, music is something I can't live without."

The girl's face darkened.

"Yeah, she's gonna be a problem," Maryann said. "We just need to find a musical troupe and get both these horny kids married—"

"MoTHer," Amy groaned and the group laughed.

Ryan sat quietly and, when he thought no one noticed, stared at Fox's breasts. Tony smiled. Evidently, going topless hadn't erased the boy's attraction to boobs.

As the glowing mountains turned black, Maryann led Tony and Fox down the canyon path to a pond above the dam where they could bathe. After soaking in the cold water and scrubbing furiously, they returned to the darkening house, to their room made from reed partitions. Sheets and what looked like hand-woven blankets covered their pallet. They slipped under the cool sheets, a first experience for the couple, and lay side-by-side, not speaking. A breeze blew from the mountains toward the sea, warming them. They rolled back the covers and lay naked, their bodies tingling. When Tony touched her, she came into his arms and they kissed.

"Take it slow," Fox whispered in his ear. "Let's make this last."

For a while it felt like they'd been transported back home, lying by Tolosa Creek in the evening air, letting their bodies find their natural rhythm and pace, breathing slow and deep, then fast when the moments came.

Afterwards, Tony settled back and closed his eyes. From above, the floorboards creaked followed by a soft giggle. The flicker of a candle shone through a crack in the ceiling. Tony reached down and pulled the sheet over them.

"Nosy kid," he whispered into Fox's ear.

"You remember when we spied on the McCloskeys when we were twelve? They had that big tent two camps down and liked to make love in the afternoon."

"Yeah, I remember. I couldn't keep my hands off you after that."

"I feel sorry for Amy and Ryan," Fox said. "They're out here by themselves."

"Not for much longer, I suspect."

Outside, a rustle of wings stirred the night air and an owl called mournfully. The wind died and from down canyon the burble of the creek filled the stillness. *Yes, a few days here will be good,* Tony thought as he drifted into dreams of the Channel Islands on the glittering horizon, across the towering seas of Winslow Homer's "Gulf Coast."

8

Captain Hanpian had waited two days. During that time, only huge drone freighters passed Sergeant Statler's police stakeout at Gaviota Pass, with no sign of a kayak or the fugitives. He'd ordered Statler to move overland and swarm Surf City. They'd found only a bunch of stoned surfers with the girls running around without tops. They spent two days searching the back canyons and the hills above the camp, but turned up nothing.

The daily vid conferences with Commander Pynard got more and more shrill. Finally on the fifth day, Hanpian had something positive to report.

"We think we've got a lead, Commander," he said into the com, "but I'm not sure how helpful it is."

"Go ahead, tell me. I'll take anything at this point. I can't believe those punks can evade us for so long."

"My staff reviewed the vid files of the train platforms from Santa Barbara to El Lay. A couple of days ago, five of the Surf City loaders got off at the northern Santa Barbara platform. Only three got back on."

"What the hell are those degenerates doing on that train anyway?" Pynard barked. "It's supposed to be sealed."

"Come on Commander, you know very well about Emerald Magic and the Surfers' trade with the District Alliance."

"Oh God, I'd hoped that had all gone away. So you think they're in Santa Barbara?"

"Yes. We've reviewed the vids of the lower State Street Clans. Other than a few muggings, they haven't shown us anything. But the kids are down there some-where, and getting help."

"And you think this is something positive?" the commander cracked. "Christ, there are parts of Santa Barbara where we have no eyes at all. It could take us weeks to—"

"Yes, but that's where we need to start. Send drones out to the blind areas first. It'll take a few days. I'll start at the north platform and work outward."

"That makes sense. Just do it."

The vid screen filled with the Commander's curly-haired head went dark and he sat back in his seat, thinking. Hanpian's Mark VII Robomaid rolled toward his vid station. It carried a dust cloth and a bottle of cleaning fluid.

"Not now, Karen," he barked. "Can't you see I'm busy?" He shooed it with his hands.

"I'm sorry, Captain." The robot's voice sounded apologetic. "I will wait until you are finished." It rotated on its base and scooted away.

Hanpian smiled. He had named the mechanical servant after his older sister who used to boss him around as a kid. Now he secretly enjoyed playing role-reversal games with... it.

The Captain studied his aerial photos of northern Santa Barbara and the train platform. "Now where would I go from there?" he muttered to himself. "Who might they know?" Another map snapped onto a vid screen highlighting City sectors that lacked surveil-lance. They included the old burned-out neighbor-hoods surrounding the platform and a broad swath of the northern foothills cut by deep canyons. "I bet they're up there somewhere," he muttered.

He fingered the control panel and clicked on another vid screen. The large airy room in the top floor of the Police Operations Center gleamed brightly in the morning sun. Tony's mother sat in a chair next to a window that overlooked de Tolosa's old downtown. The vid com sat on the table in front of her.

"Good morning, Ms. Matteson. I hope you're at ease in your temporary home."

"It's still a cage, no matter how comfortable you make it." A slight smile curled her full lips. "So how are you boys doing? Catch my son yet?"

"Well, there've been some developments."

"Ah ha. And you need me to help you how?"

"We think your son and his girl are somewhere in Santa Barbara."

The woman grinned. "Good God, they've made it that far."

"So you agree, that they're heading south?"

The woman swore under her breath. "Clever, Captain. Very clever. So were you lying about them making it to Santa Barbara?"

"No."

"So why are you bothering me about these details? Even if I could help you, I wouldn't."

"You're an intelligent woman, a teacher I've been told. If what your son told you is proven to be true, the murder charge could be dropped. You wouldn't want those kids to be running from the law their entire lives, would you? That's no kind of life."

Ms. Matteson seemed to consider his statement, then shook her head. "I don't think I can trust you, Captain. Once you have them in custody, you'll forget all about dropping the murder charge. A citizen is dead and clearing my son won't satisfy the powers that be."

Hanpian sat back in his chair, knowing that the woman spoke the truth. The evidence of murder was so clear, while the evidence of an attempted rape didn't exist. He'd been surprised that the Untouchable had disconnected the interior vid system in his house. Maybe they might take a closer look at the forensics.

But whatever the Police did, Hanpian knew it wouldn't be enough to get the mother to turn on her son.

"I don't blame your skepticism, Ms. Matteson. But think about never seeing your son again."

She snapped. "Don't you think I already have?"

"Yes, I suppose you have. Let me look into the evidence and—"

"Why are you keeping me here, Captain? When can I leave this gilded cage?"

"In a while, Ma'am, in a while."

He clicked off the com and sat staring at her shapely body, resting in the chair and gazing upon the destroyed sectors of de Tolosa. This place was her city, he realized, not his. He was the outsider, being transferred to that post from far-off San Diego. Maybe if he asked her to teach him about her home, befriend her as a teacher, he might gain her confidence and she might open up. Hanpian thought about weeks and months of chasing the two rabbits all over the State and beyond, with their capture uncertain.

He returned to staring at the maps of Santa Barbara. Hunting down fugitives felt so much easier than figuring out what made that woman tick.

9

Fox sat in bright sunlight amongst a knee-high patch of pink and scarlet flowers. She balanced the artist's board across her knees and dabbed at blotches of color on her palette. It had taken a day to dissolve the old chunks of watercolor into something useful. But the range of colors worked perfectly and she'd already completed the first washes of her painting, a brilliant flower field with a backdrop of towering mountains beneath blue sky. Maryann said she'd found the art materials in the old headquarters for the Botanical Gardens. The building stood under the oaks at the downhill end of the field, its roof crushed by a massive branch that had sheared off during a winter storm, its stucco walls cracked and crumbling. Fox had completed a pencil portrait of the structure, given it to Maryann and Glen as a gift for their kindness.

The sun shone on her bare front and back that were tanned the color of sandstone. Fox's mother had always said she must have Latina blood in her because as a redhead, she didn't freckle, didn't turn pink, but browned like a Chicana. As she painted, she thought about her parents, wandering the streets of de Tolosa looking for a new home. *Had the 'Forcers rounded up the Touchables and jailed them all? Would they live as fugitives? Would they fight back? Or would they just fade away, the story of other clans in de Tolosa?* She wiped at her eyes, not wanting tears to ruin the watercolor.

A shadow fell across her painting and she looked up at Maryann. "Come sit with me for a while," Fox said.

The round woman groaned and lowered herself onto the ground. "It's getting harder for me to stand or sit," she complained, "the damn arthritis in my back, you know. But the sun feels good."

"My father has it in his shoulders. Do you take anything for the pain?"

"Well, that Emerald Magic you gave us will help. But we have a hard time finding prescription meds."

"You should connect up with the Surfers again. They say they get their supplies from some old hospital on the west side of the City."

"Yeah, well nobody around here can tell the difference between aspirin and arsenic... and the Shut-ins are the only ones with access to the web to find out."

"That's tough," Fox said. "In de Tolosa, one of our senior clansmen was a trained doctor. He was great, especially with pediatrics. We were lucky to have him."

Maryann stared at Fox. The silence built between them as Fox continued to dab at her painting.

"So how far along are you?" Maryann asked.

Fox's hand froze above the board, her paintbrush dripping scarlet onto its white surface. "How... how... what?" She sucked in a deep breath and stared at the older woman.

Maryann grinned back. "Look, I remember what I looked like when I first became pregnant. And you have that... that look."

"I... God, I haven't told anybody... and I'm not really sure..."

"When was your last period?"

"I'm three weeks late and I've been very regular. But it might be too soon to tell if—"

"Come with me."

Groaning, Maryann pushed herself upright and taking Fox's hand led the girl to the far end of the field and into the deep shade of the oaks. From a pocket of her billowing skirt she retrieved a small packet.

"Where did you get those?" Fox asked, her eyes wide.

"Don't tell my husband, but on our last trip into the City, I got them from a State Street clansman in exchange for a couple bags of our grass."

"But why..."

"Hey look, sister. Glen and I might look, ya know, frumpy. But he can be a real stallion in the sack. And I'm still young enough to bear children."

"Yeah, and if Glen is anything like Tony, birth control is all your responsibility."

"That's right. So go ahead and pee on a strip. They may be a hundred years old but last time I checked they still worked."

Fox disappeared into the woods behind the headquarters building. In a few minutes she returned, her lips trembling.

"Well, did it stay white or is it pinkish?" Maryann asked.

"It's pink."

The two women stared at each other, then broke into broad grins. "Congratulations," Maryann said. "You're gonna have a beautiful child. But you have to tell Tony."

Fox frowned and sat on a boulder, staring at the ground. "I... I don't know if I want to."

"Why the hell not? He is the father, isn't he?"

"Of course he is. But I'm afraid he'll send me back or turn us both in to the Police. You know how boys... how men get all weird, all protective when their wives become pregnant."

"Yeah. You should have seen Glen. With Amy, he wouldn't let me get out of bed for the first couple of months. He did everything. I was livin' it up."

"I'm afraid Tony won't think I'm up to running with him. But I feel fine, feel strong. There's no reason why..."

Maryann reached forward and placed a hand on Fox's bare shoulder. "It's okay, honey. You don't need to tell him now. Wait until you two get... get settled."

"Yeah, settled."

"But Tony's gonna notice soon enough and then there's... there's morning sickness and frequent peeing. I suggest you start wearing a shirt over that magnificent front of yours. That'll keep him from suspecting for awhile. And it'll keep my son from going crazy." Maryann laughed.

The two women hugged and moved toward the field. In the distance, the high whine of a crawler pierced the stillness. They ducked behind trees and kept low. The drone with its camera pod rotating cruised past on the road above the garden. Fox stared into the open field and let out a deep breath. Only the teenagers worked the garden. Glen and Tony were nowhere in sight. Maryann held a finger to her lips. Fox nodded. They waited, sweating in the hot shade, until Maryann gave the sign and they made a dash for the house.

When the women entered the home, Tony stared at them from his soft chair. Glen sat across the room, not talking. When Fox started to speak, Glen held a finger to his lips.

"Keep it low," he whispered. "The drones will cruise up canyon to where the road dead ends, then turn around and come back. Just sit tight."

The group stayed quiet and watched the two teenagers through the door, bending to pull weeds from the vegetable patch, quiet in their work. They reminded Tony of his childhood friends before he and Fox had become inseparable. He and three other boys had run throughout de Tolosa, sneaking into buildings looking for treasure. The crawlers didn't pay much attention to them. By the time Tony turned thirteen, he knew every corner of the old downtown, every room in each abandoned building, even the ones that had barely withstood the last earthquake.

But one time, he had ditched his buddies, climbed a rusting fire escape, and kicked in the window of a fourth-floor office. The room hadn't been opened since before the Change. Its air smelled like a pup tent full of dirty clothes. Climbing inside, he stepped onto soft carpet. The sun shown through another window, through Venetian blinds that cast striped shadows across a desk, file cabinets, and a chair filled with someone's desiccated remains. A pistol lay on the floor at the corpse's feet. The man had slumped onto the desk where a dried chocolate puddle surrounded his skull, staining clumps of papers, lots of papers. Tony had thought about that man working day after day in his tiny sun-lit office until no work remained, no more life for him.

After that day, his adventures with his punk friends became more personal and not just about buildings and treasure, but also about the people who had lived and worked there. He felt that way now and wondered where he and Fox would end up. But most of all, he wished he'd snatched up that dead man's pistol.

In a few minutes the high whine of the crawler passing downhill brought Tony back from his memories. The teenagers working the garden waved at it then flipped it off, but didn't stop their work.

Glen let out a breath. "That's the second drone patrol in two days."

"When was the first?" Tony demanded.

"Yesterday, early."

"Why didn't you wake us?"

"You guys looked like you could use the sleep and I couldn't tell if it was just a normal patrol. But with this one today... something's up."

"We need to leave tonight," Tony said.

"Yeah, I'm thinkin' maybe it's time," Glen said. "Well at least you guys have a better plan than what you showed up with."

"Yeah, thanks for all the help and gear."

The couple spent the afternoon preparing to flee. Maryann retrieved an old bottle of bleach and some strong peroxide and made a mess of dying Fox's hair blonde, actually closer to a light pink. Glen helped Tony stock their backpacks with venison jerky and fresh baked zucchini bread. The couple torched their surfer clothes in the fireplace and put on denim pants and work shirts that, according to Glen, looked like the crap the Lower State Street Clans wore. "If you get spotted, the 'Forcers will think you're just a couple thugs out of your territory."

They ate a quiet dinner. Tony studied the map atlas that Glen had given him, tried to memorize the route that would take them deep into the Southland, a route where nighttime surveillance wouldn't exist or would be minimal. As the sky turned crimson, then purple, Glen and Tony moved to the garden shed and rolled two fat-tired bicycles into the house's front room. Glen bent to check the equipment, tire pressure, brake cables, gear changers, wheel nuts. They made final adjustments to the seats and clamped a tiny hand pump to one of the frames.

"It's been a while since I've ridden a bike," Fox said. "But I did a lot when I was little."

"Well, you guys take it slow and careful. The roads will be in bad shape. And these bikes are antiques, built before the end of the Petroleum Era."

"How can you tell?" Tony asked.

"When I found them, their gears and front sprockets were smeared with black grease. Nobody has used that stuff since 2025 when burning any kind of fuel was outlawed."

"Too little, too late," Maryann grumbled.

Ryan piped up. "Yeah, and then the Mid-East blew up in civil war, after their one trick pony named oil died."

Tony wondered where the teens had learned their history and hoped that Maryann would teach them well. The group watched the last rays of sunlight fade away. A half moon lit the flower field and picked out the edges of the prickly oak trees. They hugged.

"Get settled soon," Maryann said to Fox.

"We will. Don't worry... and thanks for the bikes."

A soft wind blew inland off the ocean. Struggling under the weight of their backpacks, they pushed the bicycles up the path to the road above the garden. Looking back, Tony could just make out the bare-chested quartet standing in front of their reed house, waving. He wondered how many more goodbyes and hellos there would be before they could stop running. They'd been gone from de Tolosa barely two weeks. But it felt like years since he'd listened to his mother's stories, to the chatter from the campsites, to the arguments, "discussions" his mother called them, at the long tables during mealtime. He and Fox had stayed together, but they'd lost their families, their community... and for what? None of it made much sense to Tony. But neither did spending their lives in prison, working at one of the cluster of solar electric stations in Nevada or Arizona that produced energy to power the country's massive computer network.

Tony pushed off and coasted downhill, testing the bike's brakes, with Fox riding beside him. The road almost disappeared under the trees and they rode slowly. In less than a kilometer they came to an intersection and turned south once again. Their route crossed the lower folds of the coastal mountains. They pedaled steadily and constantly used the gears, either climbing or coasting downhill with little flat space in between. Below them, a few night lights defined Santa Barbara's Untouchable neighborhoods. In the lower State Street area, an open fire burned on the roof of a building, probably one of the old hotels, Tony guessed. And then the sea, glittering in the moonlight, the remains of an old pier offshore and barely visible above the waves.

They listened for crawlers but heard nothing above the wind in their ears. Bicycling felt easier to Tony than paddling the kayak. But the tug of his overloaded backpack caused his lower spine to ache and Fox also complained about hers. They stopped every hour or so to straighten up and massage the muscles.

"I know they made trailers for these things," Tony said.

Fox stood arching her back and moaning. "Yeah, when we get south of the city we should look for one."

"We have about a two-day supply of water. We'll need to find a clan by then or find some stream with clear water. The map shows there's not much of anything between here and Ventura and I'm sure the Coast Highway is flooded."

"Should we cut inland?"

"There's no easy route there and it's even more deserted."

They moved slowly southward, riding in the center of the road whenever possible. The sparse lights of the city fell behind them. The sky started to turn gray and the onshore wind picked up. Below them, a broad terrace extended from the base of the mountains that they crossed to the sea. A maze of swamps and lagoons covered the terrace with only disconnected segments of roads passing through it.

"We'll have to stay up high to avoid that," Fox said and pointed.

"I know. Let's get off the road and sleep. We'll head south at dusk."

"Yeah, my back's killing me."

The pair rolled to a stop next to a grove of oaks and sycamores and pulled their bikes downslope, into the trees and out of sight of the road. They dug pieces of tough jerky out of Tony's pack and ate breakfast, their first food since a midnight snack. Fox winced as she pulled off her riding gloves. The constant tugging on the handlebars had cracked open her chafed skin. At the base of a huge oak they lay on the stony ground wrapped in her cloak and slept.

Tony awoke in mid-afternoon to the whine of a crawler on the road above them. Fox's eyes blinked open and Tony pressed a finger to her lips and hissed, "crawlers." They remained motionless as the drone rolled past without hesitating.

He whispered in her ear, "There must be Untouchables living in these hills and they'll have surveillance. We shouldn't move until dark."

"I'm not moving anywhere. Just let me sleep."

"Yeah, go ahead. I gotta pee."

"I already did, twice last night. Ya know, you snore like a warthog." Fox turned her back to him. Her chuckling turned into long deep breaths almost instantly.

Tony pushed himself to his feet and rubbed his back and legs. He wondered if these morning pains were what old people always talked about. He crept to the edge of the tree canopy and stared downslope. The tile roofs of the Untouchables' homes, sporting wind turbines and solar panels, dotted the slopes with long access drives cutting off from the road they traveled now.

A delivery van whooshed past, braked, and wound its way downhill to one of the houses. Tony wondered how the Shut-ins could live so far from Santa Barbara's supplyport and its distribution center. Maybe the southbound train made other stops that

Glen and Maryann didn't know about. Maybe they could rejoin the Surfer loaders on the train and get a fast ride to the Southland. But the platforms would have eyes everywhere and they'd likely be picked off at the next stop. *Better to take it slow and easy.*

He stared at Fox sleeping so soundly. She's tough, he thought, but there was something different about her, something that he'd never seen. Maybe she just looked older from being on the run. But he knew that didn't explain everything. Tony slumped onto the ground and gazed seaward, at distant waves breaking over the foundations of old houses that used to line the coast. He retrieved his map atlas from the pack and studied their route. Another five or ten kilometers south, the roads ran next to the ocean with no inland alternatives. *I hope the water's shallow,* he thought and grinned to himself, then leaned back and dozed.

Fox woke him at dusk. She chewed on a piece of Glen's jerky and mumbled, "God this stuff tastes soooo good." She handed him a long strip of the leathery meat. "I must be using up all my salt." Tony took a few bites from his strip and handed her back the remainder. The evening sky was clear, with a light offshore breeze that would keep the fog bank at bay until the wind turned in the night. Tony hoped they'd be past that narrow stretch of coastline before a blanket of fog smothered them on some open hillside with no cover.

They peddled slowly in the moonlight. Only a few Untouchable homes had night lights; but all homes had camera pods on their roofs. The flooded city of Carpinteria lay dark below them. Offshore, two massive freighters plied the channel, moving steadily toward their SoCal ports. Tony thought, if they could just get aboard one of those drones, they could really make good time, or even leave the country. He pictured himself and Fox, alone at the bow of a slab-like ship, chasing the sun westward toward China or Korea and the massive industrial complexes along the Yellow Sea. But then the crush of people would be... horrible, would steal any privacy that the couple had enjoyed. It would be like prison where every movement is watched and recorded.

Their road leveled off then turned downslope. They stopped for a pee break and to stare at the atlas, published in the 20th Century by some group named State Farm, probably a company in the Mid-West, where the government controlled crop production on massive cultivated tracts tended by drone machines.

Tony shined his hand light on the atlas. "We need to head for here." He pointed to a spot where the road passed between two headlands and hugged the coastline. "That stretch is gonna be underwater. We may get wet tonight."

Fox chuckled. "I don't mind. When we were in the kayak, all I wanted to do was get dry. Now, it's just the opposite. So long as the water's not that deep or cold, I could use a bath."

"Glen didn't mention anything about submerged roads. But then he's probably never been that far south. I bet we'll be right up against the shore break. There's no walking through that."

They rode side-by-side downhill, the cool October air drying their sweat, sucking away body heat. At the base of the mountain, they turned down a narrow lane and headed toward the coast and the freeway. To the north, ocean waves crashed onto the broad expanse of crumbling concrete. But their section crossed a hillock perched above the sea. The massive highway then dove through a cleft in the coastal mountains. They let their bikes roll free on the steep downhill run. But at the bottom of the hill they found the ocean and barely stopped in time before plowing into the surf. Tony dropped his bike to the pavement and pulled out the road atlas.

"What the hell happened to Rincon Point?" he blurted. "If it's underwater then... "

Fox nodded. "Yeah, the highway is gone along this section. At least there won't be any crawlers."

"Yeah, but we're between the mountains and the sea. Where the hell can we ride?"

Fox pointed to the looming slope in the moonlight. "See that shelf?"

Tony gazed uphill and could barely make out a narrow bench cut into the face of the near-vertical slope. "Yeah, but just barely."

"Coming down the hill, I saw that the railroad passed under us. I think that's the rail line."

They pushed their bikes back uphill until reaching an overpass bridge. Below them, the electrified line for the coast freight gleamed in the moonlight. They slid down the slope under the bridge, struggling with the bikes while trying to balance their overstuffed back-packs. The rails, inset into their concrete base, hummed in the damp night air, with less than a meter space on the outside of the line to walk on.

"We should go single file along the side against the hill," Tony said.

"Yeah, but I think we'll be hoofing it. I'm not as steady on a bike as I used to be. One slip and I'd be into the rails. You'd be eating me as jerky."

Tony grinned. "Nah, you're tough, but not that tough."

Tony led off, placing his bicycle closest to the rail and striding alongside it, his sandals touching the outside edge of the track bed. The narrow hillside bench was just wide enough for a train to pass, with few wide spots that let the pair leave their path and rest. They concentrated on each step, stopping when a cloud blocked the moonlight. They had walked for several hours when the shelf disappeared from beneath them. Tony clicked on his hand light and pointed it downward. The rail bed floated on top of a massive trestle that crossed a steep chasm. Tony kept his light on as they edged forward. After a few minutes of walking, the moonlight dimmed and Tony glanced toward the Pacific. Soft gray billows of fog rolled toward them, pushed by a cold sea breeze.

"We gotta get off this trestle," Fox complained, her voice a high girlish squeak.

Tony murmured, "Just take it easy, babe, and stay close."

They pushed forward slowly. Gradually, the mountain re-appeared on their left and the shelf slid under them. With a gasp, Tony stepped off the concrete bed onto a narrow pad of dirt and leaned against the cliff, breathing hard. Fox stood beside him, shuddering violently.

"I hope we don't have any more of that," he said. "We've come too far to turn around. And crossing these mountains at night would be impossible."

Fox continued to shake. Tony grasped her in his arms and waited until her breaths returned to their normal cadence and the tremor died. They continued. To break the tension he sang a new tune that had been rattling around in his brain for the past week. Fox suggested a new word or phrase here and there and he sang their way south. In the fog, their flat route seemed to float in thin air, disconnected from the rest of the planet, drifting somewhere beyond the moon, maybe in the asteroid belt out past Mars. They crossed another trestle, the second longer than the first, and leaned against the hillside at its far end.

"Ya know," Tony said, wheezing, "they used to put railings on those damn things."

"Yeah, I saw the same old photos that you did. But that's when men used to work the rails. We're probably the first humans that have ever walked this thing."

"And probably the last. The Police might send a drone down the rails to search for us. But I can't see anybody coming out here, especially at night."

At the end of a third trestle, Fox collapsed. "I... I can't do any more of this. Gotta rest."

Tony sat beside her and stroked her damp hair. "Just a bit farther, until we can get off the tracks and into cover."

"No. I... I... my back is killing me and..."

"Look, we must be near the south end." The sky had cleared. In the moonlight, a steep but passable slope fell away from the rail line toward the distant rumble of the sea. "We'll find some place on that slope to hole up."

He stood and tugged on one of Fox's arms. "Come on, babe. We can sleep all day... "

Grunting, Fox pushed herself to her feet and the pair trudged southward. On a slight curve, they hoisted their bikes onto their shoulders and stepped cautiously over the electrified rails. Fox crumpled when she reached the far side. Tony stood with hands on knees, his chest heaving. He hadn't heard Fox cry for so long, and it tore at his heart to hear her sob with exhaustion.

"I'm sorry, I'm sorry," she whined. "I'll be all right in a minute."

"It's okay, Fox. We've come far enough tonight."

As they rested, the moon disappeared and the gray dawn lightened the coastal mountains. Groaning, they scrambled downslope, half wheeling, half carrying their bicycles until they reached a grove of dwarf oak trees. Burrowing into the thicket, they found a clear space large enough to lie on the ground.

"You gotta eat something before you sleep." Tony handed Fox a chunk of zucchini bread. They munched in silence and took long swigs from their water bottles. Tony gathered handfuls of dried oak leaves and carpeted the ground with a thick spongy mat. Once again, Fox's cloak became their bedroll. She stretched out, groaned once and fell asleep. Tony retrieved the map atlas from his pack and crept to the downhill edge of their hiding place. They were camped a kilometer or so north of the partially-flooded City of Buena Ventura. To the south, the coast highway bridged a large lagoon then disappeared underwater. The remnants of stone breakwaters, that had once protected some sort of boat harbor, foamed with a covering sea that rolled inland to crash against the base of chalk-white bluffs topped with derelict hotels and other commercial buildings. Farther south, a river joined the ocean and had formed a broad sand delta. The entire area looked abandoned, with no sign of crawlers, which made sense: the Untouchables' houses with their spinning wind turbines dotted the hillsides above the city. That's where the Police would patrol.

A smudge on the clear morning sky caught Tony's attention. He stared directly downslope to where the freeway emerged from the sea and crossed a knoll. A house sat on the point of land next to the ocean. Smoke poured from its chimney. A tiny sailboat, not much longer than their kayak, bobbed in the sea, tethered to a makeshift dock. With the highway submerged on either side of the house, Tony knew it couldn't be an Untouchable's home since the vans couldn't get to it. He stared at the place for a long time. No one appeared outside. He returned to a snoring Fox and snuggled up beside her, his mind spinning, thinking up new routes of escape, dreaming of better days ahead as his muscles relaxed and sleep overtook him.

10

Captain Hanpian played with the ends of his mustache and scowled at the vid screens. Sergeant Statler's head filled one of them, the man's fat lips moving rapidly, spitting out words so fast that Hanpian had told him to slow down. Another vid screen showed the playback of their raid on the Santa Barbara home. *That man's a complete idiot,* the Captain thought as he listened to the sergeant. It's as if he feels our failure will be less embarrassing if he throws a few thousand words at it. He snapped off the audio to Statler's screen and watched the vid record of the raid with half-closed eyes:

A pack of crawlers surround a house made of reeds and heavy timbers at the edge of a beautiful garden. Police dressed in black jumpsuits and helmets, with faceguards lowered, storm through the front door. Inside a half-naked couple and their two teenagers sit at a table and grin stupidly at the eyes. The quartet is marched outside, while the eyes follow the search team throughout the building.

The officers find an old guitar and swab the strings for cells. The swab is taken to the portable laboratory at the back of one of the crawlers. The test results are flashed on the screen almost instantaneously: the cells belong to fugitive Anthony Matteson. Another officer sifts through the ashes in a fireplace and finds unburned remnants of clothes similar to those worn by the Surf City Clan. The officer collects more cells that are tested: they belong to Fox Slade. They also find her cells on two pieces of artwork proudly displayed on the mantle above the fireplace.

The officers hustle the renegade family into a van for processing. The van departs for the Regional Courts-Jail Complex in Goleta. The eyes continue to document the police search of the grounds, recording the imprints made by narrow tires on the trail that leads to the service road above the garden. The vid screen goes dark.

Hanpian reached forward and returned the audio to Statler's screen. The sergeant's voice filled the Captain's home-office.

"In conclusion, we missed the fugitives by a day, maybe two. They appear to be continuing south on bicycles, riding during the dark hours since our eyes along the South Coast have shown nothing unusual."

Hanpian keyed his com. "Thank you, Sergeant, for such a... a comprehensive report."

"You're welcome, sir. What are your orders, sir?"

"Hold your position in Carpinteria, Sergeant. The fugitives' bicycles will be useless south of Rincon Point. They may have abandoned them and taken to the mountains. But we need to study satellite surveillance before you make your next move."

"Will do, Captain."

Sipping his coffee, actually chicory-flavored colored water since the imported stuff cost too many credits, Hanpian moved to his home gymnasium. He peeled off his clothes and stared into the mirrored wall at his body. At sixty-three, he looked pale and sickly. His two-hours-a-day exercise and weight training routine had flattened his belly but little else. Still, he pictured himself standing naked next to the Matteson woman, pulling her into his arms, kissing her on the mouth, and then carrying her to his bed.

Shaking his head and laughing, Hanpian slipped into a pair of running briefs and keyed the treadmill for a moderate-to-difficult workout. A vid screen showed the old highway running north of de Tolosa into the mountains, uphill toward the Cuesta Ridge. He attached the machine's body monitoring sensors and started running, the overgrown highway opening slowly before him as he passed through groves of oaks and eucalyptus. As the steepness increased, he glanced at the monitoring screen and smiled, his heart rate, blood pressure, and blood-oxygen level all within normal ranges. As he ran, he studied the rail line that descended from Cuesta Ridge, passing through numerous tunnels on its way to de Tolosa.

A shiver ran down his back and he hopped off the treadmill, disconnected all the monitoring devices, and hustled back to his vid room. Keying a large panel, he called up the high resolution satellite feed digitally recorded and enhanced the previous afternoon. Huge combers crashed against the base of the mountains along the Rincon Coast, swamping most sections of the old Coast Highway. But uphill from the sea, the thread line of the railroad cut across slope, bridged deep canyons on steel trestles, and passed through the abandoned section of Buena Ventura.

"They did it again," he muttered and stabbed at the com that connected him to Statler.

"Yes, Captain, did I forget something?" the sergeant asked.

"No, no. But the fugitives used the rail line to reach Ventura. You need to get down there, pronto."

"The rail line? Really? That thing has no shoulders and the drops are... "

"Damn it, I know that. But these two have... have more guts than brains. If they're anywhere, they're on that line close to its south end, or in Ventura."

"Roger that, Captain. The fog here has played havoc with our solar rechargers, so it'll be a couple of hours until we can depart... and the routes through the mountains are treacherous. Our ETA in Ventura is 1800 hours."

"Just get to it."

Hanpian clicked off the com. "Crap, now where are they?" he muttered. He'd been talking out loud to himself over the past several weeks, ever since the destruction of the Garage. In addition to the escapees, he had a clan of displaced misfits roaming the streets of de Tolosa looking for a new home, and a fugitive's mother locked up indefinitely in her gilded cage. So far, he'd failed to capture the girl's parents, although satellite surveillance had picked up several adults moving northward through the interior valley toward San Simeon and the Big Sur coast. Once they reached those mountains, they'd be impossible to find.

He shook his head, as if trying to rattle away the bad thoughts, and studied a vid screen that displayed enhanced photographs of the Rincon Coast taken the day before. Near the northern approach to Ventura, he outlined with a finger the coastline, looking for any-thing that might be attractive to the fugitives. A squatter's cabin on a point of land next to the ocean caught his attention. But it was cut off from the roads. If anything, the pair would have followed the tracks southward across the lagoon and into town. He continued to stare blindly at the vid, until a particular detail became clear in his brain. Some sort of small boat rested against a dock next to the cabin.

Hanpian called up the real-time feed for the same area and stared at the fuzzy and pixilated images. He managed to locate the squatter's cabin and the dock. The boat had vanished.

"Shit," he muttered.

11

When Tony awoke, the sun hung several centimeters above the Pacific. He nudged Fox and she rolled onto her back and blinked rapidly, groaning. They both sat up, almost bonking their heads together. Standing, they moved in opposite directions into the oak thicket to relieve themselves. When Fox returned to their campsite, Tony had sliced some zucchini bread and laid out strips of jerky and the last of their dried fruit. Their water bottles stood almost empty. Tony sat rubbing the circulation back into his left side while staring at the map atlas in his lap.

"How are you feeling?" he asked.

"Like somebody has been beating me... and just stopped."

"Are you gonna be able to hustle today? We could always find someplace in Ventura to hole up, someplace where there's no surveillance."

"And where might that be?" Fox said. "No, we need to keep moving and get there while... while I'm still in one piece."

"Are you planning on falling apart?" Tony asked and dug her in the ribs.

"Don't do that... and no. I just feel like I am."

They finished their breakfast-at-dinnertime meal and waited for the sun to set. "What about staying there for half the night?" Fox pointed downslope to the cabin.

"Yeah, I was thinking about that. I've only seen one person come out the back door to tend a fire. She looks like one of us... definitely not an Untouchable."

"Maybe she has some water we can have."

"Yeah, maybe. But let's get down there before dark. I don't want to scare her. We'll leave the bikes here and just take our gear."

Tony hoisted the antique carbon-fiber-frame upward and helped Fox loop her arms through its shoulder straps. She did the same for him. They emerged from the oak grove and half slid, half fell down the steep slope cut by a green crease in the brown vegetation that ended in the yard of the squatter's cabin.

"Looks like a spring of some kind," Tony said. "At least we know she'll have water."

The squat dwelling sported windows on all sides; the ones facing the hillside were shuttered. Two wind turbines spun on the roof and an odd-looking array of solar panels covered half its surface. The couple made as much noise as possible moving through the shoulder-high brush, wanting to warn the woman of their arrival. At the rear of the house, a low fence with two strands of wire stretched above its top rail enclosed a yard where chickens scratched at the ground. A huge cat lay in the waning sunlight, legs extended full length, eyes closed.

Tony stood with his hand on the gate latch. "Hello, is anybody home?" he called. The cat woke, stretched and pushed through a hole in the screen door into the house.

"I said, hello, is anybody—"

The screen slapped open and a round woman with white pigtails and brown skin stormed out carrying some sort of weapon. She stopped and sighted down its long barrel at Tony.

"Now hold on, Ma'am, hold on," Tony sputtered.

"We just need... need some water," Fox squeaked.

The woman lowered her weapon and grinned. "Jeez, I didn't even know you were a girl. That short haircut and getup had me fooled."

"One hundred percent female," Fox said, "and about to wet my pants."

"Use the privy," the woman said and motioned with her rifle.

The woman carefully opened the gate and Fox stepped into the yard, slipped out of her pack straps, ran to the closet-like shed in the far corner, and disappeared inside.

"What's with the wires?" Tony asked, pointing to the fence.

The woman grinned, "You're lucky you didn't try climbing over it. The thing's electrified."

"But... but why?"

"The last couple of years the black bears keep coming outta the mountains, trying to get at the water and my chickens. The fence slows them down enough until I can get my gun and scare them off."

The woman turned on Tony. "Now, what's this all about? How did you get here? Dog and I have been watching the sea all morning and I haven't seen a single craft in close."

"We're from de Tolosa up north. We walked all night to get here from Rincon Point."

"Don't give me that crap." The woman scowled. "There's no coastal trail and no beach... only the mountains and the sea."

"Believe me, we know. We had to walk the railroad."

The woman's mouth fell open. "That's crazy. You can get yourselves fried that way."

"We know. But we had no alternative."

"So why are you running? Who'd ya kill?"

Tony felt his face burn and he tried laughing it off. "Why, what have you heard?"

The woman chuckled. "Young man, out here, I don't hear much of anything, don't get many visitors. And I can't remember the last one that came overland." She leaned her weapon against the house's outer wall, dipped a wrinkled hand into a feedbag, and sprinkled grain across the ground. The chickens clucked their appreciation. She wore a thick cloak that reminded Tony of Fox's. But the woman's garment included intricate designs, flowers of some sort.

Fox rejoined them. "That's a beautiful cloak, Ma'am."

"Okay, let's get one thing straight," the woman said sternly. "My name is not Ma'am. It's Amelia."

"I'm Tony and this is Fox."

"Fox?" The woman raised a dark eyebrow and grinned, showing two rows of tiny white teeth.

"Yes, my parents named me after the natural color of my hair."

"Good God, girl. So why did you bleach it that ugly pink?"

"That's a long story," Tony said quickly.

"I haven't had anybody tell me a long story in years. Why don't you come in out of the wind and I'll put on a pot of my famous rosehip tea."

The couple looked at each other and smiled. One large room occupied the cabin's entire interior, with areas organized for sleeping, reading and music, and preparing food. A large black dog with golden eyes stretched out in the sunlight beneath a huge window that overlooked the ocean. The dog lifted its head to stare at Fox and Tony and licked its graying muzzle with a pink tongue, its tail thumping the floorboards. An old guitar leaned against a wall. Tony's fingers itched to play it. But in one corner, a vid screen flickered at them.

"Where'd... where'd you get that?" he asked, pointing. "You're not an Untouchable, are you?"

Amelia laughed. "Good God, if you only knew. But we call them the High Lifers where I come from."

"Sounds like we all have stories to tell," Fox said.

They sat on a cushioned bench in front of broad windows, the sun turning the room a blinding gold as it sank below the horizon.

"This place was all buttoned up when Dog and I found it years ago," Amelia said. "It came with one mummified High Lifer inside. I never could figure out how he got deliveries to this place. But he might have lived here before the sea change took out the south roads."

The old woman pushed through the back screen door and retrieved a kettle of boiling water from the grill over the fire pit. The teapot she set on the low table gave off a sweet and tangy fragrance. "Where I come from, our clan harvests wild rosehips and makes a tea blend that we trade to the High Lifers for stuff we can't grow."

"You trade with them?" Fox asked, her eyes wide.

"Yeah, in SoCal, the High Lifers aren't quite as... as isolated from the rest of the world as the Shut-ins are around here. It's hard to stay isolated when there are still three or four million of 'em living in the El Lay basin."

"So why did you come to this place?" Fox asked.

"Hold on, girl. You're the ones who just walked in here off the mountain. Your story first."

Tony glanced at Fox and decided to spin their tale cautiously, to gauge Amelia's reaction before opening up with details. "We're from de Tolosa. Our clan is the Touchables and we live, ah, lived in a huge garage in the center of town."

Amelia held a hand in the air, palm outward, and then moved to the vid console in the corner. She fumbled with the command pad then turned and motioned for the pair to join her. The grainy vid feed showed photographs of Fox and Tony; Fox still had her long red hair and pale impish face and Tony lacked the dark scratchy beard he now sported.

"Is this you?" Amelia asked.

"Yeah, that's us," Tony muttered.

"It says here that you're wanted for killing a citizen."

"That's right."

"Did you do it?"

"Yeah."

"Why?"

"He had us trapped in his house and wouldn't let us go unless Fox let him..."

"I get the picture," Amelia said and sighed. "My own son, Desy, was killed by a High Lifer after she seduced him then tried to weasel our tea formula out of him. She cut the poor boy in half with a laser, claimed it was self defense. He wasn't much older than... than you."

Amelia bowed her head and slurped her tea from an earthen cup. A strong onshore wind buffeted the house as the silence lengthened along with the deep shadows inside the cabin. Finally, she raised her head and smiled.

"So where are you kids headed? There are more Police in SoCal than up your way. It seems like you're going in the wrong direction."

"Maybe we are, Tony said. "But we've heard that the communes on the Channel Islands are free of surveillance and police patrols."

"Just how do you expect to get there? The channel is over 40 kilometers across, maybe 35 at its narrowest."

Tony looked at Fox and shrugged. "We haven't figured that out yet. The first part of our journey was by kayak. Maybe we can find one in Ventura or farther south and paddle out."

"That might have worked during the summer. But the autumn seas are already stirring up the channel. You'd make it a few kilometers before a rogue wave takes you under."

"Shit," Tony muttered. Fox reached over and rubbed his shoulders. "It's all right, Tony. We'll find a place to hide. I'm sure Amelia has some ideas."

The old woman laughed. "You're looking at somebody who's on the run herself. After that bitch killed my boy, a bunch of us blew a hole in her condo door and threw her off the freeway bridge into the lagoon. She cussed us out the whole way down. The 'Forcers have been looking for me for more than five years."

"Where are you talking about?" Fox asked.

"The name of our clan is the Dungees. We live on the Marsh Islands just inland from Long Beach, where Terminal Island and Wilmington used to be before the sea level rose. The High Lifers live in Palos Verdes and in the condos attached to the underside of the old freeway bridges that span our lagoon."

"How did you get here?" Tony asked.

"Didn't you see my fine vessel tied up out front? After the raid, Freddie, Dog, and I sailed north. But just up from Santa Monica Fred wanted off. The last time I saw him he was swimming through the surf toward the mountains. Hope that old guy made it."

Amelia stood and lit several beeswax candles. "I was just about to put on supper before you guys showed up. Diane died yesterday, so I'm having roasted chicken with vegetables from my garden."

"God, that sounds delicious," Fox said. She stretched out on the wooden plank floor and rubbed her back, arching her feet, groaning.

Amelia looked at her for a moment, then smiled and went about her business. "That spring you followed downhill gives me all the fresh water I need. I have a covered hot tub next to the fire pit if you want to take a bath later."

"The 'Forcers don't have any eyes around here, do they?" Tony asked.

"If you mean vid cams, the answer is no. I've disconnected the house's old system and threw the cameras into the ocean... only keep the one feed to track the Police."

"Makes sense," Tony said. "Mind if I play your guitar?"

"Heavens no. I don't play, myself. It was Freddie's. He left it with me when he jumped ship. You know, I keep looking for him. I figure that some day he'll come up the coast and keep me company for awhile. It's only been six or seven years."

"It must get lonely out here," Fox said.

"Damn straight, it does. You're the first face-to-face human contact I've had in three years. Sometimes I feel that I've become a High Lifer, shut away from the world, from other people. But my isolation is not by choice. I know I can never go back south. I have my garden, my hens, Dog and Kitty. I fish off the bluffs just north of here. I keep myself busy."

"Never going home, we know how that feels," Tony said and looked at Fox who turned away and swiped at her eyes with the sleeve of her shirt.

Tony managed to tune the old guitar and played quietly as Amelia shuffled back and forth between the kitchen and where they sat, laying out plates and glasses that had probably never been used since the Untouchable occupied the house. When she served them their meals, they tore into them with abandon. The tough chicken had a strong flavor but was nicely seasoned. The spinach and leafy vegetables tasted refreshing. Amelia kept filling their plates until both he and Fox leaned back onto the floor, burping and smiling.

Amelia cleared the dishes and joined them on the floor. "Sorry, but my water supply isn't big enough to grow anything that I can make wine or beer out of."

"That's all right," Tony said. "I've brought something with us." Fox looked at him with a raised eyebrow as he moved to his backpack and extracted a two kilo bag of Emerald Magic and an old pipe. He rejoined the women and began stuffing the potent marijuana into the pipe bowl.

"Just what the heck is that stuff?" Amelia asked.

"It's Emerald Magic. When we stayed with the Surf City clan, they gave me a—"

"I know damn well what that is. It's more like green gold. Every clan up and down the coast wants to get their hands on that stuff. The Surfers showed up in San Pedro years ago and we traded a boatload of tea for a couple kilo bags."

"Really," Tony said and grinned. "I don't know anything about trading. But if people want this, it could come in handy."

"Damn straight," Amelia said and chuckled. "You can buy yourself passage to the Channel Islands with that stuff."

The threesome lay on the floor and passed the pipe between them. The pain in Tony's back seemed to step outside his body and sit in the corner, watching them. They didn't speak, listened to the ocean lap against the boat dock, to the occasional squawk of seabirds in the night, to the whistle of the wind under the cabin's eaves. After a while, Amelia rose unsteadily to her feet and brought them large squares of soft cloth. The threesome stripped naked and, holding candles, slipped into the backyard. Amelia pulled a heavy lid off the hot tub. The water steamed in the darkness. They rinsed in a cold tub fed by the uphill spring, then slipped into the hot water, each groaning with pleasure.

"I'm not sure I can go any farther tonight," Fox murmured, then laughed.

"Me neither," Tony said.

"You two relax here tonight," Amelia said. "Having

someone to talk with, to be with is such a pleasure. You can leave tomorrow if you must."

"I'm not looking forward to hitting the rails again," Fox said.

"Yeah, especially hauling those damn bikes," Tony said.

"Bikes? Where the heck are your bicycles? I thought you two walked here."

"We did, but we rode south from Santa Barbara to Rincon Point then pushed our bikes along the rails."

"Jeez, that's even more stupid than walking it," Amelia said and laughed. "Where are they?"

"Hidden in the oak grove uphill," Tony replied.

"I got an idea," Amelia said excitedly, "but I'm too stoned to talk about it tonight. Let's chat over breakfast."

The couple agreed. After a while, Tony floated on the very verge of unconsciousness. They climbed from the tub, quickly dried off in the cold air, and hurried inside. Amelia donned a long gown, spread cushions on the plank floor, and brought them pillows and soft blankets to cover themselves.

"You kids, sleep," she said. "I'm going to read for a while but... but don't mind me. I remember what it's like to lie in the arms of a lover."

She moved to the far end of the room and arranged herself in a padded chair. Pulling a book from a shelf she bent next to a candle and pretended to read, never turning the pages. After a short while Amelia's chin dropped to her chest and a soft snoring filled the room.

"I thought she'd never drift off," Fox whispered in Tony's ear. "I want you."

He rolled onto his side and stroked her trembling flesh until she pushed him back and slid onto him. They rocked furiously. The floorboards creaked. Fox let out a low whimper, then covered his quivering body with her own. They stayed that way until Tony started to cramp up. He rolled onto his side, back-to-back with Fox, and stared at the flickering candlelight that danced across the walls. The old woman sat slumped in the chair, her eyelids quivering, a smile stretching her seamed lips. He thought about Fox and what it would be like to live with one person until they got that old. Would they look saggy and wrinkled to each other? Would they still feel the desire? Or would they become like Fox's parents... comfortable, caring, considerate, and decrepit. Tony chuckled to himself and closed his eyes. Fox rolled over and snuggled close. But he soon grew restless. Slipping from her arms, he put on his pants and crept toward the candlelight and the sleeping Amelia.

He stared at the collection of battered books on the shelf. The title of one caught his eye, "The Change" by Frederick Sanchez, Ph.D. He reached for it, opened its cover and read in huge cursive, "To my dearest wife Amelia, without you I could never have written this." The book was published in 2053. Tony stared at Amelia sleeping in the flickering light and tried to imagine her as a young wife more than sixty years ago. He flipped through the book's first few pages until he came to the abstract.

The Change:

Most scholars believe that change is inevitable and that universes are never static. Here on earth, it is the speed and direction of change that modern man has tried to influence. Prior to 2025, most demographers believed that human history demonstrated an evolutionary process, influenced by the rise of new technologies, of man's understanding the nature of the cosmos, and his ability to improve his lot.

But beginning in the latter part of the 20th century, our evolutionary track shifted to a devolutionary one—socially, culturally, politically, and economically. What has been called "The Change" was a complex series of shifts in human behavior coupled with alterations to our world's physical environment that resulted in a new paradigm. Consider the following trends experienced by the United States between 2000 and 2050.

"What are you doing?"

Tony jumped and stared at Amelia. "I... I couldn't sleep. Thought I'd read a little."

Amelia chuckled. "Most men pass out after sex... but you... you're different."

"Ah... sorry if we disturbed you." Tony felt his face burn but he hurried on. "My Mother is our clan's teacher. I grew up with books, lots of them."

"Here, let me see what you've got there." Amelia extended her hand and took the volume from him, smiling. "Yes, this is Freddie's dissertation. I helped him with the research and getting it published. He was so handsome and... and young. We sold at least fifty e-versions. This is one of the few hard copies." She laughed and handed the book back.

Tony bowed his head and studied the text, trying to understand the information.

Population:

Population declined by 27.5%, coastal communities experiencing a 42.6% decrease.

Of the 28.8% of the households with children, birth rates declined to 0.6 children per couple, well below replacement rate.

Household size dropped to 1.6 individuals per dwelling (from 2.61 in 2000), with 59.8% of all households being a single adult.

Tony sighed. "It must have been strange before The Change, to live in cities full of people and cars."

"Strange isn't the right word. There were just too damn many of us. Things started moving faster and faster, in all directions. The Hopi Indians called it 'life out of balance' or *Koyaanisqatsi*. While each new gadget let the High Lifers avoid face-to-face contact, they became trapped in their web of electrons. I was just a kid when The Change started. It got ugly quickly, especially the high unemployment, homelessness, then the pandemics."

"Yeah, my Mother has stories passed on from my grandparents," Tony said and continued reading.

Employment and the Economy:

76.2% of the jobs are in research and development (R&D) and professional services.

Government services (primarily Regional and National Law Enforcement and health care) account for 19.6%.

Transportation and distribution of household and durable goods and agricultural production accounts for 3%.

Manufacturing/fabrication declined to 1.2% of the workforce (down from 10% in 2000).

Tony set the book down and stared out the window at the black ocean. "So did... did you and Freddie have jobs after The Change?"

"Oh sure, we were first-rate egghead professors. We both taught at UCLA, me in the Music Department... classical piano... I haven't touched one in forty years. Freddie taught cultural anthropology."

"What happened?"

"The entire University converted to online classes. All of a sudden, a single professor or a pre-recorded interactive vid could teach thousands. At the same time, the number of students dropped like a stone. For a while they kept some teachers on as tutors, but only the tenured guys. The rest of us got cut."

"Cut?"

"The British used to call unemployment being 'redundant'. That's what we were." Amelia bowed her head and swiped at her eyes. "Fred and I were in our mid-twenties and already declared useless, told that we needed to retrain in some field that would help other High Lifers earn credits. Why the hell would any of them want a music professor or a cultural anthropologist? The world became too damn pragmatic and competitive... left no room for art, for culture, for us."

She covered her eyes and wept quietly. Tony moved next to Amelia and leaned her head onto his shoulder. He continued to read.

Public Health, Energy, and the Environment:

Global climate change and the sea level rise displaced 86 million people along America's Atlantic, Pacific and Gulf Coasts. Alaska's land area was reduced by 32.2%.

Carbon-based emissions declined on the regional and national level by 94% as petroleum, coal, and natural gas-based energy technologies were replaced with solar, wind, hydroelectric, wave action, and advanced nuclear technologies.

In 2050, the average American lives 71.2 years, a decline from 77.0 years in 2000. Other than *"natural causes,"* the four leading causes of death are (in descending order) heart disease, Type II diabetes, suicide, and cancer.

Tony pointed to the last reference about causes of death. "I never knew that suicide was that common among the Untouchables, as we call them. As a kid I found a skeleton of a guy who shot himself... but I always thought it was just, ya know, a fluke."

Amelia wiped her eyes and nodded. "Yes, evidently long-term isolation from others, even with unlimited indirect contact, can drive some High Lifers into deep depression. Before Freddie and I joined the Dungee Clan in San Pedro Bay, we scavenged around the El Lay basin. We got good at picking out the High Lifer houses that were abandoned. A lot of times we'd find dead bodies inside, just like my cabin here. And they didn't die naturally. One guy blew his face off with a shotgun, the one I now use to keep the bears away."

Tony frowned. "Aren't you, ya know, worried, about living by yourself?"

Amelia chuckled and patted Tony's arm. "I'm 85. I'd have killed myself by now if I was gonna do it. Besides, Freddie will show up any day now and my memory of him is enough to keep me going until then."

A strong night wind pushed at the house, making it creak and moan. Tony remembered the stories his mother told him, tales passed on by her mother, of the chaos along the SoCal coast when the sea level rose and millions lost their homes and jobs. His grandparents had lived and worked in a beach town that rimmed the coastline. When they got flooded out, faster than anyone had expected, they fled inland, only to be chased by roving gangs of refugees who seemed intent on punishing anyone for their own misfortune. And then the pandemics hit. But being part of that 86 million displaced persons felt more real to Tony now than any statistic on a page or his mother's often-told tales. *Fox and I are running just as hard as my grandparents ever did. Who will we tell our stories to?* He picked up the book and continued reading.

Society:

The creation of robust satellite communications and the internet enabled unrestricted indirect human contact. This change has, in turn, reduced the need for— then the desire for face-to-face contact. Indirect contact has led to major reductions in personal mobility and the abandonment of most human transportation infrastructure.

Public health emergencies (e.g. the Nuevo Polio Epidemic of 2041; the Indonesian Plague Epidemic of 2043) reduced the population (primarily middle class households displaced by rising seas) by tens of millions and the demand for personal travel almost disappeared. Many sociologists believe that these health emergencies combined with decimation of the retail and tourist sectors, flooding of coastal areas, and dependence on indirect contact, have led to a form of "societal agoraphobia."

The once-robust middle class vanished as blue-collar service and manufacturing jobs were eliminated or exported to Asia and South America. The clan system absorbed a small fraction of the surviving middle class—educated households that developed survival skills yet rejected the isolated lifestyles of the dominant population group. (It is estimated that the clans account for less than 15% of the nation's population.)

Tony felt like he was reading about some alien culture on another planet. He had grown up knowing only one legitimate class—the Untouchables—and had killed the last one he'd met. *Where is the rise of the Untouchables written about? Will the clans be just some casual citation in the Country's history, or might they actually help change things?*

"Have you read enough?" Amelia asked. "That book says a lot. But you need to drink a couple liters of strong tea to get through it."

"Yeah, it's a lot to take in... but it makes sense." He scanned more pages that described the decline of religion and the arts, then read the abstract's final paragraphs.

From my analysis of these and many other factors, I have concluded that the United States citizenry has become isolated within its own boundaries. Its influence on global affairs has been greatly reduced as Asian and South American economies have flourished. Given our depressed birth rates and lack of household formation, a continued drop in population is forecast throughout the 21st Century, with the very basis for America's cultural identity unclear.

While technological advances continue through our leadership in the R&D sector, overall quality-of-life and public health indicators for U.S. households have diminished. The true irony here is that our nation's improved environmental quality—measured in terms of clean air, water, and increased bio-diversity—has been a byproduct of our social and cultural decline. It is quite possible that only the Clans have reaped the benefits of these changes, since they alone have adapted to the impacts of global climate change.

Tony slid the thick volume back into its slot, wondering how such a book had ever been published and who would read it. He stared into the candlelight and pondered the words "isolation" and "decline." His chest tightened when he thought about the scattered Touchables, wandering the streets of de Tolosa, homeless, separated from the comfort of clan life. Fox moaned and squirmed under the covers.

"You'd better go to her before she wakes," Amelia said and grinned. "It's the one thing I miss the most, having Freddie to snuggle with."

Tony hurried into the dark end of the room and slid under the covers. Fox pushed herself against him. The wind whistled a forlorn song. He lay quietly, thinking about their next move, and about the joy of returning home someday to de Tolosa.

He awoke with Amelia standing over them in the bright morning light, grinning. "Come on, you two, rise and shine."

Tony remembered the words from an old Tennessee Williams play his mom made him read. "'I'll rise—but I won't shine,'" he answered.

Amelia toed him in the ribs and moved off toward the kitchen. He rose, hastily dressed, and hustled to the outdoor privy. An old wind turbine had been mounted to its roof, making the stench surprisingly tolerable. Returning, he met Fox scrubbing at her creased face with both hands. She stumbled past him without speaking and disappeared inside the out-house. Tony washed his hands and face at the basin next to the hot tub then entered the cabin. Amelia motioned to a table where a plate filled with scrambled eggs and diced vegetables steamed in the morning air. Outside a rooster crowed, as if announcing breakfast.

"Sit down, young man, and eat. You need to build up your strength after all that..." She laughed and poured steaming red liquid into three cups and sat across the table from him.

"What is this stuff?" Tony asked, staring doubtfully into his cup.

"It's pine needle tea, has lots of Vitamin C. Put a little wild honey in it and it'll taste better."

"Where the heck do you find pine trees around here?"

"There are a few groves back in the mountains. I make a trip every few months. But it's getting harder and harder for me."

Tony nodded and sipped the pleasant liquid. "I'll leave some of our Emerald Magic with you. It should make the trip less painful."

"No, you two are gonna need your stash to trade."

"Trade?"

Fox joined the two, her ragged pink hair sticking out in all directions. Amelia left them and returned with a crude comb made of some kind of bone or hard shell. "Go ahead and keep it. I have plenty of material to make more."

"Thanks." Fox tugged the comb through her hair until it slid smoothly. She stared at Tony and laughed. "That curly mop of yours looks like a bird's nest sitting on your head."

"Thanks for the compliment," Tony muttered and slurped his tea.

"So we've got a lot to talk about today," Amelia said.

Tony nodded. "We'd better leave soon before the Police catch up."

"Have you seen them?" Amelia asked.

"At Gaviota Pass, a couple dozen crawlers, vans and jet boats were waiting for us to paddle past them in our kayak. Then in Santa Barbara, the drone patrols increased..."

"That's odd for the Police to get so agitated over an isolated murder case," Amelia said. "I've been listening in on the com for years and there's been a lot more chatter lately. But most of it's coded and I can't tell what they're transmitting."

"All the more reason for us to get out of here," Fox said.

"But you're gonna have to play it smart," Amelia said. "From here south, inland and shoreline surveillance is... is intense."

"So much for riding bikes all the way to Nirvana," Tony said.

"Don't get me wrong. It's possible to find routes that avoid surveillance. But you'll eventually get spotted. I have a better idea."

"What's that?" Fox asked cautiously.

"Take my boat."

"You're kidding me," Tony said.

"No, no, you kids can have it."

"But don't you use it to fish?" Fox asked.

"Oh, sure, every month or so I take her out a few hundred meters. But I can catch what I need from the bluffs north of here... and can ride one of your fancy bicycles there and back... will be easier on my old bones."

"But it's... it's your boat," Fox murmured. "It kind of connects you with the Dungees, with your people, doesn't it?"

"Yes... but... but it reminds me too much of my son. Since he's gone, I'd rather think about two young lovers, sailing the seas, out to start a life, to start a... a family." Amelia stared at Fox whose face darkened.

"So will that chip of a boat make it to the Channel Islands?" Tony asked.

Amelia threw back her head and laughed. "Good God, no. The November mid-channel swells are awesome, will roll my poor boat like a log down a hill."

"Well then, how are we supposed to get there... wherever there is?"

"My boat will take you to the people that can get you across channel. Have either of you sailed before?"

"I have," Fox piped up. "I spent winters sailing a 5-meter catboat on the lake near de Tolosa. That sucker would whitecap and the wind would blow at 30 to 40 knots."

"A lake is nothing like the Pacific, but at least you know how to handle a boat. What about you?" Amelia asked Tony.

"I'm a quick learner," he said.

"Good, because we got a lot to talk about and a lot to plan."

They finished their meal and moved to the reading area. Amelia pulled an old nautical chart from a shelf and spread it across the low table. She and Fox talked about the details of the SoCal coast all morning while Tony picked on Amelia's guitar and dozed. He realized that most of the shoreline would look different since the sea level had changed. When Fox had committed their route and notable landmarks to memory, the couple repacked their gear and followed Amelia down a gravel path to a small cove and the dock. The pale-green boat stretched barely four meters, had a fiber-glass hull with a slant-bottomed cockpit and a short keel. Its single metal mast was folded in a horizontal position, with the sail furled between the mast and boom. Dirty water sloshed in the bottom of the cockpit.

Fox climbed aboard and tested the tiller. Tony

followed with a bucket to bail her out. He cracked his shins painfully against the bench seats, and swore like a sailor when they struggled to right the mast. But once up, it felt rigid and locked in place. They loaded both backpacks, lashed them to the forward seats with nylon rope that Amelia gave them. Finally, Fox secured a set of paddles to the inside of the hull.

In mid-afternoon the wind freshened. They hurried to set sail, knowing that if next morning's light caught them on the open sea, they'd be in trouble.

Before climbing aboard, they hugged Amelia. "You sure you don't want to come with us?" Fox asked. "There's room in the boat, and... and she could use a Captain that knows the way."

Amelia placed a finger against Fox's trembling lips. "Thomas Wolfe was right... you can't go home again."

"But the islands, a new clan, new friends?" Fox murmured.

Amelia grinned. "Nah, I'd rather stay here with my memories and keep an eye out for Freddie. He should be showing up any day now. He'll be pissed if I'm not around."

The couple zipped up their windbreakers, pulled knit caps over their ears, and clambered aboard. Amelia scrambled to cast off the bow and stern lines. Tony moved forward and hauled on the halyard. The dirty-white sail with a rose insignia slid to the masthead. He secured the line at a cleat near its base. The sail immediately snapped taut with the onshore wind. Tony ducked as the boom swung over him, narrowly missing his skull.

"Where to, my Captain?" he cried.

Fox grinned and pointed. "South, matey, south."

12

Near sunset, Sergeant Jonas sat in his crawler and gazed westward down the mountain to the sea terraces below his vantage point at Hearst Castle, eighty-four kilometers north of de Tolosa. Ever since the Change, the grand old palace of the long-dead newspaper magnate had been shuttered. The Cambrian Clan had occupied the buildings for a short time but had shunned it in favor of the pine-covered mountain tops above the Big Sur Coast. The Castle's once-magnificent towers and guest houses showed signs of crumbling with each successive earthquake. Jonas loved the place, felt happy that Captain Hanpian had assigned him to lead the northern pursuit.

After the Garage in de Tolosa had been destroyed, Fox Slade's parents had fled the city with another couple. At Morro Bay, the couples split up. The first pair had been captured in the dunes near Montana de Oro beach. Then surveillance spotted the Slades two days later, heading north along the remnants of the Coast Highway. Jonas figured that if they made it into the Santa Lucia Mountains north of Ragged Point, they'd be gone for good.

The sergeant climbed from the crawler and moved to the forward observation post set up on a stone terrace with a panoramic view of the entire north coast. Two policemen manned the scopes.

"Tolson, do we have infrared and starlight detection tonight?"

"Yes, Sergeant. We'll be able to pick out a squirrel taking a pee."

"I must know immediately when you see anything."

"You'll be the first, Sergeant."

Jonas returned to his crawler, sealed himself inside, and keyed the audio system. Old-style jazz music from the 1930s filled the vehicle. He watched the moon rise over the Castle's central terrace to the sound of the Duke Ellington Orchestra performing Mood Indigo. But in a few minutes Officer Tolson's gravely voice destroyed his meditation.

"Sarge, it looks like they're on the move."

"Where?"

"They've just climbed from a ravine next to the highway. They're heading north, riding bicycles."

Jonas stared at the fuzzy vid feed, keyed the com and spoke softly. "Attention all units, the fugitives are on Route 1, just north of San Simeon. Units 1 through 8, close off the road between Markers 57 and 61. Units 9 through 11, roll to intercept. All units use stealth mode. We don't want to spook them."

Jonas waited until Officer Tolson joined him. He keyed the crawler's electric engine and set it to its quiet mode. Rolling off the terrace, they joined the narrow road and drove downhill through the moonlight, letting the vehicle's tracking sensors keep them on the rutted pavement. At the Coast Highway they turned north and joined three other crawlers at the southern roadblock.

Jonas murmured into his com. "Units 9 through 11, do you have visual contact?"

"That's affirmative, Sergeant. We're less than 100 meters from the fugitives and closing."

Jonas and Tolson sat listening to the open com and staring at the onboard vid as pale green-edged images of two bicyclists came into focus and filled the screen. The officers exited their crawlers. After a short foot chase across a sea terrace and into a ravine, the couple emerged in handcuffs, pushed along by a tall officer that Jonas didn't recognize. The officer placed them in a van and gave the thumbs up signal. Jonas let out a deep breath, grateful that his part of the murder investigation had succeeded. He smiled as he keyed the com and activated Captain Hanpian's link. The old bastard would be pacing his floor, waiting for his report, and scheming on how he would break Fox Slade's parents, having failed with the Matteson woman. *I hope those kids run forever*, Jonas thought as he watched Hanpian's face change from exhausted to excited when he heard the words, "We've got them."

༄

Elliot Slade slumped in the padded chair, his face bronzed by the sun, his beard and mustache sporting gray patches. His wife, Louise, sat next to him. Tall, both over two meters, they held hands. Elliot dozed while Louise rocked back and forth. She passed a hand over her forehead and pushed the tangle of dark hair away from her gray eyes. They'd been locked in an upper office of the Police Operations Center all morning. Neither had been allowed to bathe. No food had been provided.

Captain Hanpian studied them on the vid screens in his home-office while fingering the service award medal that hung from his neck.

"I'll go after the woman first," he muttered to himself, "easier to break."

He keyed his com and gave orders for Louise to be taken to interrogation, a windowless room seldom used. Ever since the penal systems had been regionalized near the end of the Change, Hanpian and his predecessors had been improvising. Most prisoners were immediately placed on drone flights to the Regional Courts-Jail Complex in Goleta. But this time, Hanpian had other plans.

With his vids flickering before him, he stripped naked and moved to the shower. Afterwards, donning his best uniform—a starched camouflage shirt and pants, black boots, and a silver-plated pistol clipped to his waist—he keyed the lock to his front door. It hadn't been opened in two years. He slipped on sunglasses and, squinting against the blinding light, rushed along a shaded path to the waiting crawler. Jonas sat behind the controls, grinning.

"It's a pleasure to see you, Captain."

Hanpian scowled. "I hate being outside. This damn heat fries my brain, and the wind wears me out. But duty sometimes calls."

From inside the crawler, he stared at his house, a small mansion on a wooded knoll, originally built to house de Tolosa's State University president. He tried to imagine what it must have been like to live there when thousands of college students crowded into buildings and walked the surrounding streets. But all CSU administrators had been moved to Sack City during the Change and the university campuses abandoned one after another. *What idiots the pre-Changers had been*, Hanpian thought, *wasting tax dollars paying for young punks to party. Online schooling became so much more efficient and avoided all those premature pregnancies and marriages.*

At the Operations Center, the crawler pulled into a basement garage. Hanpian and Jonas climbed six flights of dark stairs. On the top floor nominally used as the Command Unit, the Captain strode down skylight-lit hallways. Other officers gawked, many never having seen their commander in the flesh. At the door to the interrogation room, Hanpian turned.

"Make sure that Matteson woman is awake and dressed. I want her to see this."

"Will do, Captain," Jonas said and hurried away.

When he entered, Louise Slade raised her chin

from her chest and stared at him. Her eyes focused for a moment before going blank.

"Good morning, Ms. Slade. My name is Captain Hanpian."

"I know who you are," Louise shot back. "You're the idiot that ordered the attack on the Garage."

"Yes, I'm that idiot... although there were plenty of other idiots that night."

Louise glowered at him. "What do you want and why are we here? We didn't do anything—"

"Ah, but you did. Harboring fugitives is a crime, Ms. Slade."

Louise lowered her head and sighed. "You're talking about my daughter, not some criminal murderer."

"All murder is criminal, Ms. Slade."

"Just what do you want?"

"I want to know where your daughter and that boy are headed. We know they're moving south."

"Why should I tell you anything?" Louise stared him in the eyes, her lips trembling with rage. "Some bastard tried to rape my child and all you can do is—"

"I understand, Ms. Slade. I have already talked with Ruth Matteson and she's told us the story. It's highly unlikely that your daughter will be charged with murder. There's no evidence that she had a hand in it."

"So you'll let her go?"

"No, I didn't say that. But I have a lot of leeway in dealing with the District Attorney who decides what crimes to charge her with and sentencing recommendations."

"I could see my daughter again?" Louise said wistfully.

"I hope so, Louise. I hope so."

"What's the catch? What do you want? You're not

one of those Untouchable perverts, like the one that attacked Fox?"

"That citizen paid dearly for his perversion, a price that the Matteson boy had no right to charge."

"You know damn well us Touchables have no rights. Why should we worry about the law?"

"Because without law we have nothing but chaos."

"What do you think we have now?" Louise leaned back in her chair, a slight smile creasing her lips.

"A good point, Ms. Slade. But let's focus on what I'm offering. Do you want to see your daughter again?"

Louise's face turned pink and she buried it in her hands, her shoulders shaking. Hanpian waited quietly.

After a few minutes she sucked in a deep breath and wiped her eyes dry. "So what kind of deal can you offer if I cooperate?"

"Reduce the charges to evading arrest. Maximum of three years with a recommendation for a suspended sentence."

"So she would be free?"

"Yes, but Fox would need to stay in the District and agree to monitoring pending Anthony Matteson's trial."

"Would Fox have to testify?"

"Probably. But the District Attorney will have to decide."

"What will happen to the boy? I... I know he's all Ruth has."

"If you cooperate, second degree murder or manslaughter charges are likely with leniency on sentencing."

"God, I can't give up another woman's child to save my own."

"That's your decision, Louise. When Anthony and Fox are caught, and they will be captured, they will stand trial for the full range of charges. Neither you nor Ms. Matteson will ever see your children again. They'll likely spend the rest of their lives at the Phoenix Correctional Institute, servicing the Western Region's Solar Electric Station."

"I... I can't decide by myself. I need to talk it over with Elliot."

Hanpian frowned but remained calm. "Certainly, Ms. Slade. You talk it over with your husband. But I will need to know your answer, your information by 1500 hours today."

"But that's only two hours."

"Plenty of time to decide."

Hanpian stood and strode from the room. He moved down a hallway to his office where Sergeant Jonas joined him.

"Well, what do you think, Captain? Will she crack?"

"Oh, she's ready. I could see it in her eyes. But whether she can convince her husband to turn on the boy is another story. Bring me some coffee and something to eat. I need to check in with Sergeant Statler before I make any final deal with these... these people."

Hanpian slouched in the chair and longed for the comforts of his home-office: the fresh-brewed coffee; the familiar bank of vid screens to stare at and ponder the world; the climate controls set at 23° Celsius; the latest feeds from the UN's space drones circling some distant planet. The pursuit of the fugitives had drained his energy, become tedious, like watching the same porn vid over and over and feeling nothing. He keyed the console and Sergeant Statler's face filled the screen.

"Okay, Sergeant, give me the latest."

"Yes Captain, early this morning—"

"*Please*, keep it short."

"Yes sir. We spent last night in Ventura and were able to reach that squatter's cabin this morning. An old woman lives there, has been there for years. She claimed to know nothing about the fugitives even though we found their bicycles in an oak grove just uphill from her home."

"What about her boat? She had to know about that."

"She claims to have awakened near dawn and found the boat gone, says either somebody stole it or the rough seas tore it from its mooring."

"Did you check for cells inside the cabin?"

"That's affirmative, sir. They were there all right. But the old bat has clammed up. Won't tell us anything."

"Is she in the system?"

"No. And she doesn't have any clan tattoos or other markings that might identify where she came from. She looks old enough to be a pre-Changer."

Hanpian sat thinking. The com line hummed. Finally Statler spoke. "Ah, Captain, do you want us to bring her in?"

"No, Sergeant. She's not going anywhere. Besides we have no leverage to make her talk. At least now we know they're on the water. Just hold your position until I give you further orders."

"Yes, sir."

He leaned back in the chair and pictured the fugitives riding the waves somewhere on the vast Pacific. Reaching forward, he keyed the com and ordered enhanced aerial photographs of the entire Santa Barbara Channel. *Now, if that Slade woman will just talk we can narrow our search, pick them off on the open sea.* But he remembered the failed intercept at Gaviota Pass and bolted from his chair. The Slades had fifteen minutes until their deadline. Hanpian didn't care. He needed an answer right then and would promise just about anything to get it.

13

Fox grasped the tiller firmly and steered their cat-boat into the Santa Barbara Channel, beating against a strong wind out of the northwest. Tony bobbed and weaved, ducking to avoid the swinging boom on their starboard tack, throwing his weight against the gunwales to help level the boat. They made good headway, slicing through the sea and riding over the swells. Their boat took on water, but not more than Tony could handle with his bailing bucket.

They bore southward toward the sharp outline of Anacapa Island, its barren cliffs and highlands rising tall above the ocean. The air looked crystal clear, smelled both salty and sweet. Fox remembered old library photographs of a brown chemical fog engulfing the coastline; aerial shots of freeways clogged with cars, each belching smoke from its tailpipe. *How could the drivers not know that they were destroying the atmosphere?*

After a couple kilometers, Fox turned the boat to port. They ran with the wind, the sail eased out. The afternoon sun lit the undersides of puffy clouds scuttling overhead. The entire coastline turned golden, looked precious, making Fox grin. She ignored the chill of the wind and sea. It had been at least three years since she had last sailed. But her skills hadn't faded and she deftly steered them across swells and through the troughs.

Even along their near-shore course, the sea felt formidable and the whitecapping waves kept Tony bailing. Fox imagined what mid-channel would be like with towering combers rolling under their tiny craft. One sudden wind shift and the sea would swamp the catboat or fling the fugitives into the water, to sink to the bottom, 1,000 meters down. Just ahead, a pod of dolphins broke the surface and crossed their bow, arching their sleek backs as they swam in formation. *They seemed to be having fun. It's been so long since we've had any fun. I'm always tired and my back hurts. Uh-oh!*

She bent over the port gunwale and vomited into the ocean. Dipping a cupped hand into the water, she washed off her face and sat upright. Tony clambered across the bouncing bottom and joined her at the helm.

"What's wrong?" he demanded, his eyes wide. "You look as white as a sail."

"I don't know. But I feel okay now, feel strong. Maybe it's just—"

Before she could finish the sentence another wave of nausea hit and she complained once more to the sea gods below.

"Do you want to head for shore? We could find someplace in the swamped parts of Port Hueneme. Those old housing tracts along the beach that Amelia told us about are—"

"No, I'm feeling... feeling better. I'm the Captain and I say when we go ashore."

Tony's mouth dropped open. "It's okay, Fox. Just let me help."

"Believe me, I'll ask for you to take over if I can't manage. But get back to your bailing. We're riding low and sluggish."

The plastic bucket floated inside the catboat's hull. Tony hustled to bail her dry, only to have another wave send white water over the gunwales, soaking both of them. Fox shook off the shock of the cold wave. She let the boat slip sideways across the sea, angling toward the coast. She had wanted to stay far enough offshore to avoid any localized surveillance of Untouchable housing enclaves along the shoreline. But the afternoon wind had freshened and the waves battered their craft, shaking them like the rag doll her mother had given her as a little girl. She sucked in deep breaths, ground her teeth and clutched the tiller with both hands.

They continued to rocket southward. Onshore, the Santa Monica Mountains fell into the sea, massive humps of rock and brush-covered soil with remnants of the old Coast Highway clinging to their near-vertical faces. By sundown, they had passed Point Dum. The western sky blazed with reds, purples, and golds that made Fox long for her paints and a blank wall to destroy with color. As the light failed, the wind slacked off. She motioned for Tony to join her at the helm. Taking a water bottle from inside her windbreaker she handed it to him.

He took a long swig. "You're looking a lot better. Are you feeling better?"

"Yes, I... I don't know what that was about. But I'm good."

"So are we ready for our moonlight cruise?"

"If the wind stays like this, we should stay dry and make it by morning."

"Show me how to steer this thing and I can spell you," Tony offered.

"No, I'll rest when we get there. Right now, while there's still a little light I want to move offshore a bit. They'll have lots of surveillance near Malibu."

"Aye, aye, Captain. I'm ready with the bailing bucket."

Fox grinned. "Just shut up and get us some food. It's going to be a long night."

Fox turned the boat to starboard and angled outward to the darkening horizon. The moon hung high above them in a clear black sky. The stars burned as bright as the flashers on the roofs of police crawlers. Fox sat in awe of the night sea, savored the feeling of isolation, the feeling of being borne along by some massive rolling beast that would take them to safety yet could shake them off at any moment and send them to the bottom.

"There, that must be the Malibu Coast," she said pointing to a sprinkling of lights across the tops of the bluffs above the sea.

"Yeah, the low beach houses got swept away when the sea level rose. But those bluff top places will have plenty of eyes."

Fox sighed. "Why would any Untouchable want to live in plain sight of such beauty, yet close himself off from it?"

"I suppose they're afraid of contact with anything, even the stark beauty of this place."

"Nah. I don't buy it. Not here. They gotta be sneaking peeks at those magnificent sunsets... maybe using their security eyes to do it."

"You may be right," Tony said. "When we were inside that... that freak's house in de Tolosa, I noticed some of the vid screens showed the surrounding valley, the town, the mountains."

"It's as if the Untouchables don't trust their own eyes, ears, noses, tongues, or fingers, to teach them about the world. The vids are some kind of filter that make it... make it safe."

"Damn, Fox. That's so profound."

"That's *Captain* Fox to you." She grabbed Tony around the neck and kissed him, enjoying the salty tang of his mouth.

They bounced across the sea, clutching each other, until an errant wave wet them and sent Tony scurrying for his bailing bucket in the darkness. Fox checked Amelia's pocket compass with her hand light and set a southeastern course, across the broad mouth of Santa Monica Bay to the distant twinkling lights of the Palos Verdes Headlands. To the west, large blocks of blackness, barely defined by their running lights, plied the deep channel waters. The drone freighters' guidance systems held the behemoths to perfectly set-in courses, by part-time captains who sat behind vid screens on some distant continent. *What's the fun in that*, Fox thought, and laughed to herself.

Tony rejoined her in the stern and they huddled together. With wet clothes, the November night became frigid. They rubbed their hands together and struggled to get warm. With a shaking voice, Tony began singing an old folk song about the Sloop John B. The thought of sailing through the warm waters of the Caribbean comforted Fox, although she knew they could never reach such a distant place in their tiny boat. Some serious cracks had appeared in the fiberglass along the hull's port side. Fox had ignored them all afternoon, not wanting to think about their boat breaking up beneath them.

The wind fell off even more and the headland's lights seemed to grow nearer at a snail's pace. Tony dozed and Fox fought off sleep. After hours of trundling along, they came abreast of Palos Verdes. To the east the sky began to lighten. The outlines of the bluff-top town of Nuevo San Pedro came into view and passed to port... but not for long. From the west, a vast swirl of fog rolled in off the channel.

"What the heck is that?" Tony asked, groaning and rubbing the sleep from his eyes.

"Amelia warned me about it, called it the Catalina Eddy. It used to show up only during the summer months. But when the world got warmer, the fog stayed thick throughout the fall."

"So we're gonna sail into a strange harbor in this stuff?"

"Yes. What choice do we have?"

"We could try for Catalina Island," Tony said.

"Sure, it's out there somewhere in the fog, across a treacherous channel. And if we miss?"

"I get your point. What can I do?"

"Just listen to the sea, like we did at Point Arguello. The old breakwaters that used to protect El Lay Harbor are now underwater reefs. I'm sure we can hear the waves breaking over them."

"But where's the harbor entrance?" Tony asked, his whole body shaking.

"Somewhere in this soup," Fox replied, and grinned. "Be prepared to come about if I give the word. This little boat is maneuverable, but it's no kayak."

Fox turned the boat to port. Its sail filled then flapped in the unsteady breeze as they edged eastward into a fog so thick they couldn't see their masthead. Fox sent Tony to the bow to sing out when he saw or heard anything. Each sat tensely at their stations, waiting. The sky continued to lighten but not clear.

"There's the breakwater," Tony hollered.

Fox pushed the tiller hard to starboard and the boat swung northward into the wind, scraping its keel on something submerged. Off their starboard side, the sea churned as it surged across the old outer break-water. Fox held the catboat as close to the underwater shoal as possible. Finally, on a starboard tack, they reached the end of the jetty and the harbor opened before them. Turning landward, they edged toward their destination. The sea gradually flattened. Fox let out a deep breath and realized she had wet her pants yet again. *I won't be able to lie to Tony much longer. At least now we're more committed to seeing this through.*

A massive ship emerged from the fog. It listed sharply to port, its decks empty of cargo, hatch covers gaping. A raft of sea lions swam next to its rusting hull. They stopped long enough to stare at Fox and

Tony, as if to say, "Welcome to our harbor." Other abandoned cargo ships slid past.

"What's with all the derelicts?" Tony asked.

"They're the old container cargo ships. According to Amelia, when the harbor flooded, all the areas that supported the freight industry were destroyed. Then the drones replaced manned shipping. Only the Ports of San Francisco and San Diego could be easily adapted."

"They really look spooky," Tony said. "I can almost hear their captains barking orders, the crew hustling across their decks."

"In your dreams. It's been fifty years since..."

"Hey, it just sounds more romantic, sorry." Tony grinned and Fox grinned back.

Tony turned again and stared into the mist. Some kind of island off their starboard bow loomed before them. Tall reeds and other marsh plants covered its low shores. Another island appeared off the port side. What looked like a cluster of short logs floated toward them. Tony wiped his eyes and squinted as the logs turned into grizzled sea otters and their pups, rolling in the water, cleaning their muzzles, and squeaking to each other.

"We must be in the lagoon," Fox said. "Amelia told me that the wind would blow us to our destination. We should be close."

"We'd better be. Look up."

Above them, the fog evaporated. Blue sky and brilliant morning sunlight blasted them. Ahead lay more Marsh Islands, all overshadowed by a massive bridge and old skyways. A strange-looking train shot across the bridge and disappeared southward. On the underside of the skyways hung rows of dwellings, each with greenery trailing into the wind off their high balconies.

"Quick, reef the sail and take down the mast," Fox

ordered. "We might as well be waving my bright pink hair with that thing."

Tony hurried to comply, groaning as he hauled on the lanyard. The sail came down without a hitch. Fox left the helm and helped him lower the mast to its horizontal position.

"Now what?" Tony asked.

"Grab a paddle and go forward, starboard side. I'll handle the port side and the tiller."

"You sure you can..." Tony stared into Fox's eyes. "Aye, aye, Captain."

Paddling the catboat proved slow going but they managed to nose their craft into a narrow inlet on one of the islands, the tall reeds closing in above them. When the bow bumped land, Tony jumped out and slogged through waist-deep muck before finding a firm footing. He hauled on the bow line and the boat inched onto the soggy shore. Fox joined him and they slid the boat until the keel became wedged in the mud.

"It looks like low tide," Fox said, pointing to the water level against the inlet's banks. "When the tide comes up we can yank her farther inland."

They returned to the boat. Tony bailed her dry and they stretched out as best they could in the shade provided by the overhead canopy of reeds. Blackbirds and starlings sang them to sleep. The lurch of their boat woke them. Jumping from the bow into the muck, they again pulled the sailboat inland until they lay on the ground, groaning from the effort.

"At... at least she won't float free on us," Fox whispered.

"Yeah, but getting her unstuck will only work at high tide."

"That's okay. God, I want to sleep... but I'm so keyed up."

They ate the last of the zucchini bread that Maryann had given them in Santa Barbara and stretched out together in the bottom of the hull. Fox lay awake and thought about how she would tell Tony that she was pregnant. She imagined his grin, kisses and a warm embrace, his kindness toward her in the months to come as she grew huge. But she also imagined the opposite: accusations that she had purposefully saddled him with fatherhood, and his leaving her on that godforsaken island with a broken boat and nowhere to run. After all, Tony didn't even know his own father, didn't know what it was like to be one, acted like a creep sometimes, like when she first met him and he ran wild with those punks from the Garage. But other times, he... She snuggled against his rumbling body and finally drifted off to sleep.

14

Something shook the boat. Tony opened his eyes and stared up at the sky. The fog had returned, wetting the reeds and spattering their windbreakers with dewdrops. Again, the boat rocked. He sat upright. Six lean men stood barefoot on the banks and stared silently. They wore tattered shorts with no tops. Their shoulder muscles bulged, like swimmers' might, partially covered by their ragged hair. Their brown faces were free of whiskers.

"Where did you get this boat?" the tallest of the group demanded.

"It was given to us," Tony replied.

Groaning, Fox sat up and rubbed her face. She stared at the men for a moment before clambering ashore and rushing into the reeds. In a few minutes she returned, grinning sheepishly.

"Grab your gear and come with us," the tall man ordered.

Tony and Fox pulled on their backpacks and stepped ashore while the men hauled the catboat out of the water on its starboard side. They pushed and shoved the craft into a dense thicket of reeds that surrounded a grove of stunted oaks and willows.

"We're under constant daytime surveillance," another man said. "We need to hurry before the eddy clears."

They followed the men along a barely-visible path, slogging through waist-deep swampy areas and pushing back reeds until they came to a sizable clearing, its ground elevated. A large building made of

151

wooden beams and rusted corrugated metal walls and roof sat surrounded by dozens of woven reed houses, their walls covered with some kind of animal hide and their floors raised at least three meters above the ground. They rushed the couple inside the large elevated hall.

"Wait here," the tall man ordered and the group left, except for one who stood guard outside the door.

The couple slid out of their backpacks and set them on one of many long tables that filled the building. A raised stage occupied one end of the room. The place smelled of smoke and cooked food. Tony's stomach rumbled and he remembered they were almost out of provisions.

"What do you think?" Tony asked. "Are these guys the Dung People that Amelia talked about?"

"I can't tell. Her description fits, but somehow I expected them to... to be friendlier, like Amelia."

Tony laughed. "Remember how she first greeted us with her shotgun?"

"I suppose. Still, I don't like the way those men looked at me."

"They probably never saw a pink redhead before. Good ole Maryann did a good job with the bleach but she forgot your eyebrows."

"Why didn't you tell me?" Fox said and dug Tony in the ribs.

"I think it looks cute. Sorry."

"When they come back, let me do the talking," Fox said. "Amelia told me a lot about them and I think I'm less threatening."

"Yeah, us short guys are always threatening."

"Shut up, will you."

They sat at a table, their legs jouncing, and took in the details of their surroundings. A round man and two women wearing long cloaks, like the one Amelia had worn, entered the building, with the six others filing in behind them.

As they approached, Fox stepped forward. "My name is Fox Slade, and this is Tony Matteson. Are you Alanso?"

The round man stopped and stared. "How do you know my name?"

"Amelia told me."

After a moment of silence, the group's chatter filled the room. "Where did you... when did you meet Amelia?"

"We saw her yesterday, at her cabin on the bluffs just north of Buena Ventura."

Alanso grinned and motioned toward the table and they sat. "Amelia sailed north six years ago. She was fleeing the 'Forcers."

"Yes, she told us the story about her son's death and the revenge killing of the High Lifer. But Freddie swam ashore off the coast of Malibu and she's been living alone... doing quite well, has a wonderful garden, chickens, fresh water, and a hot tub to bathe in."

Alanso frowned and shook his head. "Freddie was her husband. He died years before Amelia left us."

"I don't understand," Fox said.

Alanso sighed. "She carried his memory with her every day, would always speak of him, as if he still lived."

"That's... that's sad. Amelia still expects him to join her some day."

"I think their meeting will be the other way around."

The group sat in silence. The older woman swiped at her eyes. Finally, Alanso smiled and leaned back from the table.

"So how did you get her boat? It was Amelia's prized possession and her rose insignia was famous along this stretch of coast, among both the clans and the High Lifers."

Tony looked at Fox. "Go ahead, tell them everything," he said.

Fox recounted their story, from the beginning, including their life in de Tolosa and their odyssey southward, with Tony adding details as she rambled on.

"So why are you here and where are you going?" the younger of the two women asked.

"Excuse my rudeness," Alanso said. "This is my daughter Blanca and my wife, Dolores. Blanca was... was close to Amelia's son."

Tony nodded. "We need to find a safe place to live, away from surveillance and the Police. My Mother told us to try and reach the communes on the Channel Islands. Amelia said you might help us get there."

Alanso smiled. "Yes, yes, that's not a bad idea. Thousands of years before the Change, just about all the islands were occupied. The Chumash lived on the northern islands; the Tongva lived on the southern ones, and a band of Nicoleño occupied San Nicolas."

"But what's on the Channel Islands now?" Fox asked.

"Well, there used to be a small group on Santa Cruz. But they left long ago."

"Yes, the Surfer Clan told us about that," Tony said, "something about no water."

"That's the problem with the islands," Alanso said and sighed. "They're really nothing more than the tops of sea mountains with little opportunity to capture rainwater. But the Zane Grey Clan on Catalina seems to have done okay. They have a wind-energy plant that they use to desalinate seawater."

"That's a strange name for a clan," Fox said.

"I suppose. A century before the Change, the author Zane Grey lived on the island. They use his old Pueblo as their common house."

"How big is their clan?" Fox asked.

"Maybe a hundred."

"How do they feel about... about taking on a couple of new members?"

"I'm not sure. We only trade with them once or twice a year, during the late spring and summer when the channel is passable for our canoes."

Tony stared at Fox and frowned. "You said canoes?"

Alanso grinned. "Yes, they're big slant-sided boats made of thick planks, just like the Chumash used to build."

"But you said the seas are only passable during..."

"I'm afraid so. We won't be going back until April or May."

Tony and Fox fell silent. Finally, Tony said quietly, "That's... that's a long time for us to wait." Fox nodded in agreement. "I noticed surveillance on the bridge and on the top rails of the skyways. Hiding here for five or six months—"

"Is a bad idea," Alanso finished. "The 'Forcers do a sweep of the Marsh Islands every few months. You're lucky because they just passed through. But the next time, they'll find the boat and you."

The silence returned. Finally, Tony stood and moved to his backpack. He rummaged inside its waterproof compartment and retrieved a package wrapped in a cloth and plastic sheeting and laid it in the center of the table. "Do you think this might buy us passage to Catalina?" he asked, staring into Alanso's eyes.

The clan chief gawked at the bag. "What, what..."

"It's Emerald Magic from the Surfer Clan. I understand you've sampled their harvest."

"Good God, yes... a decade or so back. We still tell stories about that weed. When you make love after toking up, it's the best—"

"Shut up, Al," Dolores said, smirking. "These folks

don't want to hear about your sexual prowess."

"I suppose not," Alanso said and grinned. "Tell you what I can do. Tonight at dinner, I'll ask for volunteers for a channel crossing. You'll need eight strong paddlers. Half your stash should go to the volunteers, the other half to the clan... for ceremonial purposes, you understand."

"Sounds fair enough," Tony said. "But I've got to hold back some in case I need to bargain with the Zane Grey Clan."

"You're a smart kid. I can see how you two made it this far."

"Hey, it was me doing the sailing," Fox said.

Alanso smiled. "Meanwhile, my wife and daughter will get you two some Dungee clothing and do something about that pink hair. You can't be walking around here like that when the sky clears. The 'Forcer eyes will pick you out."

"God, yet another dye job," Fox complained. "It's a wonder my hair doesn't fall out."

⌣⌣⌣

Outside the dining hall, Blanca spirited Tony away to her reed house that she shared with a husband and two children. Fox went with Dolores while Alanso disappeared into the hut of one of his cronies, "...to drink tule root vodka and tell dirty stories," Dolores muttered.

Once inside the Chief's hut, Fox told the woman, "I'm sorry but I gotta pee really bad."

Dolores pointed, "The latrine's just down the end of this line of huts. We recycle all of our waste and use it to fertilize our hydroponic gardens."

"So is that how your clan got its name?"

"I'm afraid so, not a very flattering one. But hurry off. We've got some work to do."

When Fox returned, Dolores had laid out several simple above-the-knee shifts, the common dress of Dungee clanswomen. Fox fingered the dappled gray and white material. It had close-cropped fur on the outside and felt leathery, with a coarse texture on the inside.

"What is this?" she asked.

"It's pounded harbor sealskin—warm, waterproof, windproof and great for a November channel crossing. Go ahead, try on a few. I'm a bit rounder than you but I think one should fit."

Fox sucked in a deep breath and peeled off her salt-encrusted denims. The coarse shirt had rubbed her breasts raw and she wondered how she would manage in her new disguise. Before she could try on another shift, she excused herself to visit the privy, this time forcing herself to relax, hoping it would delay the next interruption.

When she returned, she slid the shift over her head and reached for another.

"So... does your boyfriend know yet?" Dolores asked.

The smile froze on Fox's face. "Know what? What are you talking about?"

"Come on, honey. You're peeing like a leaky irrigation pipe. How far along are you?"

"I... I think I'm about five weeks, maybe more."

"Well, you're not showing yet. But that will happen soon enough."

"Look, Dolores. I don't know what I'm going to do. When Tony finds out he might send me back and go on by himself. I'd never see him again."

"You don't know that. He's come this far. Seems like he's committed to being with you."

"God, my own Mother doesn't even know. If she did, she would never have sent me away."

"You're going to have to trust him at some point.

The longer you wait the angrier he'll be when you tell him."

"I know, I know. I just avoid thinking about that."

"Having a child is something to plan for and it'll take both of you to do that, especially on the island."

"Why?"

"Well, the Zane Greyers don't have... have access to medicines like we do here. We trade our wild rosehip tea with the High Lifers for our essentials, and we also have a doctor who's a clansman. I doubt they have meds and a physician on Catalina Island."

"No, I suppose not."

"Are you sure you want to have a baby?" Dolores asked. "Our doctor could induce..."

"No, no. I feel strong. I want to start a family with Tony, start a new life where I can raise our child."

"Sounds noble," Dolores said, chuckling. "Just hold onto that thought when you've gone through hours of labor and feel ready to explode."

"No, it's not anything noble. Its just... just part of, ya know, the grand adventure that I always dreamed we'd have. Sometimes I hope Tony and I will never stop running. It makes me feel so alive to be with him, meeting new clans, new people like you. Having a baby is all part of that adventure."

Dolores shook her head and laughed. "Yes, but adventures are found everywhere, and you don't need to sail to hell and back to find them."

The two women talked about children and clothes. Dolores reminded Fox of her mother and how she'd sent her daughter into de Tolosa's abandoned retail districts to look for something to replace a worn dress or skirt, something stylish even though it may have been sewn decades before the Change.

As Fox tried on yet another of Dolores's shifts, the clanswoman retrieved a garment the color of human flesh. It had adjustable straps and a lace fringe.

"You're gonna need one of these," Dolores said and smiled. "Here, let me help you."

Dolores fitted the nursing bra around Fox. "It may feel a bit loose now but it won't be for long. You're going to get real sensitive and you'll need it to protect yourself from chafing."

"I've heard women in our clan complain about the tenderness. But I've never seen one of these."

"Yeah, it's a holdover from before the Change... but a good thing to have. I sure won't be needing it any more." Dolores grinned and continued to pull other clothing from drawers and closets for Fox to try on.

Two hours passed before Dolores opened the door to an old wooden hutch and stepped aside to let Fox stare at herself in its mirror, at the black-dyed hair, at the sealskin shift that fit her contours, but with room for expansion. She fingered the heavy cloak; it felt warm enough to fend off the bitterest of winds.

"So, do I look like a Dungee?" Fox asked.

"Oh yeah, except your legs are too pale. You'll be a real turn-on for the boys around camp."

"Great, just what I need," Fox said and smiled.

A clean-shaven man with spiky black hair and wearing sealskin shorts and a sleeveless shirt pushed past the hut's woven reed door and stared at the two women.

"So how do I look?" Tony asked.

"Good God, your hair," Fox said.

Dolores smiled. "Yeah, Blanca's sort of a wizard with hairstyles. But you still look handsome, especially since you've lost that beard."

"Yeah, I feel half-naked. But whatever it takes."

Dolores bustled around the spacious hut, putting clothing away, setting out candles, sweeping the mat floor. From a large trunk she removed a rolled mattress and spread it on the floor against a far wall.

"You kids are staying with us tonight. Just stow

your things anywhere and relax this afternoon, sleep. This mattress is stuffed with tule down... you should like it. I have to work in the garden. There's some cake on the sideboard if you get hungry." She hurried out the door.

Fox stared at herself in the mirror. Tony came up beside her and slipped an arm around her waist and pulled her to him. "Wanna try out the bed?" he whispered in her ear. "It may be our last chance for a while."

"Ah... not now."

Tony took her in his arms and kissed her full on the lips. Her whole body trembled.

"Are you all right?" he asked. "You seem far off somewhere."

"I guess I'm worried about, you know, the channel crossing."

"Yeah, so am I. But these guys are real seafarers. They know what they're doing."

"I hope you're right."

Fox sat on the edge of the bed and stared up at Tony, his hair looking like a late 20th Century punk rocker. She scanned the room, searching for something to focus on. Tony blathered on about flirtatious Blanca, about her bratty daughter and toddler son... and the husband, who had paced their hut while his wife worked on Tony's disguise. But finally his voice faded. They curled up together on the soft, musty-smelling mattress and slept.

At sundown, Dolores shook Tony's shoulder then roused Fox. He felt his stomach rumble; neither he nor Fox had eaten since breakfast... devouring the last of Glen's deer jerky.

"Bring your stash," Dolores told him.

Tony wrapped the Emerald Magic in his dirty shirt and tucked it under an arm. Outside, the compound seemed deserted. But a dull roar came from the dining hall. Inside, the smoky room reverberated with the raucous sound of men and women yelling at each other. When Fox entered, the men hooted and whistled. Fox's face darkened.

"Don't pay any attention to them," Dolores said. "It's just our way of showing appreciation."

The Dungee women also called out and voiced some kind of high yodel that Tony had never heard. He ducked his head and grinned as Dolores led them to a table where Alanso and three other couples sat, drinking. From the way they acted, Tony knew they'd been at it awhile. Dolores introduced them and they sat on the rough plank seats, marked by generations of kids scratching their initials or some expletive Tony couldn't decipher into the butt-polished wood. He listened to the couples talk, determined that some of them were on the clan's Council. They chattered about trade with the High Lifers, about the lackluster production of their rose hips on an adjacent island, about progress in securing lumber to build new canoes for next spring's fishing and trade expeditions, and building a new solar oven using old automobile mirrors scavenged from San Pedro.

A serving crew of teenage boys and girls carried in platters of steaming vegetables and smoked fish of some kind and laid them on each of the tables. The rumble of voices lowered as the clansmen con-centrated on eating with great gusto.

"We serve two meals a day," Dolores explained between mouthfuls, "just after dawn and at sunset. At noon, we snack in our huts then siesta or work in the garden."

As the food platters emptied, the servers placed brightly-colored carafes of vodka on the tables. Alanso filled Tony's goblet. "It's a bit harsh going down," he said, grinning. "But it won't give you a hangover."

"Our clan members brew beer," Tony said. "It tastes

great on a hot summer's day."

"God, I remember drinking beer in the years after the Change. Our clan was mostly scavengers back then. We found a few hundred cases of Budweiser in a flooded warehouse in Wilmington. It didn't last long."

Fox sat quietly and toyed with the remains of her dinner. She had refused the vodka, which seemed strange to Tony since she enjoyed drinking as much as he did. He laid a hand on her arm.

"Are you feeling okay?"

"I'm just nervous about... about whether they'll help us cross the channel."

"So am I."

As the night wore on, the couple sat side by side and clutched each other's hands under the table. Finally, Alanso climbed onto the stage at the end of the hall and stomped a foot on the floorboards until the roar of conversation subsided.

"Fellow clansmen... fellow clansmen. As your leader, I must ask for your help."

The room quieted until the low howl of the wind in the eaves made the only sound. "First, I'd like to introduce our two visitors. Tony and Fox came to us from the Touchable Clan up north in de Tolosa. Will you two stand?"

When the couple rose from the table, a chorus of hoots and yodels filled the hall. Alanso let the clamor die down before continuing. "Tony and Fox sailed into our midst this morning, in a catboat given them by our dear sister Amelia Sanchez."

A gasp went up from many of the older clan member at the mention of her name. "Amelia is alive and well, living north of Buena Ventura on the bluffs. So if any of you ever travel that way, be sure to stop and see her." A chuckle rippled through the crowd.

"Tony and Fox need to reach Catalina and the Zane Grey Clan. To be honest, they are on the run from the

'Forcers, have been since they left de Tolosa. I realize that the seas are treacherous, but I'm asking for eight strong volunteers to take them across to Avalon. Anyone who wants to volunteer please stand up."

Alanso looked out at the scores of quiet faces. Nobody moved. He looked at Tony and motioned to him. Tony slid the wrapped bundle under his arm and stepped onto the stage, his legs feeling like tree limbs trembling in the wind.

"There is something more you should know," Alanso continued. "Tony and Fox stayed with the Surfer Clan near Gaviota Pass on their way south. Those fine and generous people gave this couple a gift to share with those who help them."

Alanso nodded at Tony who unwrapped the two-kilo bag of marijuana. "Some of you may remember years ago when the Surfers left us a gift of their Emerald Magic." A rumble grew from the crowd. "Tony and Fox have agreed to give half their stash to the eight clansmen who take them across channel and most of the remainder to our entire clan for... ceremonial purposes."

The low rumble of the crowd grew into a roar. Men began standing up to volunteer for the mission, some of them broken and withered but speaking of fond memories of the last time they had smoked Emerald Magic. "Jose, you're too damn old to paddle these kids to Catalina," Alanso called. A gray-haired man with dreadlocks gave a gap-toothed grin and sat down. After the ruckus subsided, twelve men remained standing. Alanso selected eight and huddled with the sailors in the corner of the dining hall.

Tony climbed down from the stage and slumped next to Fox, his whole body shaking. "Jeez, I thought we were done for."

"Nah, you would have gotten volunteers eventually," Dolores said, "but the Emerald Magic sped up the process a lot."

Tony gulped his vodka then refilled his cup from the carafe. Fox still wouldn't take any. Alanso finally rejoined them. "Okay kids, listen up. You need to get ready tonight and be set to go before dawn. If the eddy is in, it'll be even better. But if it's clear skies, you'll want to be past the old oil platforms before the sun comes up."

"God, it's all happening so fast," Fox said and leaned her head against Tony's shoulder.

"Come on, we better pack our gear and get some sleep. We've had a long day and tomorrow will be another one. But we're... we're getting close."

They returned to Alanso's and Dolores's hut and stowed the food that Dolores gave them in Fox's backpack. The camp settled in for the night, candles snuffed out, voices quieted. Fox and Tony stripped quickly in the damp air and slid under the heavy covers. They lay on their sides, face-to-face in the night, breathing deep and slow. Alanso and Dolores snored softly at the other end of the hut. Fox reached out and took Tony's face in her hands.

"I have something to tell you," she murmured.

"What?" Tony asked sleepily and snuggled against her.

"I'm... I'm pregnant."

15

Captain Hanpian strode down the polished hallway of the top floor of the Operations Center, his leather-heeled boots smacking against the old linoleum. Stopping at a non-descript door, he entered an alpha-numeric code onto a keypad. The door clicked open. Elliot and Louise Slade sat in metal chairs against the wall. They stared at him, as if he had just interrupted something important.

"I'm afraid I can't wait any longer for your inform-ation. I have talked with the District Attorney and he has agreed to the terms of the deal I outlined to you before. But you have to talk now, or that deal goes away."

"I want to see it in print first," Elliot Slade said.

Hanpian felt his face burn as he entered the DA's code into his portable com unit and keyed a message. In a few seconds, a response came back and he sent it to the printer sitting against a far wall. He retrieved the hard copy and handed it to Elliot. The couple leaned forward and read the single sheet, murmuring to themselves. Finally, Elliot sat back and stared at Hanpian.

"Captain, we agree to the terms so far as they affect our daughter, Fox. But... but we can't in good conscience agree to this without knowing what will happen to Tony."

Hanpian sucked in a deep breath and let it out slowly. "Mr. Slade, only Ruth Matteson can negotiate the terms of any deal for her son. You have no legal standing to intervene on his behalf."

"That's ridiculous," Louise snapped. "If you have Ruth in custody, bring her in here and we can come to an agreement as a group. I'm not selling out my best friend's son. We need a lawyer."

"There is no time for a lawyer, Ms. Slade... and you won't be selling out anyone. Your friend can bargain on her son's behalf. But you have to look out for your daughter."

"Louise, maybe the man is right," Elliot said. "Maybe..."

Louise stared at her husband then covered her face and wept. The sound of her sobs filled the room. Hanpian ground his teeth and checked the time on his com unit. Elliot took his wife into his arms and they sat rocking back and forth, the sobs growing louder but finally subsiding.

"Mr. and Mrs. Slade, I need your answer," Hanpian said softly.

The couple looked up at him, then at each other. They nodded.

"You're doing the right thing," Hanpian said. "Now, where are they headed?"

"To the Channel Islands, to find a commune to live in," Elliot said.

"But we don't know which one... don't know anything about those clans," Louise said and began to sob again.

The Captain turned and headed for the door, leaving the Slades to contemplate what they'd done. Back at his office he summoned Sergeant Jonas.

"Sergeant, is the Matteson woman awake?"

"Yes, Captain. She has been pacing her room."

"Are the blinds open to her quarters?"

"Yes, as you instructed."

"I want you to remove the Slades from interrogation and walk them down the hallway past Ms. Matteson. Then take them to holding. We'll fly them to Goleta this afternoon."

"Are they being charged, Captain?"

"Of course, for harboring a fugitive. We can't just let them walk." Hanpian shook his head and smiled. "They were so intent on negotiating their daughter's release that they forgot about themselves."

Sergeant Jonas disappeared and Hanpian slumped into his chair. He keyed the desk com and Sergeant Statler's face appeared.

"Captain, what's the news?"

"The fugitives are headed to the Channel Islands. The only clans that live there are the Zane Greyers in Avalon on Catalina Island and the West Enders, also on Catalina. I want you to take your men to the Southern Regional Headquarters in Palos Verdes and report to Captain Peterson. He will be handling the pursuit."

"Will do, Captain. They can't be more than a day or maybe two ahead of us. The island will be like a cell with water around it. They should be an easy capture."

"You'd better hope so, Sergeant. We've already blown our budget big time on this case and Commander Pynard is menopausal over it."

The vid went dark. Hanpian pressed another key and Captain Peterson appeared, a man in his forties, blonde-haired and balding, wearing antique wire-rimmed glasses. The officers talked rapidly, using clipped police lingo to speed up the conversation.

"We'll take it from here, Captain Hanpian," Peterson said. "We have air, sea, and land resources. It shouldn't take long."

"Those punks are young," Hanpian said, "but they're also smart, were always one step ahead of us."

"Yes, yes. I've reviewed the reports... and Commander Pynard is already bitching at me about the fugitives. I'll have Sergeant Statler contact you whenever anything changes."

"Appreciate it, Peterson, and good luck."

Hanpian leaned back in his chair. *Good riddance to those punks. They're his problem now. Let Pynard ride his ass for a change.* He longed for a glass of his twenty-year-old Vinho do Porto from Portugal, his soft bed, and his collection of music vids of his favorite mid-twentieth-century band leader, Lawrence Welk. He contacted Sergeant Jonas for a ride back to his home-office. Once every two years being outside was more than enough, he thought. *There's only one loose end... the Matteson woman. I'll give her a few days to stew and then see what I can get.*

16

Fox and Tony rolled onto their backs under the heavy blankets and lay listening to Alanso and Dolores snore. Tony didn't touch her, stayed quiet, his mind racing. The silence between them grew. Blood throbbed in his temples. But he knew if he said anything it would probably be something stupid, hurtful, or both.

Finally, Fox gave him a gentle shove. "Well, aren't you going to say something?"

"Are... are you sure you're pregnant?"

"Yes. The afternoon before we left Santa Barbara, Maryann gave me a pregnancy test. It was positive... and I've missed two periods."

He bit down on his lower lip, struggling to sort out the questions that jammed his mind, the feelings that made his heart pound. Outside, a freshening wind howled around the reed hut, pushing at its creaking walls. Alanso woke momentarily, snorted something, and then quieted.

"How did this happen? I mean, I thought you were taking..."

Fox sighed. "I think my BC pills got too old... or maybe I missed a day... I can't be sure.

"Why the hell didn't you tell me? This changes everything. We could have..."

Tony threw off the covers, slipped into his shorts, and strode from the hut. Fox caught up to him in the yard where he paced the windswept ground under a full moon.

"I don't blame you for being mad," Fox said, her

voice sounding loud in the night air. "But—"

"But what?" Tony shot back. "Is this some sort of trap? Did you do this to... to make me stay with you?"

Fox stood still and stared at him. Her mouth fell open.

Tony groaned, pushed his fingers through his hair and sucked in a deep breath. "God, I'm sorry. I didn't mean..."

Fox walked up to him and gave him a hard push. "You jerk, I didn't tell you because I was afraid you'd send me back to de Tolosa... or turn us both in to the Police. I... I'm still afraid."

Tony reached for her but she twisted away and walked toward the meal hall, her shoulders shaking. He caught up to her and encircled her in his arms. She tried pushing him off but he grasped her tightly. They rocked back and forth in the night air until their bodies stopped shuddering and they separated.

"So... so how pregnant are you?" Tony asked.

Fox choked back a laugh. "I'm fully pregnant. But if you're asking how far along, I think I'm about six weeks, maybe more."

"How do you feel? I mean, can you handle all this running from the Police?"

"Well, you've seen my phony seasickness... and Dolores says I pee like a leaky irrigation pipe. But so far, I... I feel strong... and we should be on the island soon."

Tony sucked in a deep breath. He thought about the millions of people throughout history that had asked the same questions: what was best for both of them? What was best for each of them? What was best for the child? The baby... should they even have a baby? Were they being incredibly stupid?

"Listen Fox, do you really want to have a... I mean... I can understand if you don't."

She stared at him. "I'm... I'm ready, Tony. But only

if I'm with you and you want me... I mean, us."

He stared at her wide-eyed. She came into his arms and he felt the wetness of her tears on his shoulder. "Hush now," he said, "save your strength. We have a long day ahead of us. I could never do any of this without you. I never want to be without you."

They returned to the hut, slipped out of their clothes, and crawled under the covers.

From across the room came a low mutter from Dolores. "All right already. Now that that's settled, will you two go to sleep? Some of us have work in the morning."

Fox's body shook with silent laughter. Tony let out a deep breath. "Good night, Dolores."

The pair snuggled into each other's arms, their bodies tingling with desire, and made quiet love. Fox fell sound asleep. Tony lay awake, his mind churning with thoughts of childbirth, raising a kid, and doing it all on a mountain top called Catalina Island, far from any regional med center. He closed his eyes to rest for a moment and dropped off to sleep.

Dolores stood over them, holding a candle. Tony reached over and shook Fox gently. She roused herself, slipped into her new sealskin shift, and bolted for the latrine. Tony pulled on his shorts and long-sleeved shirt and followed as quickly as he could. Afterwards, they joined the throng of sleepy Dungees stumbling through the darkness to the dining hall where they ate a breakfast of wholegrain pancakes topped with honey, and sucked on tea brewed strong enough to resemble coffee. The morning crowd moved quietly about with little chatter, except for the kids, excited about their day attending the village school.

Back at the hut, Alanso wasted no time. "It's about an hour till dawn. With that strong wind, it should be clear skies. You'll want to be well past the breakwaters and into the channel by sunrise. Grab your gear and come on."

Fox looked at Tony and grinned. "At least we've got someone else to do the paddling." They shouldered their bulging backpacks and followed Alanso out of the hut and down a path through the reeds and pygmy oaks to a well-defined inlet with a short dock.

A slender canoe rested in the calm water. It had a flat bottom with steep sides made of thick planks, pinned and somehow glued together. The sides came to a raised point at the bow and stern. It looked maybe fifteen meters long and rode high in the water. Tony and Fox placed their backpacks in the storage area at mid-ship, next to some waterproof packets of tea. Alanso introduced them to the crew, a grinning group of muscular men who acted like they had already sampled their Emerald Magic payment.

Jake, the crew leader, clapped Tony on the back and grinned. "We'll have ya in Avalon in seven or eight hours. Looks like a good day, but the mid-channel swells will be something else."

"Don't worry," Tony said. "Both Fox and I are good swimmers."

Jake laughed. "If our *Tomol* goes down in mid-channel, it won't matter. The Great Whites will be nibbling on your toes long before you get tired."

"So what's the tea for?" Tony asked, pointing to the storage area.

"We'll trade it to the Zane Greyers for some of their pottery."

"Pottery?"

"Yes, you probably saw it last night at dinner—the colorful stuff that we use to serve our vodka. The Catalina Islanders have been making it since just after the Change."

The couple clambered aboard and scrunched down next to their backpacks. A tarp was pulled over them. "Since we've got clear skies, we don't want any aerial surveillance picking you guys out," Jake said.

"What about heat sensors?" Tony asked.

"Nah, there's no reason for them to use that stuff in the channel. The 'Forcers are used to seeing us, although a November crossing is... is unusual."

In a few minutes, the canoe rocked as all the crew-members settled in for the day-long haul. Tony peeked out from underneath the tarp and watched each Dungee bend and dip his paddle into the quiet sea. The canoe sliced through the water with little drama, the boat surging with each stroke. The roar of the ocean grew louder as they approached the break-waters and the harbor's mouth. The canoe began to buck as it steered head-on into the swells and the onshore wind. Seawater splashed over the gunwales and the teenage bailer scampered fore and aft across them, filling his bucket as the paddlers picked up the pace.

"At least I've learned how to bail," Tony muttered.

"At least with all this water, nobody will notice when I pee," Fox cracked.

"Eeeew," Tony said and dug her in the ribs.

They tried to relax and doze in their cramped quarters. The hours passed and the hot sun hung overhead when the high whine of a drone skimmer jerked them awake. Tony clutched Fox's trembling hand and peeked out, saw the skimmer flash above the wave tops, not more than a kilometer to the north of them. It continued westward toward Catalina Island, which now filled their seaward horizon.

"How far have we come?" Tony asked Jake, who sat on a bench closest to them, bending and rising to pull his paddle through the water.

"We're just short of mid-channel. But we've been pushed by the wind and current a bit southward and will need to bear north."

"What about that drone?"

173

"I don't like it. But one's not unusual. If we see more—"

Before he could say anything else, a squadron of manned skimmers passed westward, toward the cleft in the island where the flooded remains of Avalon lay. Jake laid his paddle down and retrieved a giant set of antique binoculars. He followed the skimmers to the island then swung the field glasses toward the mainland.

"Hell, there's a half dozen crawlers on the bridge, and I can see the shore patrol circling our island. I'm sure the 'Forcers are searching our camp."

"What... what about on Catalina?" Tony asked.

"Those skimmers will come ashore at Seven Moons Bay. They'll be waiting for us."

"Why don't they just take us here at mid-channel?" Tony asked.

"Too dangerous in these high seas. Whoever they want, they want alive."

"What about some other landing on Catalina?" Fox asked, her voice a high squeak.

"When the sea level rose, just about all the coves were taken out. The cliffs fall right into the ocean. Even if you swam ashore, you'd have to be a mountain goat to get off the rocks."

"Looks like we're between the devil and the deep blue sea," Fox muttered.

Jake grinned. "Yeah, something like that. But it's not over yet. The eddy's coming in and there's one place they won't expect us to stop."

"What are you talking about?" Tony asked.

The Dungee pointed south. Four old oil platforms rose out of the sea. The farthest three looked like bare tables with the channel swells breaking near their tops. The third platform, less than a kilometer away, stood 15 meters above the waves, its deck bare except for a boxy structure with white metal walls with no windows. The first wisps of the oncoming Catalina Eddy started to blur its edges.

"The tallest one is Platform Edith," Jake said. "We can drop you there and continue to Avalon."

"Then what?" Tony asked.

"At Avalon, the Police will search us and won't find squat. We'll sail back to Dungee Island and wait for the 'Forcers to clear out. Then come and get you guys in a few days."

"A few days?" Fox cried.

"Don't worry, we won't leave you stranded. But I don't like the way the sky is looking. Those clouds are not just part of the eddy. We could be in for an early blow and it could take us up to a week to get back here. It's risky, but it's up to you two. We can always return to the mainland."

Tony stared into Fox's face, saw her mouth tighten, eyes blaze as she nodded. He turned to Jake. "Give us all your food and get us on that platform."

The canoe turned south and picked up speed, running with the current and wind. As they drew close, Tony saw the remains of a rusting steel ladder emerge from the sea and climb one of the many columns to the deck above. Jake pointed and the crew maneuvered the canoe to ride broadside to the ladder but not too close for fear of smashing against the pylons.

Jake pulled a grappling hook and rope from a forward storage area. "I'm going to try and hook the ladder from here," he said. "Do you think you can pull yourselves up? You'll need to get above those rusted rungs before you put any weight on it."

Tony stood in the rocking boat, his arms and legs cramped from being confined under the tarp. He beat on his muscles with clenched fists to bring back the circulation. The fog had obliterated Catalina and the western horizon and the mainland disappeared fast.

He looked at Fox and she nodded. "We can do it."

Jake swung the grappling hook and it crashed against the pylon and fell into the sea. On his third attempt, he caught one of the higher rungs, yanked on the line, and it snugged against the ladder. Fox and Tony stood unsteadily and slipped into their pack straps.

"I'll go first," Tony said. Grabbing the line with calloused hands, he pulled himself upward. As the fog thickened, the wind died back. He heard the Dungees yelling encouragement as they struggled to hold the canoe off the pylons and keep the line steady. Tony wrapped his legs around the rope and yanked himself upward, hand over hand until his shoulder sockets burned. When he got within a meter of the grappling hook, he reached for the ladder. His legs caught a rung and he tested it with his weight. Releasing the rope, he clutched the ladder until his breathing slowed. Scrambling upward, he climbed onto the platform's deck, slipped out of his pack, then descended toward the bouncing canoe. Fox's pale face stared up at him, lips trembling.

"Come on, Fox. You can do it," he yelled to her. She grinned back and clutching the line began her slow ascent, wrapping her legs around the rope as Tony had done. About halfway toward the pylon, she stopped to rest. Her legs slipped and she dangled above the sea, the wave crests licking at her boot heels.

"Keep coming, keep coming!" Tony screamed into the wind as he moved down the ladder toward her. The crew hollered encouragement and the bailer looked ready to dive into the sea if Fox should fall. But she looked into Tony's eyes and swung her legs around the rope and continued climbing. As she neared his position, Tony stretched out an arm and pulled her into the pylon as the Dungees slacked off the line. She clamped onto the rails with both hands, her head down, blowing air like a whale, arms trembling. As her breathing subsided, she tilted her head back and stared into his face.

"Christ, I really gotta pee."

"Go ahead," Tony said and laughed.

He moved up the ladder, staying with Fox until they both stood on the platform's deck in the cold wind and fog. She slipped out of her pack straps. Tony flung his arms around her and squeezed hard as the boat crew cheered.

"I'm okay, I'm okay," she whispered in his ear.

"I know. I... I just love you."

She kissed him on the lips as the crew continued whooping. Jake whipped the slackened rope so that the grappling hook dislodged and fell into the ocean. They hauled it onboard.

"You guys are tough," he yelled. "See you in a few days... when the eddy is in."

The couple waved. The canoe turned northwest-ward toward Catalina. The paddlers put their backs into it. Within a few moments, they had disappeared into the mist. The cold wind chilled the couple's bare arms and legs. Tony removed the long Dungee cloaks from their backpacks and they slipped them on and buttoned up the fronts.

"God, that feels good," Fox said. "I didn't realize how cold I'd gotten. My butt feels like ice. I don't think I've ever been this cold."

Tony pulled her to his side and they stared at the swirling eddy that engulfed them. A colony of seagulls huddled in the far corner of the platform, heads tucked under their wings. A latticework of steel beams and girders formed the deck, covered with concrete, with various openings reserved for what must have been the well head, piping, and utility connections. Sections of the concrete had crumbled away, leaving rusted reinforcing bars exposed to the wet sea air. Tony and Fox shouldered their packs and picked their way across the deck toward the lone metal structure. Shaped like a brick, it resembled an old-style cargo container that the manned freighters used to carry. Windowless, a door stood ajar near one end; a second door stood closed at the other. Tony pulled the door wide and they edged inside.

"We're probably the first people here since the oil crews pulled out," Tony said.

"Yeah, can you imagine what it must have been like to live here during the last days of the Petroleum Era?"

"Not much different than our Garage," Tony said. "A small clan isolated from everyone else. At least the roustabouts and roughnecks got paid well."

Head-high metal lockers, like the ones Tony had found in abandoned school buildings, lined the walls. A long bench ran the length of the room between the lockers with a sink and cracked mirror along the far end wall. Two stuffed chairs with cracked upholstery sat side-by-side against the near end wall. Skylights let in the noon sun. The pair set their backpacks on the bench and moved to the mirror.

Tony pointed and laughed. "We look like those artists' paintings of cavemen."

"Nah, cavewomen didn't have these." She opened her cloak, exposing her sculpted legs.

"Nice, very nice," Tony said and reached for her. She sidestepped his advance and giggled. "Maybe later, buster. I don't usually put out for platform workers on a first date."

"Usually?"

Fox pulled off her cloak and hurried outside. She returned in a few moments, grinning sheepishly. Tony checked the doors to make sure that they wouldn't jam shut, then closed them to the wind. Their home felt tight and well insulated. They unpacked their provisions, stowing them in the lockers.

"With the food the Dungees gave us, we should have enough to eat for a week," Tony said.

"Yeah, but it's the water..."

"Three canteens isn't a lot."

They spread their long cloaks across the stuffed chairs. Sitting, they wrapped themselves in their seal-skin cocoons to stay warm. After eating some dried berries, they leaned back and fell asleep. When Tony woke, the light inside their cabin had faded. Fox stood before an open wall locker, staring. He joined her. Old photographs decorated the inside of its door: a toddler celebrating some kind of holiday; a pretty woman blowing a kiss; pictures of a dog and cat playing; parents; brothers and sisters; of things that joined that long-ago oil worker to his life on the mainland. Fox touched the photographs' cracked surfaces, as if trying to feel the people, to somehow connect with them. Were they angry that their husbands' and sons' jobs had ended? Did those old roustabout families form their own clan after the Change, drilling water wells after black gold became illegal as a fuel?

A wave of homesickness washed over Tony, the first since they'd left the Garage just weeks before. He thought of his mother, probably holed up in the Library, reading the classics, waiting for the Touch-able Clan's world to stop rocking... and all because of him. *I could have just knocked that bastard out. Why did I have to kill him? But it felt... felt so right when I did it.* The image of the hulking rapist filled his mind. He shuddered and opened another door. Nothing.

They checked each of the sixty lockers and found rotting pieces of clothing, a serviceable steel pot, scraps of paper, and more photographs. Tony wondered if the crew had abandoned their home quickly and why only one structure had been left behind while everything else had been cleared away. In another twenty years, all the platforms would be nothing more than bits of metal on the bottom of the channel. Good riddance? He knew the use of fossil fuels had led to climate changes that destroyed whole cultures. Yet, it was all part of that golden Petroleum Age that he'd read about. Would something like that ever happen again? His mother didn't think so since the oil reserves had been used up. But just maybe...

Before the light failed, they ate supper—slices of strong-tasting bread, more dried berries, and pieces of salted fish. Fox washed it down with sips of water while Tony took nips from a bottle of tule root vodka that Dolores must have slipped into his pack. They agreed to use the sink at the other end of the room as their overnight *pissoire* since it felt too cold to venture outside onto the treacherous deck. The wind increased, pushing at the sides of their cabin. Rain rattled against the roof. Tony placed the steel pot outside the door near a downspout, hoping to catch rainwater. They slumped in their chairs, held hands, and listened to the platform creak as the night sea thundered against the pylons and rocked them to sleep.

17

Sergeant Statler gazed on the town of Avalon from the ruins of an old home site high above the water on one of the harbor's headlands. Across Seven Moons Bay, the top of a round concrete building with a Spanish tile roof formed the other headland. The waves slammed against its massive walls, just below its upper balcony. Officer Graham, the sergeant's skimmer pilot, had told him that the clansmen called the building "The Casino," and that it had once housed a magnificent ballroom and movie theater before being flooded.

The channel had pushed its way into Catalina Island's interior, destroying the town's bay-front commercial district and the low-lying homes. Only the huge mansions that clung to Avalon Canyon's near-vertical slopes escaped the sea's destruction. But with no delivery service and the island's tiny airport closed, the pre-Change residents had fled and Avalon became a ghost town... well, almost.

Statler flipped his Rangemaster down over his eyes and stared across the bay at the promontory above the Casino. A two-story sprawling structure with tan plaster walls came into view. He upped the magnification and the building filled his screen. A hand-painted sign that read "Zane Grey Pueblo" decorated its foundation. What looked like Native American paintings adorned its exterior. He studied the building and grounds that had several levels and stretched along the headland. House cats of every color and size walked the pueblo's parapet, perched on window sills, or stretched in the sun on the brightly-colored patio, feet in the air, sleeping. The apartment windows facing the bay stood open. Inside, clansmen moved about, most small and brown, of Latino origin. Statler paused his glasses at a particular window to ogle a man making passionate love to a woman.

Aroused by what he saw, Statler shifted his view to the old chimes tower uphill from the pueblo. An islander sat on a stone wall, watching the channel with binoculars. He shifted his focus to Statler's position, grinned and waved. The sergeant waved back. The Catalina Eddy blanketed the channel. But the sky directly over the island stayed clear. The sergeant stared at the harbor entrance and watched for movement. Pelicans dove into the bay's crystal-clear water and high above, black ravens circled, their faint croaking calls drifting on the afternoon wind. Then a long slender canoe slid into view. Statler clicked his com unit.

"Captain Peterson, we have visual contact."

"How soon until they reach shore?"

"Ten minutes."

"All right, follow the plan. Alert the shore units."

"Yes sir, will report in fifteen."

Statler clicked to a different com channel.

"Units 1 through 4, we have visual contact with our target. Close in slowly but stay concealed until they step ashore. I don't want any bloodshed."

"Roger that."

The strange-looking boat moved slowly across the bay, expertly avoiding the wreckage of old piers, overrun seawalls, and derelict buildings. Eight Dungees manned the craft, all of them too big and muscular to be the fugitives. They paddled with their heads down, laboring to lift their arms, their bodies glistening. Statler studied the canoe's mid-ship cargo area. *If they're anywhere, they're under that tarp.* He watched the Dungees paddle into the canyon, passing between flooded shops and hotels, moving toward a landing next to a tower that looked like it had been used to train firemen.

"Get ready," he murmured into his com.

The canoe nudged into a low wharf and a clansman jumped out and secured the bow to a dock post. The Dungees laid their paddles down and slouched on their benches, not moving. They didn't seem to notice the camouflaged police force approaching from all sides, weapons drawn, including those in requisitioned dinghies. Within a minute it was over. The paddlers sat on the wharf with their hands secured behind their backs. Statler walked back to his skimmer and shook Officer Graham awake.

"Come on, fly me downhill."

Graham rubbed his eyes and activated the air car's controls. They slid over the bay and up canyon, landing in what looked like a parking lot for some public building which had long since crumbled into the new surf line. As he stepped from the skimmer, a group of clansmen from the Zane Grey rode up on bicycles and sat muttering to themselves. The 'Forcer team stood with their legs spread, weapons drawn.

Statler keyed his com and murmured, "Take it easy boys. These creeps are just curious. They have no weapons." He strode onto the dock. "All right, who is in charge of this detail?"

The tallest of the boat crew pushed himself to his feet. "My name's Jake. We're from the Dung People Clan on Terminal Island."

"I know where you came from. We've been watching you since you left before dawn."

"So what do you want from us?" the Dungee asked.

"What's under the tarp?" Statler asked, smiling. He drew his sidearm, grabbed a boat hook lying on the rough planks, snagged the tarp covering the midsection of the canoe, and pulled it away. A carrot-topped teenage boy stared up at him, blinking and rubbing his eyes.

"Who the hell are you?" Statler demanded.

"I'm the fricken bailer. What's it to ya."

The clansmen laughed. Statler felt his face grow hot and he unbuttoned the top button of his starched shirt. "What are you transporting?" Statler pointed to the packets wrapped in plastic and bound with twine.

Jake grinned. "Rose hip tea. Do you want us to brew you a pot?"

The Zane Grey clansmen chuckled.

"What is the purpose of your trip?" Statler asked.

"We trade with Rafael here and the Zane Greyers. They like our tea and we like their pottery."

"That's right, officer," a slender brown man with a graying goatee said. "We've been trading with the Dungees for years. You should know that."

"But it's November. Why are you here now? You're lucky you made it alive."

"Well officer, we ran out of pottery," Jake said, and the Zane Greyers exploded into laughter.

Sergeant Statler groaned to himself. *Why do I always get the wise-asses?* He remembered the incident at the Garage in de Tolosa, right before he'd ordered it blown to bits. Three teenagers had stayed inside the parking structure, taunting the Police from its third level. After it became clear that the fugitives had escaped, listening to those punks had been the last straw. *At least no one will ever find their bodies, covered in tons of broken concrete and twisted re-bar. But that pussy Captain Hanpian had to find someone to take the fall for the failed mission; and Commander Pynard needs her pound of flesh.* Statler knew his demotion from lieutenant to sergeant satisfied the higher-ups and that only his success in capturing the fugitives could ever correct his blunder.

"Release these men," Statler ordered.

Groaning, the Dungees pushed themselves up and unloaded the canoe onto a cart that two of the Zane Greyers pulled uphill along what was left of the canyon road, heading toward their common house. The Dungees followed at a slow pace, their arms hanging loose by their sides. Statler climbed into his skimmer and Officer Graham flew him back to their stakeout on the headlands.

He keyed the skimmer's com. "Captain Peterson, this is Sergeant Statler reporting."

"Well, do you have them?"

"No sir, they weren't on the boat."

"Are you sure they were on that particular canoe when it left Dungee Island?"

"Well, no sir. But it was unusual for them to be crossing in November and I am—"

"Save your breath, Statler. Could the Dungees have made a quick drop somewhere else on the island's landward coast?"

"We've had skimmers patrolling it all afternoon, and there aren't any good places to come ashore and survive the surf and rocks."

"Very well, maintain your positions until further orders."

"Yes sir," Statler said and moaned to himself. Another night crammed inside the skimmer's cramped cockpit, watching the Dungees, and now the Zane Greyers, away from his vid screens and his five-year-old Cabernet. As the wind buffeted the skimmer, he stared into the fog and thought about the last month. As a lieutenant, he'd been on track to take over as District chief when Hanpian retired or kicked off. Now, it was anybody's guess who would get the job, and he'd have to compete with kiss-asses like Sergeant Jonas, the weirdo who liked the outdoors and would rather beat off on a mountain top than watch the latest porn immersion vids. But more likely, Commander Pynard would bring in someone new from outside the District anyway. *Why the hell should I care*, he thought, and leaned back in his seat and dozed.

$$\backsim$$

Across the bay from where the Police had taken up surveillance, the clansmen wound their way along the steep road that climbed the canyon slopes toward the Zane Grey Pueblo. The Dungee crew stopped often, their bodies near exhaustion. They had paddled hard after dropping the fugitives off at Platform Edith, trying to make up for the lost time so as not to raise suspicions with the 'Forcers, who Jake knew would be waiting for them in Avalon. The mid-channel swells had swamped their canoe. One of the paddlers had helped the bailer keep them afloat.

Near the Pueblo, the clansmen left the road and climbed a series of winding steps cut into the steep headland. The stairs led to a paved patio next to the building. The Dungees fell to the ground and leaned against the low perimeter wall, gasping. Several women brought pitchers and goblets and poured each paddler a drink, refilling their goblets as often as requested.

"What is this stuff?" Jake asked one of the women. "It tastes sweet and tart at the same time."

The woman smiled at him shyly. "It's a mixture of lemon and lime juice blended with our tequila."

"Where do you get..."

Rafael, the Zane Grey Clan Chief, slumped onto the patio next to Jake. "You Dungees aren't the only ones we trade our pottery with. The West Enders are a tiny clan at the other end of Catalina. They tend orchards on the hillside above the old Banning House, irrigate the hell out of those trees with spring water."

"And the tequila?"

"Years before the Change the slopes above Avalon were covered with prickly pear cactus. When everything got hotter, we replaced them with blue agave that we took from the gardens near the Wrigley Memorial."

"It tastes potent," Jake said and grinned.

"It's a hell of a lot better than that disgusting vodka you guys make."

Jake sighed. "I'd love to get my hands on lemons and limes. But the West End is just too long a haul from Dungee Island. Maybe you guys could trade some of your fruit supply for our tea."

"I think we can work something out."

The pair leaned back against the wall and slurped their Margaritas. A company of brilliant green parrots with red bands above their bills flew over the patio and settled in the swaying eucalyptus trees next to the pueblo.

Jake pointed out the birds. "They're new. When the heck did they show up?"

"We think they're from Mexico or Central America. They arrived last year about this time and never left."

"Damn, this place really is becoming tropical."

Rafael grinned. "Yeah, the heat is good for the Margarita business and we started making really beautiful glazed tiles of parrots, like our ancestors did during the early 20th century. But forget about all of that. What are you guys doing out here? It's fricken November and I can't remember the last time you made such a late crossing. And why did you drag the Police with you?"

"We were helping two fugitives from up north, from de Tolosa... a couple of good kids that killed a High Lifer."

"Well, where the hell are they?"

"We had to leave them on Platform Edith before the

eddy cleared and the 'Forcers searched our canoe."

At the mention of the oil platform, Rafael pushed back the bandana that encircled his forehead, stood, and stared into the channel, wide-eyed. "You... you left them out there?"

"Yeah."

"Didn't you see those clouds?" Rafael pointed to the sky, at the massive thunderheads rolling past, sliding over the channel toward the mainland. "That's just the front edge. When the storm hits, the sea will wash right over those platforms."

"Don't you think I don't know that?" Jake snapped, then relaxed against the wall. "It was either that or bring them here... and you know what would have happened."

"Jeez, at least they'd be alive," Rafael said. "The storm's gonna blow for a couple days."

"They have food for a week... and they're tough. You should have seen the girl climb the rope onto the platform."

"Christ, this story gets better and better." Rafael grinned and downed the remains of his Island Margarita.

"They wanted to come here and join your clan, away from surveillance and the Police."

"Not a bad idea. We don't get many new members, especially young ones, and our numbers have been dropping for the past few years. Some of the old timers get island fever and try to reach the mainland in their dinghies. We never see them again."

"It's too late for the fugitives to join you now," Jake said. "Even if we could get them here, the 'Forcers will be all over this place like flies on—"

"Don't worry, I got some ideas," Rafael said and smiled. "But those kids must be something special for you guys to go to all the trouble."

"Well, they did provide us with an incentive," Jake

said and withdrew something from his satchel. He opened a cloth bag. "Take a whiff."

Raphael bent and sucked in a deep breath through his nose. When he leaned back he broke into a face-splitting grin. "Is that..."

"Yeah, Emerald Magic."

"We're gonna party tonight," he said and hurried inside the pueblo to arrange for sleeping space for the Dungee seamen in the common room, and make sure that the clan buttoned up the place tight against the oncoming storm.

∿∿

The last glow of the sun had faded when Sergeant Statler's vid com buzzed. He touched his headset. "Yes, Captain Peterson."

"Any sign of the fugitives?"

"No sir. I don't believe they're on the island."

"What about the Dungees?"

"They're holed up in the Zane Grey Pueblo. They've got the place shut tight and we have no eyes inside."

"Can you get someone close? Maybe we could at least get audio, see what they're up to."

"It would be difficult, sir. The pueblo has no unexposed approaches. Plus..."

"Plus what, Sergeant?"

"It's starting to rain. We better get off the island ourselves before we get trapped here. It really looks like a mean blow, maybe even hurricane strength... at least that's what the satellite feed is showing."

"I know that, stupid. I have the same vid in front of me. Get your ass back to the Palos Verdes station and await my orders. I still think the fugitives hunkered down on one of the Marsh Islands in San Pedro harbor. But nobody will be going anywhere during the storm."

"Yes sir," Statler said. "ETA in 20 minutes."

Statler clicked off his com and leaned back in the skimmer's seat, letting out a deep breath and shaking his head. Officer Graham looked at him, waiting.

"Back to the mainland, Graham. We're done here... for now."

18

Tony woke with a jolt. Fox clutched his arm, her nails digging into his flesh. She climbed from her chair and joined him in his. They scrunched into the over-stuffed seat with their cloaks pulled over their heads. Outside, the night sea sent waves breaking against the oil platform's bottom cross beam; and every few minutes, a thundering wave slammed into the side of their metal cabin, causing it to creak and groan.

As the minutes dragged past, Fox's trembling body calmed. Tony patted her hand then rose, clicked on his hand light and moved about the room, checking the tie-downs to the platform's deck. The welded and bolted connections looked well preserved. But he worried about what the underside of the deck looked like after being doused for years with corrosive sea-water. A huge wave might break them loose, slide them across the platform, and send them tumbling into the Pacific. He checked the doors. Both held tight. He returned to Fox and snuggled into her arms.

"We're still dry. But that storm sounds mean."

"Yeah... yeah it does," Fox muttered, her body vibrating again like a plucked guitar string. "I'll bet it'll be a hurricane before it's done."

"Great. At least that's one problem we didn't get in de Tolosa. But SoCal is now just like Florida, and every year the storms come farther north from Mexico."

"I wonder how the Dungees handle it?" Fox asked and shivered.

"You saw how they built their huts and meal hall high above ground level. I'm sure the tidal surges really mess up the entire lagoon."

"Tony, do... do you think they'll come back for us?"

"They will if their boats aren't on the bottom of the channel. We just need to be... be patient and think about our next move. The sea is gonna do what it wants. I'd rather worry about the Police and where to go next once the Dungees come for us."

"I know. I'm just glad you're here now." Fox kissed him. They wriggled out of their sealskin clothes and undergarments, trying to keep the cloaks over their naked bodies as they made passionate love, their cries drowned out by the crash of waves against their cabin.

"I... I don't want to hurt you," Tony murmured into Fox's ear, "or the baby."

Fox laughed. "Are you kidding? Shows how much you didn't learn about pregnant women. Yeah, parts of my body feel tender... but I also feel different, ya know, more... more excited." They continued their lovemaking until he fell into a sleep so deep that not even the waves could keep him awake.

Tony slowly opened his eyes to gray light pouring through the skylights, along with a steady stream of rain. Ankle-deep water sloshed across the cabin floor. He was glad they had stowed their gear in the lockers. Sometime during the night, Fox had returned to her chair and lay curled up on its cushions, wrapped in her cloak and snoring. Tony walked to the sink and peed, then tried opening the far door. It felt jammed. He put his shoulder against it and shoved but it wouldn't budge. *The waves twisting this metal box are messing up the doors.* He tried the other door. With a little shove it opened.

Outside, sheets of seawater streaked across the platform, and disappeared into the gaps in the concrete. Their water pot had washed away. The seagulls had abandoned their refuge, the deck now sporting new holes with twisted re-bars. Tony slid outside and edged along the wall of their cabin until he could face seaward. Catalina Island stood dark and brooding on the horizon, obscured by curtains of slashing rain driven by a fierce onshore wind. Phalanx after phalanx of combers rolled toward their platform. It shook and swayed with each collision. The sea looked more white than gray. After a few minutes of staring into a storm sea where no human could survive, Tony returned to the door and gave it a tug; it wouldn't budge. He banged on the heavy metal sheeting and could barely hear Fox on the other side, her body thudding against the panel with no success.

"Stop it, Fox. You're gonna hurt yourself," he screamed.

A huge wave slammed into the far side of the cabin, lifting it ever so slightly. *The damn tiedowns along the seaward edge are failing. Our little box twists every time a wave hits.* He continued to tug at the door until the effort took his breath away. With his chest heaving, he scanned the deck, hoping to discover some other shelter that had magically appeared overnight. But if anything, the deck disintegrated with each wave-set. He remembered what Jake had said about the Great Whites nibbling at their toes and shuddered.

Another wave slammed into the cabin just as Tony tugged on the door. The wall twisted and the door sprang open, exposing a wide-eyed and naked Fox. Tony grinned and ducked inside while holding onto the doorknob. He used his antique Swiss army knife to dismantle the latch. Attaching a piece of nylon cord to the knob, he tied it to one of the bench posts to keep it loosely shut.

"That should hold off the storm without locking us in or out."

"Don't worry," Fox said. "I have no desire to go outside anytime soon, except maybe to..."

Tony laughed. "I'll hold the door for ya."

They slouched into their chairs and talked about where they might run next: south to the cargo piers in San Diego where they might sneak aboard a drone freighter bound for Buenos Aires or the South China Sea; find a small canoe of their own and continue to Mexico where murderous clans lived and the Police wouldn't follow; return to Amelia's place and hide out in the coastal mountains until the baby came; find some other rock in the sea where they could live out their castaway lives eating seagull eggs and seal meat. None of it sounded good and after awhile they stopped talking. Tony sang songs and listened to the wail of the northwest wind. He imagined it sounding like the ancient Greek sirens, calling to Homer's brave Ulysses and his men to join them and suffer death in the sea off some rocky coast.

The days and nights passed slowly. Tony wished he had brought some books from de Tolosa's Library to read. Fox used the stub end of a pencil to draw his portrait over and over, or whip out sketches of Catalina Island from memory, or of their oil platform refuge, but filled with roustabouts getting undressed after a hard day's work. Tony borrowed her sketchbook and tried his hand at drawing her nude. When he showed her his attempt, she choked back a laugh.

"You know damn well my breasts aren't that big."

"Just wait, they will be," Tony said and grinned.

On the fourth day, the wind backed off. Tony ventured outside and studied the sky. The clouds had broken up and the thick bank of the Catalina Eddy formed out to sea, ready to fill the channel with gray wispy soup. As the platform stopped rocking, they untethered the door and flung it open, hoping the water covering the floor would drain more easily. It didn't.

By the fifth day, they were socked in with fog and running low on drinking water. Tony had managed to collect some in his canteen from the leaking skylight. But it tasted salty and they wouldn't drink it. They lost track of time and bearings. After a while, he had to study the waves to remember which direction the coastline lay and where Catalina might be in the thickening fog. They slept as much as possible, conserving their strength but feeling weaker with each passing day.

By mid-afternoon of the sixth day, they sat in their chairs, staring dully out the propped- open door at the fog-shrouded platform. Out of the mist walked a tall man wearing long shorts and nothing else, picking his way between the holes in the concrete. Tony rubbed his eyes, expecting the figure to disappear. He had imagined someone coming for hours as his grasp on reality continued to slip.

"It's Jake," Fox murmured.

Groaning, they pushed themselves up and stepped outside their cabin. A broad grin spread across Jake's face. He hugged both of them. "Well what are ya waiting for?" he cracked. "We got the boat pulled up ready to take you off. Why aren't you ready?"

Tony and Fox stared dumbly at him for a moment before bursting into action. Fox cleared out her locker, leaving behind only her sketch of their cabin filled with naked roustabouts. Tony figured that she had left it for the next castaways that occupied Platform Edith.

In less than five minutes, they closed the cabin door for the last time and followed Jake across the deck to the rusted ladder. Tony's backpack felt like he carried a dead body, maybe his former childhood self that he wasn't quite ready to discard. Staring downward, he noticed that only two or three rungs remained of the ladder. Whoever had thrown the grappling hook had done one hell of a job in snagging it.

Tony went first, wrapping his legs around the line

and lowering himself smoothly into the canoe. Fox followed without any drama. They huddled in the cargo area, filled now with pottery and bottles of some yellowish liquid. Above them, Jake took one last look around then dislodged the grappling hook and tossed it into the sea. Grinning, he jumped off the platform, disappearing under the cold green waves. But in a moment he surfaced and with a few strong strokes reached the canoe and climbed aboard.

"After last night's party with the Zane Greyers, I needed a bath," he said grinning.

"So where the heck are we going?" Tony asked. "The Police must be watching the island."

"Yeah, they've got skimmers parked on all the headlands and mountain tops surrounding Avalon. But that's not where we're taking you."

Jake handed Fox a bottle of the yellow-green liquid. "Have some of this, it will wake you up. It's just sweetened lemon and lime juice."

Both of them took a long swig, their lips puckering then curling into smiles. The paddlers turned the canoe toward Catalina Island, at least where it should lie hidden in the fog, and began stroking in earnest. The couple and Jake talked over the plan that he and the Zane Greyers had cooked up.

"Are they sure there's a trail?" Tony asked.

Jake nodded. "Yeah, one of the ZGs hiked it a couple of weeks back. It's definitely passable, but only to those who have been cross-bred with mountain goats."

"Naa, naa, that sounds like us," Tony said, making more goat sounds that cracked Fox up. The couple left Jake to his paddling. Tony offered to help the carrot-topped teenager bail the canoe but he refused, grinning at them as if they were somehow honored guests that shouldn't be expected to exert themselves after such a harrowing stay on Platform Edith.

With the onset of the Eddy, the wind had died and the rough seas calmed. The canoe slid blindly through the water at amazing speed. The paddlers seemed to be enjoying each stroke and several times they broke into songs that Tony didn't know but tried to memorize. Several hours passed. Before the light began to fade, the sound of surf pounding Catalina's north shore filled their ears. They turned westward and skirted the island, a desolate rock-strewn coastline bordered by steep cliffs and mountain slopes covered in grasses, wind-twisted oaks, and chaparral.

"The Zane Greyers told us Toyon Bay should be close to that point we just rounded," Jake said and continued paddling.

"Is there a beach there or what?" Fox asked.

"Good God, no. Toyon Bay is its old name. The beach and encampment were all wiped out when the sea level rose. But most of the trail leading to the ridgeline is still there. And there's a grove of ironwood trees on the lower slopes that you can camp under for the night."

"Sounds like you know the place well," Tony said.

"I was there fifteen years ago when I first started coming to Catalina. It's a beautiful spot, but no water."

"You were paddling fifteen years ago?"

"Hell no, I was a punk bailer back then, full of piss and vodka. My parents didn't want me to join the canoe crews, wanted me to stay with them and tend the gardens, or help at the school. But the sea got into me. It's the same with the rest of the crews. They'll die before they give up their paddles."

The crew worked in silence. They approached a broad-mouthed cove that ended in a tiny stone-covered beach, not much longer than the canoe and backed by near vertical slopes. The boat turned perpendicular to the shoreline and the paddlers picked up speed. At the surf line they caught a low wave and the

Dungees paddled frantically until the canoe ran up the shingle and stopped. The crew jumped into the water and dragged the canoe farther ashore.

"There ya go," Jake said. "You won't even get your feet wet."

They climbed out, the crew stretching their backs and legs and grinning at the couple. Jake pointed up the mountain toward the towering ridgeline. "You'll find the old trail up that way. There's no surveillance on the island so you can travel during the day. But if ya see any skimmers, lay low and move at night. That chaparral will hide ya."

"Thanks for the food and for everything," Fox said and flung her arms around Jake. The rest of the crew hooted and hollered, until she did the same with each of them.

"You saved our asses," Tony told Jake. "I will always remember you walking across that platform in the fog, coming to get us. I hope the Zane Greyers are right about the West Enders."

"Hey, if the West Enders turn out to be assholes, you can hop a return trip with us next summer. Maybe the 'Forcers will have given up by then."

"You don't know Captain Hanpion and his minions," Tony said and shook Jake's hand.

Jake handed Tony a full canteen. "Here, you better take this. Climbing that mountain you're gonna get real thirsty."

Tony nodded and clipped the canteen to a pack strap.

The crew passed a bottle of the West Enders' Margarita Mix between them. Tony suspected it was spiked with the ZG's tequila. They clambered back into their canoe and pushed off, waving to the couple and singing.

Fox and Jake watched the paddlers disappear into the eddy. They shouldered their bulging packs and headed up the mountain. Climbing a steep grassy slope on all fours, they entered a grove of ironwood trees with red peeling bark and toothed leaves, like nothing Tony had ever seen. They walked on ground covered with decades of bark litter and leaves.

"Let's camp here for the night and start early," Tony said.

Fox grinned. "Good idea. My legs are still wobbly from our days on the platform."

"Yeah, well my legs are still wobbly from..." Tony made a crude motion with his hips.

Fox punched him in the arm and slipped out of her pack straps. They rummaged around in Tony's backpack and found the blanket woven by the Zane Greyers out of goat's hair. They spread one of their sealskin cloaks and then the blanket on top of the tree litter at the edge of the grove. The wind had died and the air felt warm, almost like summer. They sat on the sloping blanket and stared at the channel. The fog lifted ever so slowly until they could pick out the Dungee canoe, a speck on the flat ocean making for the mainland. The shadows grew long across their mountain. The sun dipped below the island's central ridgeline. Across the channel, gold light reflected off buildings in the bluff-top towns of Nuevo San Pedro and Palos Verdes. In a few minutes the entire mainland turned golden, the sky clear all the way to the San Gabriel Mountains.

"Now if the Police will just stay on the mainland and leave us alone," Tony muttered. When Fox didn't say anything he looked into her eyes. Tears streaked her cheeks and her shoulders shook.

"What's wrong, Fox? Is it something I said?"

She shook her head but continued to sob silently. Finally she sucked in a deep breath and shuddered. "I... I just miss my parents. This place is beautiful... but we will never see them again. I wish my Mom were here when I have... have the baby."

"I know how you feel," Tony said. "All I can remember is my Mother telling me never to come back to de Tolosa."

"Never is a long time," Fox said.

"Yeah, well I'm not giving up on the idea."

Fox leaned her head on his shoulder. They watched long lines of pelicans skimming over the channel's electric blue water until the light dimmed and the gray dusk settled in. A drone freighter as long as two city blocks passed at mid-channel, heading south. The couple munched on some of the Dungee bread, gnawed on hydroponic carrots, and sipped the Margarita Mix until their stomachs felt full, for the first time in days.

"I'm starting to feel more and more like an Untouchable," Tony muttered.

"What the blazes are you talking about?" Fox asked and turned to stare at him.

"We've been outside in the world, feeling every-thing... everything except the friendship of our clansmen. I miss that. Even if the West Enders take us in, Jake said there are only about ten families. We'll be... be outsiders for a long time. Look at us. Our hearts are from de Tolosa, but we have wild mint tea from the Dunites, Emerald Magic from the Surfer Clan, cloaks from the Dungees, tequila from the Zane Greyers, and hair dye jobs from everyone. We've been welcomed by clans and friendly loners. But we don't belong anywhere. We're fugitives, outcasts."

"I'm homesick too, Tony." Fox said softly. "We'll have to make our own home, one as good as the one we've lost. But we can only do that when we stop running. And that's gotta be pretty soon." She grinned and patted her belly. "Have you noticed? I'm starting to show a little."

"We'll be stopping soon," Tony said. He lay back

onto the blanket and pulled Fox next to him. "We're running out of places to hide and we're on an island. If the Police think we're here, they'll swarm this place. We'll just have to wait and see if they believe Jake's story that we were never on that canoe."

The San Pedro Channel had turned from a red, green and purple sheen to dull gray as the sunlight failed. Security lights twinkled on the mainland. Tony pulled the other cloak from Fox's backpack and covered them. *What a day, from freezing on a fog-shrouded oil platform to lying under the trees on a beautiful island mountainside.* Fox moved closer to him. Her warmth and the smell of the sea in her hair calmed him, pulled him into the dream-filled sleep of a castaway.

19

They had started at dawn, scrambling up the barely-visible trail, and had made it a third of the way up the mountain when the skimmer flew past. Fox heard it first while peeing in the bushes and let out a yell. Tony dropped to his knees and crawled under a clump of lemonade bush. A drone paralleled the ridge-line road, not more than a kilometer from their position.

"Are you all right?" Fox called.

"Yeah, just stay put. There may be more."

The chaparral covered the mountainside with a thick gray-green carpet that looked soft and inviting from a distance. But up close, it was murder to push through on foot. They had stuck to the trail and hiked as fast as they could. But now...

They waited in silence. In a few minutes the high whine from another skimmer broke the silence, this one traveling from west to east along the island's length. Once it passed, Tony scrambled on his bare knees across the rough shale slope and joined Fox at her hideout under a stand of gray-barked toyon, his chest heaving.

"So much for no surveillance," he muttered.

They waited in the stifling shade, the sun burning in a cloudless sky. More high whines could be heard from a greater distance but they couldn't see any skimmers.

"I wonder if they'll send crawlers to patrol the ridge road?" Tony asked.

"Why would they when they can see everything

from above?"

"Yeah, Jake told me that the vid feeds from those things are instantly analyzed. If they had spotted anything we'd know about it."

"So... what now, oh Great Leader?" Fox said.

He ignored her crack. "I think if the skimmers had picked us out they would have slowed or circled back around. But one skimmer could be a coincidence, two might be a pattern. I say we stay put, and move out at night."

"Really? Some of these canyon drops are more than a hundred meters. Wandering around in the dark..."

"I know, I know. But once they spot us, we have no place to run. We'll take it slow and easy."

The pair crawled farther into the stand of toyon, into the deep aromatic shade, and removed their packs. Tony folded one of the cloaks and laid it on the rocky ground for them to sit on, legs folded beneath them. A gentle wind blew out of the northwest. At their leeward position on the mountainside, it stayed almost perfectly calm. The sun baked the chaparral, which gave off strong fragrances that reminded Tony of the hills above de Tolosa. They dozed. Fox woke every half hour or so to take sips of water and Margarita Mix. Their supplies were disappearing at an alarming rate.

"We'll have to reach the West Enders in a couple of days," Tony said, "or the buzzards will have us for breakfast." He pointed to the black and white birds sailing the thermals gracefully above the ridge road. *Some of them look huge enough to be California condors. Maybe they'll pick us up and fly us out of here. I always wondered what flying felt like.*

The hot day passed slowly. For lunch, they chewed carrots and sucked on pineapple guavas, squeezing the last drops of juice out of the tart fruits that came from the Zane Greyers' orchards.

By dusk they felt cramped but rested. Fox sat

propped against a twisted trunk of the toyon, snoring. Tony crept up to her and touched his lips to hers. She opened her eyes wide and kissed him hard, biting his lip.

"Don't do that. You scared me," she complained and hurried off.

They downed a handful of crunchy pea pods and a chunk of stale bread for dinner, washing them down with Margarita mix. Tony checked his hand light to make sure the sun had fully recharged it. They waited for the moon to rise before leaving their hideout. Under a star-studded sky they pushed uphill, grunting and cursing as they stumbled over rocks and protruding roots. After falling several times on bare knees or getting raked by the brush, they stopped and replaced the Dungee clothes with their scratchy denim pants and shirts.

It took several hours of constant uphill drudgery to reach the ridgeline. Stepping onto the road, Fox took off her pack and shirt and let the night wind blow across her sweat-soaked body. Tony did the same. They sat on their packs and passed a water bottle between them.

"That was one killer climb," Fox said, wheezing.

Tony nodded. "It should be easier from here on out if we stick to the roads."

They put their heads between their knees and sucked in deep breaths. When the black spots with yellow centers cleared from Tony's eyes, they stood, slipped on their shirts and shouldered the packs. Walking along the road, even one that had major washouts, felt like walking down a flat beach compared to climbing the mountain.

"If we hurry, we can make the airport by sunrise and hole up there," Tony said.

"Sounds good, just so there's a flat spot for me to lie down. My lower back feels like somebody kicked me."

"I'll give you a good rub before we sleep."

"Yeah, I'll bet," Fox said.

They walked single file, Tony leading with his hand light, picking a route between potholes. They hiked for hours without speaking, keeping the pace steady and aggressive. As the sky to the east began to lighten, they turned southward at the intersection of two roads and picked up speed, racing the sun. Another uphill turn led them to the abandoned airport. A round-tailed plane with one of its two massive engines missing rested in the tie-down area. Tanker trucks sat with their doors flung open, as if the drivers had just left them to grab something to eat at the derelict cantina nearby. A square control tower rose into the dawn sky, its windows broken out, the pavement below covered in glass beads.

"I wonder why they abandoned this place?" Fox asked. "I'd think the 'Forcers would want to keep it going."

"Remember, there are no Untouchables on the island, so there's no need for the Police. That's why if we see skimmers or crawlers, we know they're looking for us."

"Oh joy."

They sat on a rickety bench on the cantina's covered porch and listened to the freshening wind blow through the window openings. Before the eastern sun peeked over the San Gabriels on the mainland, they climbed three flights of stairs to the top of the flight tower. Inside the operations room, Tony cleared the rubble from the floor next to a wall and made a bed with their cloaks and blankets.

Fox stared eastward along the abandoned runway toward the mainland and pointed. "I can see why nothing much lands here anymore."

The eastern end of the short landing strip had

slumped away and fallen into the adjoining canyon, leaving a ragged edge of asphalt and concrete. The rest of the airstrip had splits in its pavement. *Still, the skimmers could land here easily. We'd better hope they don't get curious.*

As the air warmed, they lay on their bedding, Tony with his back to the wall and Fox in his arms. He massaged her lower back, the muscles tight and trembling, until his hands began to cramp.

"Maybe we need a little help," he said, and unpacked their remaining stash of Emerald Magic. He rolled a thick joint. After less than a half dozen tokes, Fox lay asleep in his arms, her body soft and pliable. He sat with his back to the wall, enjoying the remainder of the joint until his eyelids drooped. He snuggled beside her and watched the sun rise above their tower before dropping off.

⌣⌣

Sergeant Statler grumbled to himself in the morning heat. After the storm had passed with no sign of the fugitives, he'd hoped that Captain Peterson would drop the whole pursuit. They had searched all of the Marsh Islands in San Pedro Bay and found nothing. If the punks had used some kind of water craft to get there, it must have been scuttled by the Dungees. Or the fugitives had never been there to begin with. But Peterson had his damn gut feelings and had ordered Statler back to Catalina.

"All right, Graham, take her up," he ordered his pilot. He keyed the skimmer's com set. "Units 1 and 2, prepare to move out."

From the headlands that surrounded Seven Moons Bay and the flooded town of Avalon, the three skimmers rose to the ridgeline and flew westward in a chevron formation, bracketing the ridge road. The previous day's patrols, both manned and drone, had turned up nothing. But Statler wanted to check out the airport, the old planes, the control tower.

In fifteen minutes, they hovered above the destroyed runway and descended in formation onto the tie-down area.

"Will ya look at that thing," Statler said and grinned. "It's gotta be an old DC-2."

"A what?" Graham asked.

"That aircraft is more than 150 years old. Its massive engine probably weighs more than our entire skimmer."

The two other skimmer crews huddled around Statler's craft awaiting orders.

"Okay, I want Gerard and Sutliff to search the old hangers and storage buildings. Lees and Ames take the cantina and don't sample any of the booze. If there's any still there after eighty years, bring it back to me." Statler grinned. "Graham and I will take the tower."

The six men fanned out across the airport. Statler took his time inspecting the DC-2. As an aviation aficionado, he'd never seen one before, only online images from Nuevo Wikipedia. After climbing aboard the old passenger liner, which apparently had been gutted and used for freight transport, he rejoined Graham and walked toward the square control tower. On its ground floor they found nothing but rotting office furniture and paperwork. The same was true of the next two floors. On the top level, he reached for the Control Center's door. His com rattled in his headset.

"Yes, Captain Peterson, how can I help you?"

"What the hell are you doing at the airport? Your units searched it two days ago. I want you to get your men back here immediately. We've found something."

"What have you found, Captain?"

"A sailboat on the bottom of San Pedro Bay, not far

from Dungee Island."

"Is finding that sailboat significant, sir?"

"You're damn right it is. That craft wasn't there on the last satellite scans of the area done a week ago. When we raised the boat, the sail insignia was in the system. It belonged to a fugitive Dungee who disappeared years ago. Somehow, this boat is related to our fugitives. We're interrogating their boat crews and should know soon enough."

"What do you want me to do, sir?"

"Get your men back here immediately. You need to organize an island-wide sweep. I'm convinced that the Dungees transported our fugitives there and that the clans are hiding them. We'll need ground, air and sea units. I want every canyon, cove, and cactus patch searched, then searched again."

"But sir, an island-wide sweep could take weeks... and at least three days to organize. Are you sure we shouldn't—"

"Jeez, how hard can it be? It's a damn island. Just get back here and do it. You're wasting time. From what I understand from Captain Hanpion, this is your screw-up to begin with. So you have to fix it."

"Yes sir. ETA at base in 20 minutes."

Statler glowered at Graham then barked, "Don't just stand there, move the fuck out."

～✕～

Tony awoke to the high whine of skimmers. He peeked out the window and saw three of the domed machines landing in the tie-down area. 'Forcer crews clustered around one of the craft then scattered. Two of the camouflage-uniformed officers strode toward them. The one with the sergeant stripes looked familiar, looked a lot like the idiot that had organized the assault on the Garage back in de Tolosa. Tony hustled back to Fox and shook her awake. She opened her eyes and groaned. Tony placed a finger to his lips and whispered, "They're here."

Fox pushed herself up and stared into Tony's eyes, as if it would be the last time. *Stupid, stupid, stupid—holing up in the one place with only a single way out. Maybe we can climb onto the roof; maybe we can jump onto the balcony below; maybe we can rush the Police and get away before they could fire their stun guns. But if they hit Fox with one of those things, the baby...*

The sounds of boots stomping on the stairs made him jump. Fox clutched him around the waist and shuddered. Tony stared at the control room door, willing it to stay shut. The footfalls of two men sounded on the landing. They stopped. Fragments of a one-sided conversation filled his ears: "Is finding that sailboat significant... what do you want me to do, sir... an island-wide sweep could take weeks... and at least three days to organize... ETA to base in 20 minutes."

Tony held his breath and felt Fox do the same. The 'Forcers descended the stairs, then silence. Tony's heart hammered against his chest. Fox scooted away from him, her face red and trembling, a puddle forming on the floor. Tony crawled to the window and peeked out. The crews moved toward their skimmers. Without hesitation, they boarded, soared into the air, and headed across the San Pedro Channel toward Palos Verdes.

"Come on, we gotta move," Tony said.

"Yeah, well I gotta change first," Fox snapped and dug into her pack and pulled out a sealskin shift.

"If they've pulled off the island, we can move during the day, make better time."

"But what for?" Fox asked. "If they sweep Catalina, where are we going to go? Going to hide?"

"I don't have a clue," Tony said soberly. "I'm hoping

maybe the West Enders will have some ideas. Jake said they're first-class survivalists and smart. They've had to be ever since Two Harbors got flooded and the isthmus became a raging strait, separating Catalina and the Enders from the new West Island."

"Maybe West Island would be a good place to—"

"No way," Tony said. "The Police will cover that in their sweep. We need to get out of here, and fast. This is not how I pictured this whole thing happening. This was supposed to be our refuge, not where we get caught."

They forced themselves to eat fruit and some of the last of the Dungee's bread. Taking long drinks of the Margarita Mix, they repacked their gear and left the airport, rejoined the main road and moved due west. They followed a gently-sloping ridgeline downward to the island's seaward side and a green cove. The road turned to the north and disappeared into the cove's surging waters, forcing the fugitives to detour around the shallow bay along the lower slopes of the valley. By mid-afternoon they had rejoined the road and made good time, climbing steadily, always on the lookout for stray skimmers. But the skies stayed quiet and the fugitives concentrated on moving.

Maybe it would be better for Fox to be caught, Tony thought as he trudged uphill. *At least the authorities will take care of her and provide medical support when the baby comes.* But he forced those thoughts from his mind, knowing that he'd take the fall for the Untouchable's murder and never see her again, never get to know his child. It felt strange thinking about being a father since, in his heart, Tony knew they were both still punk kids in many ways. But this odyssey of theirs had changed them, hardened them, made them more determined to stay together, to form their own clan of only the three of them, if need be. That idea made Tony smile.

"What are you grinning about?" Fox asked, panting.

"I was just thinking of you and me on a tropical island, me as Robinson Crusoe and you as my Girl Friday."

"You mean, you and me and the kids," Fox said.

"Damn. I knew there was a reason why we couldn't walk around naked."

"That, and third degree sunburns on parts that shouldn't be burned," Fox said and laughed.

They sucked on the tart lemon-lime drink and continued onward. They had almost reached the head of the long valley when the daylight began to fail. The green and gold hillsides turned a reddish-copper color then gray as the sun fell into the sea and disappeared. A cold wind blew from the west and they slipped on their cloaks and continued hiking, their breaths rasping in the near-darkness. As they crossed the saddle at the head of the valley, a low roar filled the evening silence. Downslope and due west from where they stood, a narrow passage of ocean separated Catalina from West Island, the swells roaring in from the open Pacific and merging with the San Pedro Channel. *This is the strait that Jake had talked about, how not even the Dungee canoes ventured across it because of its swift currents.*

Downslope from them, the last rays of light shown off the rooftop solar units of a sprawling building, set on the knoll overlooking the strait and San Pedro Channel. Smoke poured from one of its chimneys.

"There, that must be the West Enders' common house," Tony said, pointing. "Let's approach them carefully and I'll call out when we get close."

"Hold that thought while I visit the bushes," Fox said and un-slung her pack and disappeared into the brush that bordered the road. Tony removed his pack and thought that she would have lost her shyness by now, but suspected some proprieties would never diminish. The sky darkened to black. From up the road he heard a strange sound, a snort of some kind. He stared into the darkness. The back of his neck went numb and he shuddered. Directly ahead stood something head-high, a massive black smudge on a black background. Tony fumbled in his pocket for his hand light as the sound of hooves pounding along the road came toward him. He clicked on the light. A pair of mean-looking eyes below a set of curved horns charged directly at him. He pointed the light into the beast's face, hoping that it would stop or change course. But it seemed to pick up speed. Tony turned and dove off the road's shoulder into the brush. With a teeth-rattling crash, he landed on his side and rolled downslope until he was stopped by something hard. The pain hit him, then darkness closed in and took it away.

Someone shone a light in his face. In the distance he heard his name being called. Gradually, the voice came nearer. Fox's face leaned close to his.

"Tony, are you alright, my God..."

He struggled to sit up, dizzy, as if from spinning in circles like they used to do as kids back at the Garage. Bending forward, he vomited into the bushes. Fox stroked his shoulders. He ran his hands over his upper body and arms. Nothing was bleeding; nothing felt broken. But when he felt his legs, a fire-hot pain shot upward from his left calf and his hand came away wet and sticky from his torn denims. Fox flashed her hand light on the leg. It had struck a boulder and lay at a slight angle.

"That doesn't look good," she said, her voice shaking. "I... I think you broke it."

Tony took in deep breaths and tried to smile. "Hey, it's fixable, it'll just need—" A hot knife of pain shot upward into his groin and he doubled over, groaning.

"What can I do? What can I do?" Fox asked, her voice almost a moan.

When he had caught his breath Tony answered, "Go kick that buffalo's ass that ran me off the road. Jake said they were nasty, but..."

She smiled. "Nah, that's your job. Just use your right leg."

Tony leaned against a manzanita bush and tried straightening his damaged limb without success.

"Better leave it alone," Fox told him. "What should we do?"

Tony ground his teeth against the pain and closed his eyes. "I think you're really our Great Leader now. I can't decide. You must do it."

"I'll go for help. The West Enders aren't far away and..."

"But the buffalo are still out there. Why don't we wait until morning when it's light and..." Tony sucked in another breath, wrapped his arms around himself and rocked back and forth.

"Forget it. We can't wait here all night in the dark while you're... you're in such pain."

"Maybe not. We'll both be feeling pain on this trip." His smile turned into a grimace as another electric wave shot up his leg.

Fox took off her cloak and spread it across his chest. She left him for a few moments and returned with Tony's hand light and gave it to him. "Stay here and don't try to move. That house wasn't more than three hundred meters downslope and right next to the road. I'll get help."

Before he could say anything, she disappeared. He listened to her fast footsteps fade into the distance. The cold quiet closed in, leaving him to his unrelenting pain. He clicked on his hand light and managed to pull the left leg of his denims upward toward the knee. Halfway between the ankle and the knee, the shin was bloody, with a massive bruise already forming. But the leg wasn't quite straight. Tony tried to shift it into alignment, but the pain took his sight away and he came to lying on his back, panting. *Where's that bottle of whiskey and a leather belt to bite down on when ya need it,* he thought, remembering the Western novels his mother had given him to read as a kid. Whiskey and a belt seemed to be the cure for most ailments that befell a cowboy hero. Whiskey? We have some tequila from the Zane Greyers, he remembered. But it's in my pack on the road. For a moment he thought about crawling upslope. But just the thought made his leg throb. He leaned back against the brush and began counting the seconds, trying to estimate how long Fox had been gone. Every few minutes he heard grunts from the grassy slopes above the road and figured the buffalo had settled in for the night. Jake had told him the story about how the massive bison had been shipped to Catalina to be part of a western movie filmed during the early part of the 20th Century. How they'd been left to roam free and breed like rabbits... big rabbits. Tony laughed to himself and was rewarded by another jolt of pain.

He kept counting. When he reached 1,500, he became worried. What if Fox got lost in the dark, ran into another mean buffalo, or got waylaid by weird clansmen that Tony knew nothing about? His mind conjured up stories; and the more he counted the more real they became. At 2,000, he heard voices on the road. The glow of firelight lit the tips of the brush around him.

"I'm here, I'm here," he yelled.

"We hear you. Just sit tight," a man's voice called.

Three men dressed in what looked like buffalo hides pushed through the brush toward him. For a moment, Tony thought part of the herd was coming to finish him off. But the men knelt by his side. A fully-bearded fellow pulled back Tony's cloak to look at the injured leg.

"You must be Tony. My name's Peter, and these ruffians are my sons, Mark and Paul."

"Thanks... thanks for coming."

"Well, your wife is very persuasive. I have a feeling she's a hard woman to refuse." Peter grinned and so did his sons.

"Is she okay?"

"Oh yeah, she's being looked after by my wife. I'm sure they'll be well acquainted and the best of friends by the time we join them."

"How... how do you think my leg looks?" Tony asked.

"Well, my wife's are a lot prettier. But I've seen worse. Mark here broke his leg when he was fifteen and it set up just fine. I think I still have the crutches somewhere. But let's get you to the house before that buff comes back to investigate."

Tony screamed when Mark, a massive brute well over six foot, pulled him to his feet and carried him over a shoulder. They hauled him upslope to the road where they laid him on a stretcher. Peter shouldered Tony's pack.

"Christ, what do ya have in this thing? I'll bet it weighs as much as you do."

They hustled along the road, Peter carrying a torch; it gave off pungent smoke that smelled like medicine. In a few minutes they came to a path that led to the single story building with many wings and windows.

"Take him into the parlor and lay him next to the fire," Peter ordered. "We don't want him going into shock."

Tony could only moan and grit his teeth. The jolting ride along the road had almost made him scream. Electric lights lit the parlor's wood-paneled walls and open-beamed ceiling. But the heat came from a roaring fire in a stone fireplace. Stacks of what looked like driftwood flanked it. The warmth felt good and Tony relaxed his muscles and the pain backed off just a bit. In a minute, Fox stood over him.

"Are you all right?" she asked. "I wanted to go back to you with the men, but Cynthia insisted that I—"

Tony reached up and placed a finger on Fox's full lips. "Hush, you are wonderful, a great commander and chief."

A lean woman with silver hair left loose to flow over her shoulders stood next to Fox. "Your wife has told me all about your adventures. But rest easy, you're safe for now. Let's see what we can do about that leg of yours."

She had a whispered conversation with a pretty teenage girl who left the room, but returned with a wicker basket and a washbasin filled with water.

"All right, let's get those trousers off of you," she ordered.

"Let me," Fox said.

She unbuckled his belt and slid the baggy denims down his legs then pulled them off, Tony groaning the entire time. Cynthia spread a towel under the injured leg, dipped a rag in the basin of hot water and gently washed the blood and dirt away from the break then cleaned the entire leg.

Peter knelt next to his wife and ran a hand along the lower leg bones. "Feels like you broke the tibia, but the fibula feels intact and the ankle's sound. It'll be easy to set since the bone didn't break the skin."

"But all that blood..." Fox pointed.

"He just scraped the hell out of his shins slamming into that boulder."

Peter's sons stood beside him, watching intently, as if the whole affair had become some form of academic instruction.

"Aren't you gonna give me something for the pain?"

Tony asked, his voice shaking. "I have some of the Zane Greyers' tequila."

"Yeah, that'll do."

Fox interrupted. "What about some of our stash?"

The room quieted. "Just what do you have?" Peter asked.

"We have some Emerald Magic from the Surfer Clan up north."

"Christ, that stuff is legendary. But let's not give the boy anything until we're done here. It'll help him sleep. The leg's alignment doesn't look that bad."

Peter sat on the floor at Tony's feet and grasped the broken leg with one huge hand that easily encircled the calf. With his other hand he grasped Tony's heel.

"Okay, now this is going to smart."

He gave the leg a gentle tug and shifted the heel slightly. Tony let out a high-pitched scream. He half rose up off the floor then sank backward. The light faded to blackness. When he came to, Peter was wrapping the last swaths of wet fabric of a cast that ran from above his knee to the ankle. Fox mopped his face with a wet cloth and Cynthia laid a blanket across his bare chest. Somehow they had stripped him down to his drawers after he'd passed out.

"Where... where did you get that stuff?" he asked Peter and pointed to the drying cast.

"Years ago we traded the Zane Greyers a half side of buffalo for a bag of gypsum that they got from the mainland, I think Palos Verdes somewhere. We can make our own plaster with it."

"How did you learn..."

"My grandfather was a physician before the Change. He used to come to Catalina on vacations and stay at the Banning House, that's where you are now. I've got all of his medical books, and he showed me some things. I do okay."

Cynthia butted in. "All right, you men clear on out

of here and let these folks rest. You'll have plenty of time to gab at breakfast. You boys drag that couch over here so Fox can sleep near her husband."

"What about the Emerald Magic?" Tony asked groggily.

"Save it for tomorrow when we all can enjoy it more," Peter said. "Rest easy." He herded his family out of the parlor and closed the door.

Tony sucked in a deep breath and let it out slowly, resting against a pillow that someone had magically slipped under his head. Fox knelt beside him and took his hand.

"Does... does it hurt badly?"

"Not bad. But you might get that bottle of tequila out of my pack. I could use a nip."

Fox retrieved the prize and tilted the container to his lips and he gulped and half-choked down a few mouthfuls. "Yeah, that's good. Just like the Wild West."

"What are you talking about?" Fox asked.

"Nothing, nothing. But thank you for helping me and for... for telling them that I'm your husband."

"I thought it would be easier than trying to explain... I didn't know whether they would become upset if they knew that we weren't..."

"No, I'm glad you did. I've wanted to talk to... to ask you if you wanted to be my wife for a long time."

"Typical man. It takes a broken leg and a few shots of tequila to—"

Tony pulled Fox's face to his and kissed her. "So what do you think?"

"Yes, I'll be your wife. But I'm pregnant and, damn it, I gotta pee again. You'll have to find somebody else to fight off the buffalo."

She slipped from the room but returned in a few minutes, took the cushions off the sofa, laid them on the floor next to Tony, then snuggled against his good side. The fire crackled in the night, its orange and green flames casting dancing shadows against the wall before the driftwood burned down to ashes. Tony took another nip from the bottle and lay back. The West Enders, at least the ones they'd met, seemed wonderful. But the Police would be back on the island in two or three days, and might be scouring the west end and even West Island within a couple weeks. *Just where the hell could they run, and me with this damn broken leg. Maybe this is where we end it.* He took another shot of tequila and shut his eyes. The leg throbbed but he didn't care. There would be no more running... but maybe...

20

Tony woke to Fox shaking his shoulder gently. He moaned. His entire body ached and he reached for the tequila bottle but someone had taken it. The parlor door stood open and a warm wind filled the room. A covered outdoor breezeway extended from the parlor along a row of doors. Families emerged from their rooms and talked with each other as they walked to the far end of the passage and entered a dining hall. They dressed in animal skins and moccasins, looking like cavemen or maybe early Native Americans before the Europeans arrived.

"Come on, honey, get up. It's breakfast time," Fox said.

Tony pushed back the blanket, hoping that the previous day's misadventures had all been a bad dream. But the cast, the dull pain in his left leg, and his thick head reminded him that it was all real. He sat up. Fox struggled to help him dress. They decided that the Dungee shorts and cutoff shirt were easier to slide into than his bloodied denims. Fox retrieved a set of wooden crutches and helped him stand. He practiced walking around the parlor.

"Not bad. So long as I don't put my weight on it, the leg feels pretty good."

"Yeah, Peter said to stay off it for at least a week, then walk on it for short periods."

"Heck, in a week we could be in jail. I'll have plenty of time to rest there. Can you show me where the privy is? Quickly!"

Fox grinned. "You're really gonna like this one."

They left the parlor and passed along the breezeway as the West Enders stared. At a door near the far end of the hall, Fox ushered him inside. "There it is," she pointed. "Just push down the little handle when you're done. I'll wait outside."

"I've seen these things in abandoned buildings," Tony said, "but never used one."

"Cynthia told me they have a solar unit that pumps well water into a huge tank higher up the mountain. It flows downhill through pipes into this house. These guys know what they're doing."

Tony grinned. "Great, now get out."

When he rejoined her in the breezeway, all the West Enders had moved into the airy dining hall, talking, laughing and eating what looked like some kind of fried eggs and slabs of dark meat, washed down with tea and glasses of white stuff. When the couple entered, Peter and Cynthia waved them over and Tony hobbled his way through the crowd. They sat at a round table with Peter's family. The two hulking sons, Mark and Paul, grinned at him with mouths full of the greasy meat. The shy teenage daughter stared at her plate.

"So how does that leg feel this morning?" Cynthia asked.

"It feels strange but doesn't hurt that bad. Thanks again for helping me, for helping us."

"That's a tight-fitting cast," Peter said. "It should hold everything in place until the tibia has a chance to knit."

A small boy brought two plates of food and set them in front of Fox and Tony. The couple stared at the meal uncertainly.

"Go ahead, it won't kill you," Peter said and laughed. "We raise our own chickens for eggs and meat. The white stuff in the pitcher is goats' milk. Those steaks are from a buffalo we killed earlier this week. A few times a year we thin the herd a bit. Just think of it as revenge for what that buff did to you last night.

Cynthia chuckled. "If you'd come a couple months back, we'd probably have served you wild boar. Since the Change, those feisty pigs have overrun West Island. Last summer, we joined up with the Zane Greyers, took a hunting party over there to bring back pork chops." Tony and Fox looked at each other, then used metal knives with worn serrated blades to slice into the buffalo. It had a mild taste—not nearly as gamey as the venison the Touchable Clan sometimes ate. But it required a lot of chewing to get it down. Hunger overpowered them and in a few minutes they'd cleared their plates.

Tony sipped tea and listened to the chatter of the families in the dining hall, about work in the citrus groves, shore fishing off the bluffs near the abandoned Marine Science Center, trade with the Zane Greyers, child rearing, education, and the love lives of friends and enemies. Hearing these details made him long for his own clan. He could tell Fox felt the same way because she swiped away tears and sniffed loudly several times.

As their adventure continued, Fox seemed to grow stronger, braver, yet more emotional. Tony figured the pregnancy played havoc with her hormones. In de Tolosa, the clanswomen cared for and comforted wives during pregnancy and childbirth. But as he and Fox ran from the Police, he would need to help her through it. *What the heck do I know about any of it? What if she gets sick? Has a problem delivering the baby? What if... if she doesn't make it?* Thoughts of losing Fox tore at his heart. A tangle of fears clouded his mind. But Peter's friendly voice brought him back.

"I have some people I want you and Fox to meet in the library."

"Sure, lead the way," Tony said. "You deserve an explanation for why we're here."

"Fox gave us a few tantalizing details last night. But she seemed so worried about you that we didn't press for details. But if what she said is true about the 'Forcers, we'll all need some answers quickly."

As if on cue, everyone at the table rose. Peter and Cynthia escorted them from the dining hall to a door next to the parlor. Inside the sizable room, floor-to-ceiling bookshelves lined three walls. A bank of windows overlooking the rolling San Pedro Channel covered the fourth wall. Padded chairs and sofas divided the room into reading areas.

Tony inspected the books. "Wow, this is quite a collection. One of my favorite places was the Public Library in de Tolosa. I miss the adventure of finding something good to read."

"Well, you've come to the right place," Cynthia said."

"How did all this get started?" Fox asked.

The foursome slumped into chairs and Cynthia began. "During the Change and the rise in sea level, the Latino gangs south of the 405 Freeway were at war. Most of our West Ender Families originally came from Long Beach and San Pedro. Many of them taught at the State University or were professionals in law, medicine, or engineering. They got caught in the cross-fire between gangs and searched for a refuge."

"But why not find someplace on the mainland?" Tony asked.

"The Dung People had already claimed the Marsh Islands in San Pedro Bay, Wilmington and the lower parts of Long Beach were underwater. The Lost Ones— ah, the people that never leave their homes—had taken over the Palos Verdes Peninsula and the flyways above the bay, where security is tight. Our leaders back then figured that Catalina Island would be a good sanctuary since it was far from supply routes and consequently no Lost Ones would want to live here."

"But why not go to Avalon?" Fox asked. "It's supposed to have more... more stuff."

Cynthia smiled. "The Zane Greyers had already claimed it. Most of their Latino families had lived in Avalon for almost two hundred years—brought there from Mexico in the 1920s to work in the Wrigley's tile and pottery factory. Where you're from, there probably wasn't much competition between the clans. But in the El Lay basin, all the little groups struggled to find safe havens and develop some sort of mutually-beneficial trade arrangements. It's worked out over the past fifty years... but there were plenty of bumps along the way."

"And this place?" Tony asked.

"Before the sea level rose, there were two harbors, one on each side of the island. Back then a narrow neck of land called the Isthmus joined Catalina with what we now call West Island. The Banning House was an old seaside inn. Yachtsmen used to sail their boats from the mainland into Isthmus Cove, get drunk at the Reef Saloon, then climb the hill and stay here over-night. The rise in the sea level created West Island and the strait, destroying the village. Only these buildings and the old laboratories at the Marine Science Institute are left."

Tony looked out the window and down at where the tiny community of Two Harbors must have stood, covered now by the swift green seas of the West Island Strait. The door behind him opened and two couples entered and joined the foursome. One couple was older than them by a few years; the other looked their age.

Peter rose. "Let me introduce Claire and Stanley, Elizabeth and Richard. This is Fox and Anthony from the Touchables in de Tolosa. Tony, I invited them to hear your story. I think the six of you may be able to... to help each other."

Tony looked at Fox. "Why don't you tell it. It's tough for me to sound heroic with this bum leg. Plus you're prettier."

"Just wait a few months," Fox said and smirked. She leaned back in the squishy-soft chair and recounted their adventures. "So we came here in hopes of joining your clan. But the 'Forcers followed us and... and now we can't stay."

Tony raised his casted leg and set it gingerly on a low table. "Anyone who is caught helping us will likely be charged with aiding fugitives. What we really need to do is disappear for a few years until... until my wife has our child and the Police give up their search... if they ever do."

Peter cleared his throat and spoke to his fellow clansmen. "That was a great tale. When Fox gave me the short version last night I immediately thought of you and your children. Stanley, why don't you speak?"

Stan leaned forward in his seat, a small guy like Tony but with dark skin and straight black hair. "Our two families were born and grew up at the West End. We've lived here all our lives. But we want to... to settle our own place, to develop our own ways. You must have people like us in your clan in de Tolosa."

Tony laughed. "Are you kidding? Fox and I were those people. It seems natural for some clansmen to leave home and become, you know, independent. It makes the homecomings all that much sweeter."

Stan continued. "Our problem is that none of us know much about boats or sailing. Frankly, the sea scares the hell out of me. But you two have... have plenty of experience and aren't afraid of the waves. If you could help us, we can help you... sort of a personal trade agreement."

Fox looked at Tony and nodded. "What do you have

in mind?"

Stanley's wife Claire rose from her seat, went to a bookshelf and pulled a small volume from the collection. "Have you ever read this?"

Tony and Fox stared at the book titled "Island of the Blue Dolphins."

"Yes, I read it when I was maybe ten," Tony said.

"Well, that's where we want to go," Claire said.

The other West End couple nodded in agreement. Peter rose and pulled a nautical map of the Channel Islands from a shelf and spread it on the table.

Stan pointed. "We are here and want to get to here."

"But... but why San Nicolas Island?" Fox asked. "Of all the Channel Islands, it's farthest from the mainland. From what I've read, there's not much there."

"Maybe we're just being romantic," Elizabeth said, "but we're looking for a... a blank canvas. You know, some place where no one lives where we can create our own community."

"But, San Nicolas is supposed to be so... so desolate, with only a little water. And we'd be sailing against the wind and currents."

"We know," Elizabeth said, "but I'm an artist, and desolate places can be the most beautiful."

"You got that right," Fox said and smiled.

Peter and Cynthia stood. "It sounds like you folks have a lot to talk about. Let us know how we can help."

As the door closed behind the older couple, Claire cut loose with a giggle. "Don't let those two fool you. Stan and I have an eleven-year-old hormone-crazed son who's hot for their daughter. They'd love to get us off island."

Fox stared at the woman. "Isn't that kinda young for—?"

Elizabeth broke in, "That's one thing you should know about us West Enders. We... we definitely enjoy sex." Her pale face framed by light brown hair turned pink and the rest of the group laughed. "But... but we respect the partnerships that men and women have entered into."

"Heavy on the 'entered into' part," Stan said and he and Richard laughed.

The group talked through the morning and only broke for a small mid-day snack of fried chicken and bread that tasted amazingly like the Dungee variety. They discovered that Claire and Stan had two children, a boy and a girl, and Richard and Elizabeth were expecting. When Fox asked them how they handled birth control, the women laughed and pulled packs of birth control pills from their sealskin satchels. Evidently the West Enders' Margarita Mix could be traded for just about anything. Also the regional government made contraceptives available as a way of encouraging the clans to manage their numbers.

"Have other West End members left Catalina?" Tony asked.

"Good God, yes," Claire said. "Even West Enders get island fever. But most head south to the Fish Clan in La Jolla or the San Diegans. But the four of us are... are different. Sometimes I think we're more like the Lost Ones. We enjoy our solitude, but aren't lonely because of it. At the same time, we like the outdoors and the company of others, just not big crowds but the more... more intimate kind, you know, face-to-face, not connected by some machine, no matter how sophisticated."

That night in the parlor, Fox and Tony pushed two sofas together and lay on their backs, staring at the open-beamed ceiling. For a long time each seemed lost in their thoughts and didn't speak. As normal, Fox started.

"So what do you think of the idea?"

Tony sighed. "It beats getting captured by the Police and hauled off to jail. Plus, if we're going to go *anywhere,* we'll need help. I won't be able to do much until this leg mends."

"Yeah, but San Nicolas Island?" Fox shook her head.

"I know, I know. That place is blasted by wind most of the year, has little water, and even less land to plant anything. It's perfect if you like a steady diet of sea lion meat and seagull eggs."

"But we wouldn't have to stay there forever, ya know... maybe for a few... a few years until our child is big enough to travel." Fox stretched her arms into the darkness, then massaged her belly. "What do we really know about those four West Enders and their kids? If we go along with this scheme, we'll need to trust them."

Tony chuckled. "I suppose they're asking themselves the same thing. I mean, look at us. We're not exactly the paramount of civilization."

"Speak for yourself," Fox said and dug him in the ribs, which made his leg twitch and he groaned in pain.

"I'm sorry, I'm sorry." She snuggled against his good side. "Is there anything I can touch that will make it better?"

"Well, on the plus side, they do like sex," Tony cracked.

"And it'll be good to have help when my time comes." Fox sighed and kissed him on the lips.

Tony listened to the roof above them creak in the night wind before sleep took him once again onto the back of the rolling sea, where combers pushed them toward a wind-swept beach where he struggled through the surf but never quite reached land.

∽∼∾

In the morning after breakfast, Fox left Tony in the

library to read everything he could find on San Nicolas Island and to study the sea charts. She followed the two West End couples along a path that wound eastward across the flanks of the hills then dropped to the landward side of Catalina, to a tiny cove protected by headlands. Near the top of the bluffs stood old concrete buildings and a parking lot, the faint stall striping still visible after more than 50 years. The couples rested under the eaves of one of the buildings. Fox guessed that Elizabeth was about as far along as she was, just starting to show.

"So what's the story with this place?" Fox asked the group.

Claire answered. "The University of Southern California operated a marine institute here. But it shut down after the Change and all instruction went online. Any undersea research is now done by drone submersibles from the mainland. We sometimes see them passing through the West Island Strait. They're about the only craft that can do that."

Stan grinned. "Yeah. A few years back, some idiot captain tried to steer a drone freighter through the strait. It dragged bottom on the landward end and foundered. A lot of the cargo washed up at this cove and is stored inside the buildings."

"Yeah, we now have a century supply of condoms," Claire cracked and the group laughed.

They descended a trail to the cove. Richard moved to a pair of large doors on a leaning wooden building and opened them.

"There she is. Probably hasn't touched water in sixty years. But we've been working on her, with help from Peter... he's our clan's mechanical genius."

Fox stepped inside and stared open-mouthed at the boat that rested on its gunwales on an ancient trailer with flat tires. "What the heck is this thing?"

Stan smiled. "We think it's called a panga boat,

used to smuggle drugs and illegal aliens north from Mexico."

Fox ran a hand along its fiberglass hull as she circled the craft. "It's huge."

Richard grinned. "They used to carry tons of marijuana and dozens of people. All that ended when California legalized grass in 2024 and the federal government gave up on its war on drugs."

"Can you roll her over for me?"

The couples looked at each other then shrugged "Sure, but you've gotta help," Elizabeth said.

After much grunting and groaning, they flipped the craft. Fox took a mental inventory of its specifications: twelve meters long; a two-meter beam at midship; high pointed bow; flat stern where some type of engines used to be mounted; a flat but deep bottom; six benches, one forward bench having an opening for what must have been a mast; two benches with oar locks for four rowers.

"Have you ever found the mast and sail for this thing?" Fox asked.

"No," Richard said. "But we do have the oars."

"Huh," Fox muttered. "A sail would let us tack into the wind. My back already aches thinking about rowing this thing to San Nicolas Island." She pictured a crew of eight in the boat, her at the tiller with Tony as pilot, the two couples manning the oars and their children, one fore and aft, bailing seawater like crazy.

"What do you think?" Claire asked.

"She's big enough. Have you ever taken her out?"

"Ah... no," Richard said. "But we've done a lot of planning for the trip, what we'd bring, what we'd leave behind."

"Yeah, well she probably moved just fine under motor power. But rowing... I'm not sure, especially beating against the wind and currents. Let's roll her down to the cove and see if she floats."

After a mercifully short struggle, the panga boat floated on the calm waters of the cove. Fox tied its surprisingly-strong bow and stern lines to the pylons of the remains of a wharf and climbed aboard, inspecting the hull for leaks. *She's dry now, but if we hit rough seas, this old tub could break up beneath us.*

"Do you think she can make it?" Claire asked.

"Well, Tony and I sailed into San Pedro Harbor in a boat only a third as long as this one. Yeah, if we pack her right, she should be fine. But are you guys in shape for..."

Elizabeth pushed a sleeve of her shirt above a bicep. "Oh yeah, we've been training for two years now, hoping someone would come along to help us. You... you and your husband seem perfect."

"Yeah, well at least my morning sickness has passed and I'm not peeing as much. But Tony's going to have to hold out here as long as possible to give that leg a chance to knit."

"I know," Stan said. "But we can move into the Marine Institute labs, pack the boat with provisions, and be ready to get out of here the minute our scouts spot any Police crawlers or skimmers. I just hope it's during the day."

"Yeah, me too," said Fox and grinned.

They slid and heaved the boat back onto its trailer and rolled it uphill into the shed. The couples and Fox climbed the hillside, moving slowly toward the Banning House, discussing every detail of their escape. Fox wondered how the Police would plan their sweep: would they start at the east end and work west? Or divide their forces and start at both ends and work toward the middle? *Every day we stay on Catalina will help Tony. But we could get trapped. Whatever we do, we'll... we'll have to go at night. I want to be well clear of this island before the sun rises and the Police can pick us out on the open sea.*

21

Captain Hanpian sat in his home-office in de Tolosa and stared at the flickering vid screens, showing mostly porn, but also a series of reports from Captain Peterson. Peterson had promised to keep him informed of the status of the pursuit and, so far, he had kept his word. Hanpian felt especially pleased when Peterson and that incompetent Sergeant Statler had agreed on an island-wide sweep. *I know those punks are there*, Hanpian thought. *If I have to fly down there myself to bring them in, I will.*

The Captain daydreamed about how the capture would take place, how satisfying it would be to clamp handcuffs around the murderers' skinny little wrists and to lock them up. A buzz from his voice-only com interrupted his reverie.

"Captain Hanpian, this is Sergeant Jonas."

"Yes, Sergeant."

"Sir, do you have an idea about what you want to do with the Matteson woman? We've, ah, been holding her here for weeks. But we're not really set up for long-term incarceration."

Hanpian groaned to himself. The woman couldn't provide any additional information and all she could be charged with would be harboring fugitives. The judge would probably let her off with time served. Yet somehow she excited him and he found himself watching porno vids that included gray-haired shapely women.

"Captain, are you there?" Sergeant Jonas called.

"Yes, yes, sorry. Prepare Ms. Matteson for release...

but first I'm coming down to talk with her one last time. Put her in the corner office, the one with the view of the mountains."

"Yes sir. Anything else?"

"No, except that I passed on a recommendation for commendation for your success in arresting Fox Slade's parents. That was nicely done. I just wish your counterpart Statler would have the same luck."

"Yes sir, and thank you. You know I've always respected your leadership and hope some day to work as your second-in-command lieutenant."

"I've already made that recommendation to Commander Pynard," Hanpian said. "She should get back to me any day. I really need somebody to help me run the division."

"Thank you, sir, for your trust."

Hanpian disconnected the com and sat back. *That Jonas was always a real kiss-ass. But so is Statler, except he's more of an inept one.*

〜〜

Sergeant Jonas dispatched a crawler to pick up Captain Hanpian at his home. Moving to the woman's room, he entered. Ruth Matteson looked up from a book then continued reading.

"Ms. Matteson, come with me," he said softly.

"Why? Where are we going?"

"The Captain has ordered your release. But before you leave us, he wants to talk with you."

"About what? Look, I saw the faces of the Slades after you idiots interrogated them. I know they gave up my son's whereabouts. What did you promise them? That Fox would get off with some minimal charge? What more do you need from me? You want me to draw you a frickin' map?"

The woman's face darkened with anger. She

pounded her fist on the table and paced the floor, slapping at the walls with her cane and muttering.

"Just be patient, Ms. Matteson. This will all be over soon."

He took her gently by an elbow and guided her down the hall to the corner office. She had grown slimmer in the weeks that she'd been locked up. But if anything, it made her look more beautiful. Jonas appreciated the Captain's obsession, even if the prisoner had a bum leg and was pushing fifty. But the woman would have nothing to do with any of them, seldom spoke, spent her days reading ancient law books that lined the shelves in her room, or staring out the windows at the hillside homes and the Cuesta Ridge towering above de Tolosa.

As Jonas walked back to his station, Captain Hanpian moved down the hallway toward him.

"She's ready for you, sir. But be advised, she's really angry."

"Yeah, well so am I. We've been messing with this murder case for months and now I have to depend on Statler and that idiot Peterson to close it."

Sergeant Jonas sat at his station, grinning. *The Captain is in an especially foul mood. He and the Matteson woman should get along just fine.*

～⁄ ⁊

Ruth Matteson sat on the hard metal chair and stared out the office window at the Santa Lucia Foothills that rose above de Tolosa. She studied the hillside where her son and Fox Slade had spent peaceful afternoons painting, trying to make the homes of the Untouchables disappear into the background. But today a hard rain streaked the windows. The image of Fox's mother walking down the hallway, weeping as she passed Ruth's room weeks before, filled her mind.

Ruth knew that look... one of betrayal... a look made by a person who has made an impossible choice. She had wanted to reach out and comfort Louise, then bash her skull in. How could she ever look that woman in the face again?

All the trouble, all the pain, because some creep had tried to rape her son's woman. She ran a hand through her thinning hair, her dreams of teaching her future grandkids the joys of the world fading. An immense sadness washed over her and she slumped over the table and sobbed. In a few minutes her breathing steadied and she took a handkerchief from the sleeve of her cloak and dabbed at her eyes. The door creaked open and Captain Hanpian stepped into the office. Ruth clenched her fists and hid them below the table. She would not waste her emotions on this man. He was not worth it.

"What do you want?"

Hanpian sat at the table across from her. "I just wanted to see you, to talk with you before you are released."

"Released?"

"Yes, I recommended that the District Attorney drop all charges against you. She has agreed."

"Why would you do that? Do you expect me to thank you?"

"No, of course not. But as hard as it may be for you to believe this, I am still interested in justice. Fox Slade shouldn't become a victim again. She too will be released once she returns to face reduced charges."

"And my son?"

"He will need to serve jail time. But there are many options for bringing charges and for sentencing that we can explore."

"We?"

"Yes... ah, you and I."

"Why would you even consider leniency for someone that killed one of your fellow Untouchables? What more could I possibly give you?"

Hanpian extended a soft white hand across the table and touched the edge of Ruth's cloak, then ran a finger down her tear-stained cheek. "You are a beautiful woman, Ruth. If you are kind to me, I could be kind to you... and your son. You don't have to live in the streets, you know."

Ruth felt her face go cold and the back of her neck tingle. She pushed herself back from the table and stood, her legs trembling beneath her.

"You... you son of a bitch," she muttered.

"Now Ruth, there's no need to—"

"You're just like the pervert that Tony killed. What's with you creeps? Does the porn just not work for you anymore?"

"Now that's not very kind. I was just trying to be—"

"I know what you are, Captain. You disgust me."

"I was just offering to help your son..."

"He knows how to help himself," Ruth said. Grabbing the heavy metal chair, she heaved it through the floor-to-ceiling window. The glass exploded and she moved to the opening.

"*Step back from the window,*" Hanpian bellowed and reached for her, clutching her cloak.

"So is this what you want?" Ruth whispered and kissed him on the lips. Feeling his body relax, she grabbed a firm hold on his starched uniform and pushed backward through the window opening. His screams sounded high and girlish as they fell five stories, head first into the concrete.

22

A week of frantic preparation passed before Tony and Fox felt they were ready. Every night, the West End couples, their kids, and he and Fox launched the panga boat at Little Fisherman's Cove and rowed into the San Pedro Channel. The four West Enders manned the oars. Their children acted as bailers. On the first trial run, they almost swamped, turning the boat sideways to a cresting wave. But with each successive trial, the crew gained confidence and became adept at coordinating their rowing strokes and following Fox's commands. After each session, the crew soaked in the communal hot tub. Tony wondered what it would be like when they rowed for two days straight with no hot tub bath afterwards.

"So what do you think?" Tony asked Fox as they stretched out on their sofas, groaning softly.

"I actually think Claire and Elizabeth are the stronger rowers. And Claire's boy might be able to spell her if the seas are calm enough. How's your leg?"

"I walked on it for a few minutes today. It hurt but the pain didn't last. I just wish I could do more."

"Don't worry, if we run into rough seas we'll need more bailers... and you're an expert at that." She dug him in the ribs.

"How's your... your symptoms?" Tony asked.

"Being pregnant isn't a disease, you jerk."

"Sorry, I didn't mean..."

"I feel good, feel strong. But I also feel like eating an entire buffalo. We'd better cram the boat with food. We'll have two pregnant women on board."

"Not to worry. I think we have a ton of stuff already, and we haven't even loaded our backpacks."

"Yeah, she'll ride low in the water."

Tony sighed. "It's gonna be a tough haul—at least eighty kilometers. I've studied the charts. We'll need to bear northwest and let the wind and the currents push us into San Nicolas. If we miss her, there's nothing but open ocean..."

"Yeah, yeah, I get the picture."

"Once we reach the island, I think we need to hole up at the abandoned airport at its east end. There should be some dilapidated buildings where we can hide the boat and decide where we want to set up camp."

"What about surveillance?"

"The Navy abandoned the island fifty years ago, when the need for a missile defense system disappeared. No one lives there now. I think if we lay low for a few months, we'll have a chance. Nobody sails that far out, except the drone freighters—and the island isn't that close to their shipping lanes."

"Yeah, well I'm still worried about running the West Island Strait," Fox said. "It'll save us a bunch of kilometers in rowing but those swells are monsters."

"I know, but I'd rather test our abilities sooner rather than at some spot on the open ocean."

"Fair enough."

The following day, the boat crew made final preparations. The West Ender scouts reported that the 'Forcer sweep had reached the airport, moving westward, covering every canyon and cove. They would reach the Banning House by noon the next day, if not sooner.

That night, Peter and Cynthia held a farewell party in the parlor. The entire clan turned out. Near the fireplace, a dozen musicians played drums, various stringed instruments, and antique brass horns, the music louder than anything Tony had ever heard. Peter called it jazz. Within an hour the clansmen staggered around the complex, drunk on potent Margaritas. But the boat crew stayed sober and looked nervous. Elizabeth complained of stomach pains and Claire's son whined about having to leave his friends. The reality of the West End families leaving their clansmen for some rock in the ocean out of sight of the mainland started to hit home. Tony remembered the night he and Fox left the Touchable Clan and hoped none of the West Enders backed out. It would be easy for them to do, but would result in capture and jail for him and Fox.

As the evening wore on, people wished the voyagers good luck and drifted off to their rooms. Fox and Tony lay on their sofas and watched the last of the fire burn down.

"I wish we could have stayed here," she murmured. "I really like these people."

"Yeah, well, maybe in a few years we can come back. Or maybe they'll send more West Enders to live on San Nicolas."

"That's a lot of maybes."

"Fox, you know, if... if you want to stay here, I'll understand. The Police are looking for a couple and not a pregnant woman. I doubt they'd even recognize you. Plus, you didn't do anything. I was the one who killed—"

"Stop right there. You're not getting rid of me after all we've been through. Besides, if I left it up to you to steer that boat, you'd end up in Cabo San Lucas."

"Yeah, yeah, I suppose you're right. But if this doesn't work out, we can always come back, or try someplace else. Maybe Santa Cruz Island might work for a small clan of three. Maybe we should just head for South America."

"Enough with the maybes," Fox said. "I'm through

with running for now. I need to have this child, take care of our baby, and teach her art and music."

"So you're convinced our child is a girl?"

"Yes... I don't know why, but yes."

They listened to the distant crash of waves against the headlands. Tony closed his eyes and tried to sleep but couldn't. Fox rolled onto her side and faced him. "Can I ask you something?"

"What?"

"Why did you hit him twice?"

"What are you talking about?"

"The Untouchable in the house above de Tolosa. When you hit him with the pitcher the first time, he looked stunned. I could have pushed him off and escaped. So why did you hit him twice?"

Tony stayed quiet for a long time. "I... I'm not sure. I was mad. I guess I wanted to kill him."

"You'll want to forget that part of our story if the Police ever catch us. But if I could have, I would have done the same thing."

"Great. The family that slays together, stays together."

"Isn't that a proverb?"

"I don't think so," Tony said.

They slept fitfully. In the early morning darkness the others joined them in the parlor. Peter and Cynthia brought breakfast. They ate in silence, the only sound being Cynthia quietly sobbing over her food while Fox tried to comfort her. Under a full moon they wound their way downhill to Little Fisherman's Cove and the boat shed. They rolled the panga on its trailer down-slope to the wharf and tied the boat to it securely. Returning the trailer to its shed, Stan and Richard lifted another smaller boat onto it, just in case the 'Forcers might suspect that a boat was missing.

They boarded and sat at their assigned places. Then Stan bolted from his seat. "Wait a minute, wait," he yelled and scrambled onto the dock. Running up-hill, he disappeared inside the marine science building. He emerged carrying a battered guitar case tied shut with lengths of rope. Clambering aboard, he stowed the case under his seat, lashing it to the bench.

"Good God, Stan, how could you forget the Gibson?" Tony asked, grinning.

Stan grinned back. "I don' know. I guess I'm just eager to leave."

The crew checked their provisions to make sure nothing else had been left behind accidentally. When all were settled, Richard cast off the line and they drifted toward the West Island Strait. Tony looked upslope and could make out a figure standing with a torch on an outside deck next to the Banning House. He took his hand light and blinked it at the West Ender, who waved his torch in a goodbye.

Entering the strait, Fox turned the boat into the oncoming swells. The rowers worked hard. But for every meter of forward progress, they slipped back half a meter. They kept at it, each sucking in then blowing out great gasps of air. The bailers kept pace with the water splashing over the gunwales. At dawn they reached the seaward mouth of the strait, where the open ocean funneled into the narrow channel between Catalina and West Island. Fox steered the panga boat directly into the surge and yelled at the rowers to put their backs into it. They shot forward and slammed into the first swell, the bow rising high in the air before crashing downward into the trough.

"Row, damn it, row," Fox bellowed and the boat shot forward and slammed into the next breaking swell. But somebody must have dragged an oar be-cause their boat veered to port. Fox tried to correct it with the tiller but the next wave caught them and poured over the starboard gunwale, swamping the craft. The bailers went crazy trying to lighten the sea load. Richard and Elizabeth stowed their oars and helped with the bailing while Claire and Stan tried to keep the boat headed into the swells. Another wave swamped them and the boat sank to her rails.

"We've got to lighten her," Fox bellowed. "Richard, overboard with ya."

Richard stared at her, then dove into the sea.

Fox gazed at the crew, then grinned. "Hold the tiller and keep her pointed into the waves," she told Tony.

She stood, removed her cloak, and prepared to dive.

"*No, don't,*" Tony screamed.

Before he could grab her, she jumped over the starboard rail. But instead of settling against the hull like Richard had done, the current took her around the stern. She drifted south and away from the panga, swimming hard and fighting the current. The rest of the crew bailed madly until the boat slowly rose. Richard climbed aboard. The rowers took their seats and kept the panga heading into the swells. Tony narrowed his eyes against the spray and searched for Fox, but she'd disappeared.

He stood at the helm and yelled. "Starboard rowers pull!"

The boat slowly turned to port. Tony braced himself against the stern with a crutch and scanned the roiling sea as they ran with the wind and current. The minutes ticked by. He saw only waves and whitewater. *I can't lose her now, not after all this.* He shook himself, wiped his eyes and continued his frantic search. A dark mop of something bobbed on the top of a swell. It looked almost like the head of a sea lion, except the head had a red fringe.

"Fox!" he bellowed and she twisted in the water and shot an arm into the air.

"Portside pull!" he yelled and the boat turned toward their waterlogged captain.

As she came alongside, Fox grabbed the gunwale and Richard yanked her into the boat.

"Portside rowers pull!" Tony yelled again and they surged westward, the bailers once again frantic with their work.

Fox scrambled to the helm and slumped onto the bench next to Tony, choking and gasping for breath. He retrieved her sealskin cloak and wrapped it around her. Her arms and legs looked bluish and he rubbed them with one hand to bring back the circulation.

"Damn it, Fox. The Captain is the last one to abandon ship."

"I had... no other choice," she muttered.

Tony encircled her in his arms and kissed her trembling lips. The rowers grinned at the couple. Once beyond the mouth of the strait, the sea flattened and became a polished pond. The morning sun rose above the mainland and warmed them.

"Row, row, row your boat, gently down the stream..." Elizabeth broke into song and the others picked it up, repeating the round as if they'd been doing it all their lives. Tony looked eastward toward Catalina. They had already put distance between themselves and the island. A tiny black dot, like some annoying sand flea, skimmed over the top of the island's mountain ridge and landed above the Banning House. He pointed it out to Fox.

"All right mates," Fox called. "The 'Forcers have reached the west end. Time to get the heck out of here."

The singing stopped and the boat picked up speed, making good time while the wind slacked off and the waves flattened. They pulled hard throughout the morning and into the afternoon. Tony relieved Elizabeth for a while and Claire's son spelled his mother, while Fox called the cadence. The men's faces looked gray but determined as Catalina Island and the mainland slowly disappeared. No skimmers or water craft followed them. They sailed free and un-tethered into the rolling arms of the Pacific, a clan of seafarers in an open boat, hoping for landfall but at peace without it.

23

Sergeant Statler and Officer Graham sat in their skimmer on a mountaintop overlooking the West Island Strait and the Banning House. The morning sun shone golden on the machine's bronzed canopy. Statler yawned and stared at the com panel. He received a call on Captain Hanpian's frequency. *I haven't heard from that old buzzard in days*, he thought. *I wonder what he wants, probably angry that I haven't kept him informed about the latest developments.* Statler keyed both the audio and vid connections and was surprised to see Jonas's head fill the screen.

"Yes, Sergeant Jonas, how can I help you?"

Jonas pointed to the collar of his uniform, to a bright set of lieutenant bars. "That's Lieutenant Jonas, Sergeant."

"What's... what's been going on, ah, Lieutenant?"

"Well, a lot has happened since you've been on your wild goose chase in SoCal. I've been promoted to lieutenant for capturing Fox Slades's parents. I realize that it's your old position but... but I hope we can still work together. I really need you back here to pick up the slack in field operations. Plus I'll need you to teach me the administrative work."

"Why are you using Hanpian's com frequency?"

"I guess Captain Peterson hasn't told you. That Matteson woman, the boy's mother, jumped out a fifth floor window at the Operations Center, took Hanpian with her... a face-to-face header into the street."

"So who's in command?"

"I am, Sergeant. Commander Pynard confirmed my

appointment yesterday."

"Shit," Statler muttered.

"What was that, Sergeant?"

"Nothing, sir. Nothing."

"So when do you think you and Peterson will wrap things up?"

"Soon, Lieutenant, very soon."

"Good. Contact me when you depart SoCal."

The vid screen went black. Statler sat in his seat and burned with anger, disappointment, resentment. He popped open the skimmer's door and stepped into the cool morning air. To the east, the sun turned the San Pedro Channel into a pond of green gold. To the west, the open Pacific looked like a varnished lake. He strode through new grass to the edge of the promontory, lowered his Rangemaster over his eyes and scanned the channel and West Island, finding only sea lions and a pod of dolphins. He increased the magnification and made a quick northwestern sweep. Something bounced between the swells, twelve kilometers out. He increased the magnification to its highest level. A small boat holding eight people shimmered against the sea. At the helm sat a woman with a fringe of red hair. A small man sat next to her. They held hands.

"Go kids, go," Statler murmured.

The com on his headset beeped and Captain Peterson came on the line. "What have you found, Sergeant?"

"Nothing, sir. Not a damn thing."

9 781951 384524